Cambri

WITHDRAWN
FROM STOCK

CW00421023

OSTELAR

BAY OF EMPIRES

THE TRI-TIPPED
SPEAR

PASSAGE
OF ISTRYAN

ARCHDUCHY
OF OSBERGIA

THE FORK

INVEREID

AVERCAR

SOUTHERN OCEAN

THE BIGHT

REI

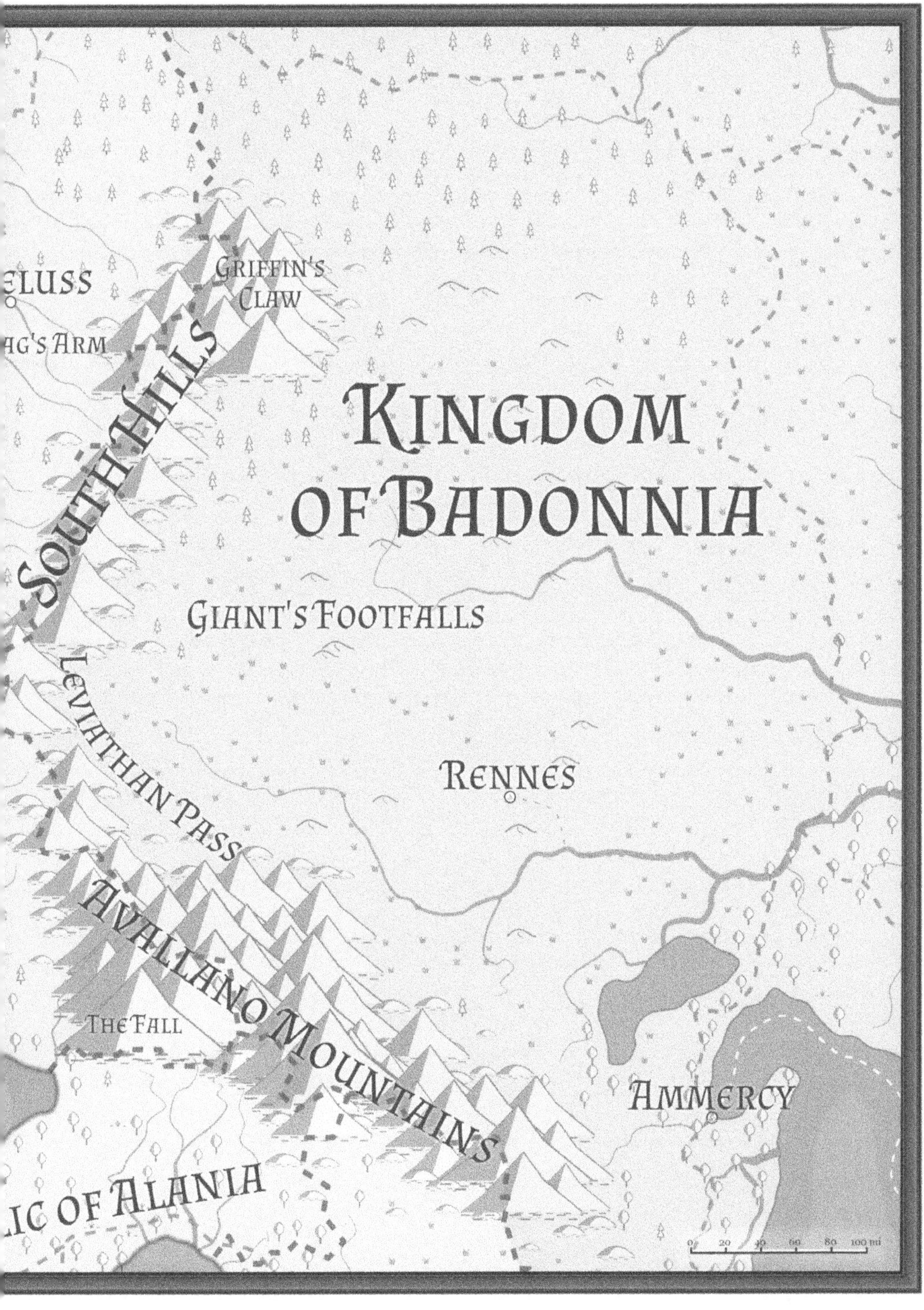

ELUSS
GRIFFIN'S CLAW
AG'S ARM
SOUTH HILLS
KINGDOM OF BADONNIA
GIANT'S FOOTFALLS
LEVIATHAN PASS
RENNES
AVALLANO MOUNTAINS
THE FALL
AMMERCY
LIC OF ALANIA
0 20 40 60 80 100 mi

THE SWORD OF MERCY AND WRATH

A NEW ADULT DARK FANTASY

NC KOUSSIS

NCK PUBLISHING

Copyright © 2022 by Nikitas C Koussis

The moral right of Nikitas C Koussis to be identified as the author of this work has been asserted in accordance with the Copyright Act of 1968.

All rights reserved. No portion of this publication may be reproduced, stored in a retrieval system, or transmitted in any form or by any means, electronic, mechanical, photocopying, recording, or otherwise, without written permission from the publisher or copyright owner of this book.

All the characters in this book are fictitious, and any resemblance to actual persons, living or dead, is purely coincidental.

Cover art and title design by MiblArt Design

See more at www.nikitaskoussis.com and sign up to the newsletter to get a free story!

For Shannon

CONTENTS

VOLUME ONE

Demon. Wukodlak. Turnskin. Shapeshifter. *Versipellis* in High Istryan. These terms describe the same creature—man or woman—afflicted with Sigur's curse. The curse was the punishment for all the descendants of the traitors who sided with the Great Fiend, the Harbinger, the Devil.

The demon is terrifying and unsettling in its monstrous magnificence. They are shapeshifters who take the form of a giant man-wolf on two legs, with wicked teeth, thick manes, and sharp claws. Those afflicted possess the strength and stamina of ten men, the ability to leap vast distances and run at great speed, and the ability to return from the dead.

Sigur's worshippers, especially those of His priesthood, are pact-bound to hunt down the creatures. The Order of the Golden Sword are Sigur's hunters par excellence, given authority by their counterparts within the church, as the Will of Sigur. The Order eschew all forms of temptation, be that body or mind, and leave behind mortal concerns such as war or politics. They do this for the immortal soul of mankind. The cursed beings are evil incarnate, and it is the duty of all good men to hunt them until there are none left.

— *Modern History of the Istryan Empire,* vol. II.

The relationship of the Sigurian Church and the Order of the Golden Sword is contentious, and one that the Church disavows and relies upon in equal measure. The Order acts with impunity, scouring through various lands, recognizing not any human authority, claiming that they are the embodiment of the will of Sigur himself. They respect not the natural laws of due process, or of fair hearing, exterminating towns wholesale if they believe it will root out 'heresy'. The greatest and most present example in recorded history are the mass pogroms that took place over a five-year period from 784-789 Aetate Discordiae. The whole continent was brought to its knees with infighting, suspicion, and lawlessness. Brother turned on brother, neighbor on neighbor, all in the pursuit of 'purity'.

In preparing for their work, the Order employs obscure and magickal weapons, traps, and poisons. The identity and existence of this arsenal are closely guarded secrets. Given that they often kidnap and indenture talented thinkers (alchemists, smiths, engineers, and others), it is no surprise that they have developed some advantages over other forces of the time.

— *Truth, or A Regard for the Fanatics of Sigur, Anonymous*

I

TRISTAIN

TRISTAIN KNEW IT WAS a bad day to piss off his knight and master. Leon's powerful kick sent him sprawling into the barrels behind. The knight's sword crunched into the mail at his side. He gasped sharply as pain shot through his ribcage. Tristain raised his shield weakly, expecting a blow. But nothing came, and he stumbled to his feet.

"Know your range, squire," Leon's voice carried from across the yard. "If you're close enough to hit them and you haven't, they'll be sure to hit you."

Enough talking, Tristain thought, grinding his teeth. Just hit me already.

Leon had his sword and shield by his side. Tristain charged. His opponent's sword swept upwards, and Tristain blocked. Flipping his sword for the reply, Tristain missed. Leon had already moved back. They circled each other.

"Where are the weak points, lad?" Leon's voice was muffled by his faceplate.

Tristain knew the answer, of course, but Leon liked to test his memory in the heat of battle.

"Armpit, groin, neck, back of the knee, and ankle," he yelled, punctuating each word with a step forward. Leon maintained his distance. Still, they continued to circle each other. "Why are you holding back?"

"You're not ready, Squire."

Not ready, my arse.

Moving in fast, Tristain brought his sword low. The knight's feet looked unsteady. He'd finally caught Leon off-guard. Tristain reversed, bringing the sword back up. Changing his footing, he ran the flat of his blade along his opponent's curved helm. He pivoted, hooking the sword behind Leon's head. He pushed, sending Leon over his outstretched leg. The crashing sound reverberated through Tristain's helmet.

Leon's red beard seemed to explode from his face as he threw open his visor. Stunned, it took him a second, then he howled with laughter.

"I yield, I yield!"

Planting the tip of his blunt training sword in the dirt, Tristain helped Leon to his feet. "I thought you had me, Sir."

"Cheeky fucking sal'brath." Leon swore in Hillard, the language of the people from the South Hills. It meant fish-breath; how everyone from the mountains thought of people not from the mountains. "Where's my flask?"

A servant boy had it on hand. Leon unbuckled his helmet, throwing it aside. Throwing back his neck, his muscles flexed as brown liquid ran down his chin. The Hillman was shorter than Tristain, but twice as wide, and all muscle. Tristain could sometimes beat him in a sword-fight, but in pure strength, Leon had him beat all the time.

"You're learning," Leon said, wiping his face.

Tristain smiled at that. Still, he wished the knight would take him more seriously. He wasn't going to get better and stronger if Leon took it easy on him. For a man given the moniker Leon the Strong, he could be irritatingly cautious.

Inside their canvas tent, Tristain racked his armor and washed his face in a small basin, then changed into finery. The son of a count had grating expectations, sometimes. Tristain's chest filled out his forest-green doublet, snug from two years of Leon's training, while russet-red hose hugged his muscular legs.

He wiped his hair. Dirt got everywhere—in his underwear, in his ale, on his clothes. The army had burned the fields months ago, and the land was still barren, little more than a dust-bowl.

He eyed the small writing desk, its papers in a scattered pile—his half-written letter to Selene sticking out like a rude gesture. *What can I say to her? That I haven't found a way yet?*

"I'm going for a walk," Leon's voice came from behind. Tristain turned. Shaved head and flowing red beard, Leon was a large man, twice as wide as his squire, wearing the clothes of a lowborn knight—loose-collared linen shirt and black trousers. "You coming?"

Tristain nodded. The letter could wait.

"So," Leon said as they passed a barracks. A woman whistled a tune ahead as she hung out soldiers' linens, while a pair on patrol walked past, spears in hand.

Tristain waited for Leon to say something. A minute of stony silence, and they reached a small hill, where they saw the besieged city open out in front of them. Rennes' walls stood stark and silent as the sun set behind them. Below them was a flat area set with outward-facing spikes, facing towards the city. Beyond the spikes, deep and hungry, laid trenches that would cover the assault. Tristain wasn't sure why they waited so long. Three long months had passed since they arrived, and still no word on the timing of the assault. *Mayhap they expect the city to starve before then,* he thought. *And they'll surrender without a fight.*

The sky turned hues of pinks and oranges. Another night in a foreign land arrived, and Tristain was no closer to his goal of finding employment as a household guard than when the day started.

"Sir." Sharp wind whipped unshorn black hair across Tristain's face. "Is there a particular reason you think I'm not ready?"

Leon stiffened. He took a sip of his flask. "You're what, Tristain... sixteen?"

Tristain clicked his tongue without meaning to. "Eighteen, sir." *He should know that... I've been his squire for near on two years.*

"Ah, I forget sometimes. And tell me, what do you want, money, fame? If you're looking for either, just look at me: ten dozen pieces of silver to my name, and a busted back. They call me the Strong, but sometimes I can't reach my arse to wipe."

Tristain stopped himself from saying something smart. Around them, the sounds of dinner picked up, crashing pots, cooks barking orders to servants, soldiers joking around campfires.

Leon gave him a look of resignation, before taking another swig. "You think I'm spineless, lad, too afraid that I'll hurt you? Don't give me that look. I know what the men say, when they talk over their fires, when they think my back's turned. They say I've lost my touch. And yet... they will die, and yet more before this war is over."

Tristain sighed, folding his arms. Below them, a campwife, the women followers of the army who cooked, cleaned, and served the soldiers, chased a servant boy out of her kitchen.

"If you won't push me, Sir, how am I going to prove myself?" He tried his hardest to keep the anger out of his voice.

"I didn't say that, lad. The squad's on patrol duty tomorrow. You'll be in the van, riding with me."

That drew a smile across Tristain's face. Riding in the vanguard, Tristain would look important to anyone that saw. If he looked important, he might look important enough to sponsor or hire as a personal house guard. If he was a house guard, his master would offer his mother somewhere to stay as a matter of course, if he could get them away from his father.

Once, he dreamed of being a lord of a mighty estate, like his father, fighting tourneys for his own glory, and fighting in wars for the glory of the empire. How high he'd ride into battle, how nobly he'd spirit a lance into the empire's enemies...

Leon belched as he drained the contents of his flask. "Let's get back." He started down the hill, then stumbled. Tristain grabbed him and kept him from falling.

Leon wiped his own face, chuckling. "Ah, you're a good lad. It's what I always told Erken: you treat your elders with the respect they deserve." A dark look flashed across his face.

As they walked back to the tent with the white eagle banner, Tristain thought of Leon's son. Erken was his name, a lad of sixteen, and much like other boys his age, wanted nothing more than to make their fathers proud. Tristain knew little of what that was like, but people often talked about legacy and family glory, and he understood the sentiment. His father had talked about it enough for a lifetime.

Erken had died in a battle in the Giant's Footfalls, thirty miles to the north. The army's last major battle before the siege, they had fought hard to gain a hill defended by archers from the Kingdom of Badonnia, the empire's age-old foe, and whose lands they had occupied. The empire had lost over a quarter of their forces—a thousand men in total to gain the hill, and the Badonnians were forced to retreat, fleeing behind Rennes' walls. Leon's son had been one of the dead.

Tristain placed Leon in his bed and quaking snores filled the room. His flask rolled on the floor.

Tristain sighed. As long as he had known him, Leon never abstained from drink, enjoying an ale or strongwine with dinner as folk do, but these days it seemed he never found a single moment without it. Though Tristain now smiled as he thought about what the knight had said to him. Riding in the van tomorrow. He was happy to have the chance to prove himself.

As he turned to get dinner from the kitchens, he heard shouting and cursing. He stuck his head out the door.

"You've heard?" a soldier in his breeches yelled, running in the parade ground's direction.

"Minstrels!" the other said, close behind.

The parade ground was at the center of the camp. Turned into a veritable city by the many and varied folk that tailed an army, it touted tents and pavilions of bright colors, rugs, armor, supplies, anything and everything. For the right price, of course.

It seemed far from the stark hill dotted with catapults, far from the noise of the drilling grounds, far from the row of latrine pits. The scent of char-grilled meats and smoky spits drifted into his nose. The sweet sound of a harp played quickly filled the air, accompanied by a quicker lute and faster drumming. From what Tristain heard along the way, a troupe of minstrels had arrived, causing a great stir.

As he entered the grounds, he had a good view of the musicians, but what really drew his eye was the general and the surrounding lords. The general, Duchess Ilse Adolar, stern of eyes and jaw, carried the face of someone accustomed to hard decisions and the weight of the world on her shoulders.

As the musicians started their next song, Tristain walked over to the general. He pushed down the knot in his gut.

"...we'll have to smooth things over with the Order, I'd say," he overheard someone say as he approached.

"No," a man in fine mottled silks and velvets said. "I'd say this is precisely what they need. They're getting a little too comfortable. They should serve the empire, not work for the highest bidder. Ah, someone approaches."

Tristain bowed. "Your Grace, my lords. I am Tristain Florian Oncierran, son of Sebastian, and heir to Invereid."

"Well met." The duchess tipped her head. "I believe you are Sir Vorland's squire, are you not?"

"Yes, Your Grace."

"Ay-ay," the minstrels' herald said, a man with a peacock feather sticking from his peaked hat. "And for the next song we have Glamis of the Tower, a sad song to be sure, but a treat for the ears."

They sang of Glamis, a man who sought power and strength above all other men. Defeated by a better fighter, he turned to the Great Devil out of spite, and became something more than a man—a terrifying wolf, killing his daughter and his wife.

"Very prestigious, to learn under Leon the Strong," the man in silks said as the harps and slow drums started. He was short, plump, with slick blond hair and a beak-like nose. "How goes it? Has the strength of the man himself rubbed off on you?"

"I believe we haven't met, my lord," Tristain said.

"No, I don't believe we have. Count Andreas Pagehald of Verania. Vredevoort leads my troops, but I pay them. Though I'm here because who better to monitor my own holdings?"

Tristain's eyes lit up. The regiment from Verania was the largest and would've cost thousands to pay. Surely, he would have more than enough to pay for a single household guard. But whether he would want to take the risk of upsetting his father... There was also Vredevoort: the vicious man had led the disastrous battle in the Giant's Footfalls, where thousands had died. And Erken, Leon's son. Though Tristain would work for Pagehald directly, not Vredevoort, so it might not have been all that bad.

Cheers filled the air as the song finished. People rose from their seats, tossing silver pieces, while young boys ran around, gathering the silver up in their arms. Tristain thought it was a decent rendition, though the strings were out of time with the singer.

"Now, we have our own real-life Glamis here," the herald said, pointing to an obscenely hairy soldier. "You're more hair than man, my friend." The hairy one waved his arms defensively. "Oh, I don't envy your mother if you were born like that! Throw him in the river, they must have said, the midwife's cursed him!"

"Count Pagehald—" Tristain went to speak, turning back.

"Yes, I remember it now," the man said, leaning on his back leg. "Your father gave me a thrashing in the August Griffin Tourney ten years ago, I believe. He always had a temper, that one. What news of him?"

"I do not have any, my lord. He was in good health when I left two years ago. It is little wonder, so far from civilization here."

"Indeed. I receive writs and reports to sign but once a moon. I sometimes ask if the sun does not set backwards here. And yet, our esteemed Grand Duke wishes to claim these lands? For what purpose?"

"You forget yourself, Andreas," the general admonished.

"Apologies, Your Grace. Excuse us. I wish to speak with Tristain privately, if you'll permit."

The duchess bent her head slightly as if her neck, stiff from carrying a stone jaw, could only bend so far. Tristain and the count bowed in return, and took to a nearby table. The count dismissed those seated with a wave.

"Tell it true, young man." Pagehald ran a hand under his smooth double chin. Though he wore a long tunic with flowing sleeves and a loose belt, it did very little to hide the plump. The days of the count's tourneys are long behind him. "What's your plan after this godsforsaken war?"

"To serve, my lord. My greatest desire is to serve an honorable household."

"Ah, color me intrigued. I would've placed heavy bets on you having dreams of fame and glory. After all, few men of your age want to set down roots in one place."

"I have responsibilities to take care of, my lord." *Let him think I have a mistress and children to support, to keep from prodding further.*

The man nodded. "Hm... I understand all too well, and I'm not unsympathetic to your position. You should come for a visit after we wrap up this nasty business in Badonnia. My estate makes the finest wine north of the Bight."

"Thank you, my lord," Tristain said, trying and failing to keep a straight face. He felt like dancing on the tables, kicking over flagons of ale in time to the music. He pushed down his excitement for now. It was only a small step ahead, and he would have to make it through the war first. But one step at a time.

"And don't forget, my friends, to tip your campwives," the herald said to the crowd. "Or give 'em the tip!"

After the count bid him farewell, Tristain sauntered off to bed, the sounds of the revelry fading, but his good mood remained strong. Guilt spiked through his chest as he planned; he was just using the count. The count seemed like a decent man, and yet Tristain had very little interest in being his guard. It was simply for the position, and all the details that came with that. A place for his family to live, where his mother and Selene would finally be safe.

But a familiar pain in his left hand, where his father had shattered his pinkie with a mallet, followed the guilt. Rage persisted over the years, though he barely remembered the specifics. Not because his memory failed him, but because there simply were too many occasions to count. He'd almost become inured to it by the end. It was only when Bann died six years ago did Tristain become the heir and the golden child. Then, his father's rage turned on Selene, the family's ward, and their mother. He couldn't forget that, even if he tried.

Selene was more than the daughter of a noble family—she was Tristain's sister in all but blood. He would do anything to protect her. The courts offered no recourse, because Selene's family did not wish to pursue a count for recompense. And like many others, they cared little for daughters—first sons were kings of their home. Everything else was dispensable. Squeezed by circumstance, Tristain had only left her to find a position that would allow them all to get away. He welcomed the pain in his left hand. It was a reminder of what he would do, what he was capable of, to get her free.

After he perfected the ending of the letter to Selene, he climbed onto the straw bed at the foot of his knight's armor, steel glinting dully in the light of a tallow candle where scarce an inch remained. For the first time in months, he slept soundly.

2

THE DEMON

THE NEXT MORNING, TRISTAIN rode alongside Leon, high in his saddle, bright-eyed and bright smile on his face. The knight Leon led his fifty spearmen, taking the dusty road that took them past the latrine pits, past the catapults, past the outer palisades, their spikes decorated with the grisly heads of deserters. Out they went, past the last lookout tower, and towards the forest to the south. The forest was named thus on a map, if a few stark trees on their lonesome could be called that. A hot, dry breeze blew over them, making the journey clammy and uncomfortable. Still, nothing could ruin Tristain's good mood. His horse flicked its tail back and forth, shooing flies. Running his hand along the beast's braided mane and down along its side, he felt the smooth leather of the saddle at his thighs, the strong back of the animal girding his spine as they rode.

"What are you so chuffed about?" the corporal Caen said, speeding his feet to walk alongside the horse. Tristain counted the corporal among his friends in this place, though he was still lowborn. From the flat farmlands of the Spear, Caen was lean and strong, with the callused hands of a farmer who worked a plough from childhood. His skin was sun-wrinkled, and though he was eighteen, the same as Tristain, he looked much older.

Tristain chuckled. "Nothing, Corporal. Can't a man be merry?"

"In this place? In this heat?"

Tristain shrugged.

"And what's the plan with that?" Caen said, glancing at the pole with the white eagle banner. "Gonna' find it's home in someone's gut?"

Tristain narrowed his brows. "Has there ever been a single moment when you've been serious?"

"Nope, and I ain't gonna start today."

When the sun drew to its zenith, they stopped by a stream, far from the siege camp now. Tristain, naked apart from his breeches, dipped himself in the shallows with the rest of the men. His gear was in a pile on the bank. He dunked his face, washing like the others. The lieutenant Gida stood guard at the shore, her eyes narrowed over the hazy horizon.

A mirage of the South Hills shimmered in the distance over the Footfalls. Tristain knew it was false because it looked only a few miles away, when it was really over fifty. *Fifty miles to the Hills, to the Leviathan Pass. Fifty miles from home.* Four day's march from his homeland of Osbergia, the largest province of the empire. Taking his horse and running would be a stupid idea; he'd be caught within hours. Even if he got away, the keep at the Pass was the Empire's, and they would ask questions, delaying him long enough that any pursuers would likely catch him. That didn't stop the thought from occurring to him. *To see Mama and Selene again...*

Tristain sat by a nettle bush. He sighed, wiping greasy hair out of his face. Something tapped his leg as Leon sat down next to him.

"Squire," he said, alternating sips of ale with bites of bread. Strung around his neck, over his polished but scratched breastplate, was a small wooden chalice, a token of Ginevra, the Goddess of Mercy and Motherhood. Tristain let it hang. He would've asked anyone else about it, but even after two years, the knight still hadn't opened to him. The most he'd gotten out of him about his son even, was an angry tirade about Vredevoort the Grim, the one who'd led to Erken's death. He remembered asking Caen about it.

"That one earned his name for a reason," the corporal had said. "Vorland fought to have Erken reassigned, but Vredevoort told him ain't no way.

In the Footfalls, Grim sent his men to secure the hilltop, throwing wave after wave at the Badonnians. Hundreds died, Erken with them. I think he blames himself."

"Why would he blame himself for that?" Tristain had asked.

"Why would any father?"

Leon sent two spearmen on perimeter guard, eyes peeled for any enemy approaching on the road or over the dusty plains. Though they didn't expect any Badonnians out here, their army having secured the corridor between the Pass and the siege camp, it didn't hurt to be careful, especially in enemy lands.

Caen whistled, drawing his attention. "I saw you've finally finished that letter."

Tristain laughed, incredulous. "You rifled through my things? Have you no sense of privacy or respect?"

"Privacy? You never stopped talking about it. I had to see it for myself. What happened?"

"I spoke to the Count of Verania. He offered me a position in his household guard. That's what I was writing about."

Leon chimed in with a tone of approval. "Household guard? Respectable. You ought to do well."

"Wait, Pagehald?" Caen interrupted. "The Count of Verania?"

"Yes."

Caen looked like he was trying his hardest not to crack up with laughter. "You've been 'ad, squire."

Tristain frowned. "Corporal?"

"Verania has more debt than a brothel has whores, and he spends plenty on them, rest assured. You'll be fightin' off debtors and cutthroats for the rest of your life, short as that'll be."

"Bastard," Tristain said without meaning to.

"I know nothing of this," Leon said gingerly from his cup. "But then we don't run in the same circles." Leon slapped his leg. "Ah, Tristain, I'm sorry. But I'm sure he won't be the last lord with an offer. If I were a lord gilded..."

From the perimeter, a private came running, running like the wind, his boots ringing hard on the sunbaked ground. "Sir... Badonnians!" he yelled between breaths.

They rose to their feet, spears clattering and swords rasping. Bread and ale spilled on the ground, and the men arranged themselves into a formation. The private reached them, his knees buckling and his breath sharp and loud. Tristain looked around. Nothing but a sultry breeze came charging at them, and the only sound was rustling trees, not the whistle of arrows.

"Speak, Sasha," Leon said firmly. "Where are they?"

"I saw hoofprints, sir. Hoofprints by the gully, where the mud still lies. Got to be six or seven at least, stopped to give their horses some water." The men relaxed, breaking formation, some of them moaning about a cowardly private and their ruined lunch. The private Sasha, a skinny lad of sixteen, turned beet red.

"Six or seven? They're probably traders or village folk. Have you lost your nerve, lad? We march on."

E VENING FOUND THEM TRUDGING along the east road back to the camp when they came across an alehouse. Tristain's belly rumbled. The air was still, and the alehouse quiet, but he could smell roasting meat and fresh bread. *We should keep moving, get back to camp...* but his mouth watered. He imagined ale that didn't taste like piss and bread that wasn't made of turnips.

"Awh, I can smell the chicken roasting from here," Caen said. Murmurs of agreement rippled through the men.

"We should march on," the lieutenant replied. "Find a well-hidden spot to camp."

"Ah, come on, Lieutenant. One ale won't hurt."

"We could meet you later, Lieutenant," Tristain helpfully added. "It would be less conspicuous travelling in smaller groups if the enemy is indeed out there." The men crooned in agreement. *And I could use a bath, too, if they have one.* His eyes lit up at the prospect. *I haven't had a proper bath in months.* The baths at the camp were always too cold, or filthy, or more often both.

The lieutenant turned to the knight. "Sir, I really think—"

"Ah, Gida, it's fine. Take half the men, and return to the camp. Besides, I don't think all of us'll fit inside. We'll be there before you know it."

The lieutenant sighed, thinking it best to just drop the matter, and took half the men, who grumbled as they left. The ones continuing on spat as they left, grumbling that they should enjoy a drink, too. Twenty-five unlucky souls trudged down the road and over the twilit horizon.

Tristain tapped his fingers on the reins as he hitched the stallion. Gida had a point. Perhaps it would be best to keep moving. Or maybe the Badonnians would find them, and Tristain could prove himself in battle. *A sure-fire way to be knighted.*

After a loud tussle for the first baths and settling himself in the warm tub, Tristain thought of Pagehald's deception. The lavender scented water rippled around his chin, wisps of steam curling up from the surface, soothing his muscles. His mind was hard at work. *Had the count really deceived me? Maybe Caen's lying... maybe he doesn't know the truth, and they're just idle rumors. Lowborns do love a good tale. But if I say no to the count... the seed has been planted. I'll have to save face somehow, let Pagehald down without causing offence. And I'd be no better off than yesterday.*

He pulled himself out of the bath, hungry and thirsty.

Flicking wet hair out of his face, Tristain took a seat with Caen, Leon, and a big, fat-faced ox-looking private named Herrad, and called for an ale. He needed one.

The innkeeper had, smartly, not turned the men away. Twenty-five blades with the potential to become pointed at his throat was a forceful argument. He wasn't happy about it, though; slamming their tankards and food onto the table. The scowl on his pockmarked face seemed a permanent fixture.

Someone carried a set of dice on them, so they enjoyed a few games and a few ales. Loud chatter filled the room. *You'd almost forget there was a war.*

"The corporal here was just telling me about the Spear," the knight said.

"Yeah. Guard Captain Hostein. He was celebrating, 'cause he'd just captured a mighty outlaw, a savage who raided near on ten villages, raped women, killed babies. You know, real scum. So, the captain was a celebrated man. He was a good-looking one, too. Everyone was thrilled to see him. The alehouse kept the booze flowing. The count came down, shook his hand. The baron, the sheriff, they all came down to shake his hand. In fact, Hostein was so popular that towards the end of the night, a few of the village wenches took him upstairs. These girls weren't known for their... timid nature, if you know what I mean. But it was deathly silent downstairs. An hour later, they came back down, untouched as their mothers would have 'em. 'What's happened?' the barkeep asked. They laughed and said, 'He's a looker, but he's about as much use as milk shoes.' And from then on, they knew him as Hostein Milk Dick."

They burst out laughing.

Caspar, Herrad's brother, the man's equal in hairiness and ox-ness turned to face them from the table over. "What's this? Herr, you told them the story about the wench from Taneria?"

"Yeah, right," Caen cut in. "It's what they all say, right? A bit a' wine and Tanerian women are less fickle than an aging whore."

"Don't they also say that men from Triburg have worms for cocks?" Maria said from the next table over, sending laughter through the room.

"Herrad might, but I ain't," Caspar replied.

"You've spent some time comparin'?" Andrea added.

"I don't need to take this from some wench." Caspar pushed himself free of the table, sending ale and chicken carcasses scattering. Both Andrea and Maria drew their weapons, rising to their feet. Lombas the Small laughed, his horselaugh shaking the room. The chubby tavern wench on his enormous lap laughed as well.

"Knock it off, lackwits," the knight bellowed, silencing the room. "Enough fuckin' chatter. It's time to get serious. Who here says they can take me? Squire!"

Tristain laughed, waving his arms.

Caen jabbed him with his elbow. "Come on!"

"Alright, alright... you might regret it, Sir," Tristain replied, to cheers among the men.

They threw back ales. One strongale, two, three. Caen patted him on the back. Tristain felt bile rise in his throat. He wasn't sure if he should be grateful for the support. Four, five, six. Feeling the liquid slide back up, he snapped his mouth closed. He thought it might come out his nose and his ears. The room spun wildly. Leon was unfazed, putting away his seventh.

It was no use. The liquid came flowing out of his nose. Choking, he opened his mouth, coating the floor in foamy beer and stomach acid. The men cheered, slapping him on the back.

"That's no fair," Tristain cried, throat strained. "You haven't got a bottom in that belly!"

The men laughed.

"Alright, alright," Caen yelled. "Who's next?"

Herrad challenged Caen, and the big lad from Triburg won handily, then Maria launched into a story.

"So, back home, right," she said, laughing. "The boys used to throw rocks at us, me an' Andrea. It was their way of getting attention, I think. Why are you boys so hopeless at just talking to women...? Anyway, one day, one of the real big boys, you know, two feet taller than anyone else and cock as big a horse's... you know the ones."

They laughed, looking pointedly at Lombas, the giant lad taller than most by a foot, and he shrugged his boulders for shoulders.

"So, Andrea and I took him out to the forest for a bit of payback. The poor lad probably thought we were gonna' let him prod us. Well, we might've but... anyway, we went for a swim in the creek, tellin' him to take off his clothes, then we would join him. So, he leaped into the water, prick flailing about like a godsdamn eel. Andrea got in with him, all naked-like, while I hid his clothes in the tallest tree I could find. I'm a fair hand at climbing, you see. I came back, told him we were leaving, and Andrea got out and ran. We didn't look back. We ran so hard that we nearly collapsed." She became breathless, laughing until tears ran down her face.

"Then what? Tell us," Caen said, grinning.

"We..." She couldn't stop laughing. Tristain smiled as he took another sip of his ale. "We hid behind the alehouse, n'... he came runnin', right to the center of town, naked as the day he was born, covered in red, angry blisters, from his neck down to his toes. Leeches got to him! Even his prick had a few on 'em! He was furious! But he never threw rocks at us again."

They all laughed.

The innkeeper said something in whispered Badonnian to the chubby woman, and she hopped off Lombas' knee.

"We're closing, sorry," the man said in a heavy accent, face pinched.

"What kind of alehouse closes?" Caen said.

"It's fine, Corporal. We've overstayed our welcome," Leon replied. "These kind folks fed our bellies and warmed our bodies. We should be on the road."

As someone opened the door, a strong, wet wind blew over Tristain. The weather had turned.

"Argh, it's raining," Maria said. "First rain in a fuckin' month and it's when we're on the march."

"All the more reason to get to camp, wench," Herrad replied. Maria slapped him playfully with the back of her gloved hand.

Tristain unhitched his horse, truly feeling the effects of the strong ale now. He nearly lost his footing as the beast buffeted him. Rain dripped down his padded jacket. It fell hard now. Thunder rumbled in the distance. The sky darkened.

A man screamed. Tristain turned, drawing his sword. He hadn't realized until that moment just how dark it was and he blinked, trying to resolve the dark in front of him. Lightning lit up the sky, and it was as bright as day for a moment. The light dazzled him, but through the intense dark blue and white, two figures lay on the ground, dead. Eight grey-plate forms stood abreast above them. Red-gold cloaks on their backs. Steel drawn.

Tristain flinched as the sky went dark again. They were the party from the road. Not a hunting party, or traders, or footsoldiers, but heavily armed Badonnian knights.

One of them bellowed, "*Allae!*"

Heavy crashing footsteps sounded over the rain. Bellowing curses and war cries, they were lit up by the sky again. Swinging their weapons in wide arcs, men fell around them, crashing against the ground in wet heaps of mail. Tristain swallowed, throwing himself forward into the blackness. Someone beat aside his sword like it was a mere toothpick, and a plated fist smashed into his jaw. Pain wracked his ear and face as he fell.

A bright fork of light rippled around the knight's raised longsword. Tristain could only watch as it came down like a headman's axe. Then someone crashed into the knight. The Badonnian clattered to the ground. Tristain's wits found him. He scrambled, his fingernails clawing up muck and blood.

A heap of mail crashed next to Tristain. It was Caen, his face twisted in pain. His temple ran with a gash of blood. Around them, the brawl became closer and tighter. A plated boot stomped on Tristain's ankle. He felt something snap. He groaned, feeling his jaw stiffen from the punch he'd taken. Pushing past the pain, he crawled out, dragging Caen with him, sword in the other hand. He strained, elbowing his way across the unforgiving mud.

At last, they were free, and Tristain set the corporal aside. He tested his jaw, feeling the stiff muscles and sore teeth. Felt like he might've even lost a few.

Tristain pulled himself to his feet, feeling a sharp tingle through his ankle. He breathed, trying to calm himself. It worked, and his eyes were adjusting to the blackness, making him feel slightly better about the screams and death around him. *Maybe there's a chance... if I can fight back.* He looked down at Caen. *You won't die here.*

He remembered Leon's lessons. The stances. He moved into a back guard, sword edge aligning with his stronger rear leg, his weak leg forward. A red-gold-cloak charged at Tristain. Lightning rippled behind his foe. He scanned for weak points. Leon's words echoed in his mind. *Armpit, eyes, groin, back of the knee.*

The air ruptured as Tristain slashed. The blow was deflected, as he expected. Tristain evaded the counter, trading blows. He feinted an attack from above, turning his blade in the air. The knight blocked high, then found Tristain's blade in his armpit. The man howled, dropping to the ground. Tristain had hit his target, the axillary nerve. Bits of food leaked from his opponent's faceplate—he'd thrown up from the pain. He wasn't getting up soon.

More of Tristain's squad fell around him. The Badonnians caught them by surprise, and they were drunk. *Much longer and we'll be finished.* He watched as Leon wrenched a knight's helmet off, snapping the buckle. He roared, burying his dagger into the base of his foe's skull.

It made Tristain sick. Death and horror unfolded in front of him. Half of his fellows were dead, glass-eyed on the ground. Straining, his lungs yearned for fresh air. Despite the rain, the air felt cloying and sticky. No longer able to stomach what was happening around him, he dry-heaved.

A horseman came charging out of the darkness and knocked Tristain straight on his ass. The rider whooped as he wheeled the horse around, waving his sword wildly. The man yelled in Badonnian, grinning at Tristain as he got to his feet. *Shit.* Three knights were drawn over. They laughed as they closed in.

"Where do you run," one yelled as he stepped forward and began a flurry of blows. Tristain deflected them all. On the last blow, Tristain feinted a cut low. The man blocked low. Tristain flicked up. The point went straight through his neck, sending him limp. Tristain moved back into guard, pushing his fear and nausea aside.

Two more pounced, forcing him backwards. He countered, disarming one. As he recovered, the other's sword bit into his arm. Tristain howled, retreating. His back sidled up against a tree. The two closed in, and there was no escape. One moved in with a spear, batting aside Tristain's weakened sword arm. He plunged the point in, pinning his shoulder to the tree. Tristain cried in pain, dropping his blade.

An officer stepped forward. The captain, from what Tristain could judge by the deference offered by his comrades, if they had such a thing as deference in Badonnia. He grinned as he approached.

"You," he said, speaking with a heavy accent, "a lord's son from your skill, I gather."

Tristain spat at him.

He chuckled. "But you die like the rest."

"Sigur fucking curse you," he swore back. "You won't get away with this."

"Your army will perish. All you wester *pudans* will die for nothing, and nobody. You will lie in the dirt. Forgotten by all but wolves. Not even your mothers and wives will miss you, because we will take them for ourselves."

"I'll kill you, bastard. You watch."

Laughter broke out.

"How can you kill me... if I kill you first?" He stabbed Tristain in the gut. Ice gripped his stomach and pain shot up through his body, doubling him over. Only the spear kept him upright. He grasped weakly at the blade, thinking somehow that removing it would stop the pain.

The captain looked at him incredulously. "Why don't you die?"

Tristain groaned as the captain pulled the sword out. Blood bloomed under his jacket. Fear bubbled in his stomach. His breath became sharper. Two others moved in to do the dirty work. Stabbing, cutting, hacking. His vision became hazy, narrowed.

He looked down, seeing himself from above, from the top of the tree. At the men taking turns to butcher his body. Thumping into his flesh, the sound of wet metal rang out, but it meant nothing to him now. He felt an overwhelming calm.

Then something took hold, wrenching him back into his body. Searing heat swelled through his feet, up and up through his legs, then his chest, and out through his head, as if he was standing on a pyre. Shooting pain went up his spine. Time slowed, drawing out the excruciating agony. His vision went white with pain.

His teeth were the first to change. They tore through his gums, growing and growing, until they were finger-long and distended his mouth. His jaw went slack, then broke, the pain causing him to drool. Between his eyes, nose and jaw shifted outwards, forming a broad snout. Through the pain, he saw his killers stare, stepping back in horror. Inside, he tried to think, tried to pray. *Gods! Please end this!*

No mercy would come. He was captive for every single excruciating moment. Thick black fur sprouted from every pore, like thousands of porcupine needles. His padded shirt ripped at its seams and his mail twisted as his chest ballooned. The speartip was pushed out as the skin wove itself back together. His head pounded as he looked up. It was like having his skull torn open. Claws as sharp as a wildcat's forced themselves from his fingernail beds.

His eyes adjusted, the pain subsiding at last. He could see in the darkness as if it were daytime. The smell of the captain's breakfast of ale and beef sausage drifted into his nose. The change took five seconds, yet it seemed like an eternity. He roared. The very air seemed to shudder.

"*Garou!*" The Badonnians scrambled away, yelling and shrieking in fear. Instinct took over. He saw his prey and grew hungry. A scream filled the air as he leaped for the captain.

3

SELENE

Selene was terrified to think of how loud her breath was. Desperately, she wanted to quiet herself, and so smothered at her mouth and lips. Deeper and deeper she shrunk, pushing, sinking herself into the darkest places of the wardrobe. Voices muffled through the wood, voices full of hate and anger. Selene's chest constricted painfully at the noise.

"Of course, he's yours," her mother guardian's shouts rippled through the door. They seemed to pace back and forth, their voices getting louder and quieter.

"You weren't pregnant when I left, wench," her father guardian roared, voice thick with irritation. "I was gone for the better part of a year, and I come home to find you've had a son!"

Tears worked their way out of Selene's eyes painfully as their voices went quiet again. Praying to the Gods, she wanted an end to it, for one of them to storm from the room, as their arguments usually went. But for all her praying, Selene was trapped.

Her mother's voice came around again. "...bringing this up every moon. Why don't you believe me?"

His vile threat sounded across the room. "I should've killed him in the crib."

"You know what—I'm glad he's nothing like you. Why would I ever want him to be like *you*? I *wish* he wasn't yours."

Selene heard nothing more. The weight of the silence pressed down on her more than all the suffocating blackness around her. She pressed her ear against the door, hoping to hear something, anything.

A piercing scream sent Selene reeling back against the wood. She threw her arm out, shoving herself from the wardrobe.

A great, hairy beast loomed over her mother guardian's limp body. Selene's breath left her though she wanted to scream, *No!* Strained eyes flicked over the monster and the violent scene before her, shivers running through her legs and arms and hands and neck, bowing her knees, and bringing her elbows in tight. At last, her voice found her, and she howled at the woman's twisted, unmoving face, fresh blood settling on her dress of silk.

The creature of mottled grey and misshapen man and wolf turned its icy gaze on Selene, fixing her to the floor, her muscles refusing to listen. Lowered to the floorboards, he stalked towards her, nasty and hideous. Bared, curved teeth brought to a savage point. Bright, silvered eyes of blue, like repulsive pools of acid. Deep, cruel snarls filled her ears. Selene flinched as the creature reached out slowly for her.

She ran. A sharp pain tore across her back, but she kept running. Out of the room, down the hall. She heard the tumbling of heavy feet behind her. Gasping for breath, she felt the creature just behind her, feeling inches away from horrible agony.

Bursting through the front door, she screamed for help. She felt something rough and strong close around her calf. She fell hard. Her temple and ear wracked with sharp pain as they slapped against the dirt of the yard. In a daze, she thought she heard people shouting. She rolled over with a groan. Claws dug into her arm. Agonizing, blinding pain ripped through her very core. She drove her head into the ground, trying to escape, trying to focus on anything but the searing throes of anguish she felt. Convulsing, she felt like even boiling water or a hot poker could not hurt this much. The edges of her vision frayed, darkening with hot excruciation. Then her world went dark.

Trying to clear the edges of her swimming vision, she blinked. She needed to look over herself, wrenching her head up. A silent, pained scream escaped from her mouth. She shook like a leaf. The big blacksmith Tomas lay on the ground, dead, while her father guardian's half-burned monstrous form lay sprawled out next to him. Only then did she notice the smell of burning flesh and singed hair. The beast wasn't moving, for now, but she had to pull herself away. Who knew if it would come back to life? She tried to pull herself away but felt a weight on her shoulder. And below that, nothing. With a clatter of iron, the still-hot half-made blade fell off her left arm as she pulled with her other arm and pushed with her feet.

Shouts and curses came from behind her, in front, all around. She felt it, an unstoppable wrenching and twisting hole digging deeper into her stomach. She blinked, in a blur already to the stables, her heart beating faster and faster. Her mind screamed to get on her horse. She tried to use her arms to pull herself up, but it wasn't working. The air was impossibly warm and stifling.

Using a small step, she flung herself, flopping headfirst onto her horse's unsaddled flanks, and her arm flailed behind loose and limp. Wild eyes and even wilder screams from the yard. *Oh Gods... I have to run! What if... what if there's more of them?* She strained, hooking one leg over and using her thighs to pull herself upright. The horse took off, knowing what its master wanted, and she closed her right fist around the creature's mane, fingers white, holding on for dear life.

The landscape moved in a blur around her. The horse followed a path only it knew for a time, only it kept track of. Heat rose in her chest as her vision blurred. The air grew stifling again. The world spun, and she was on her back. Pain hit her in waves. She lost feeling in her other fingers and her toes. Above her, an old man in a black robe leaned over, concern on his face. The man kneeled down, long grey hairs falling over his face. *Old... old man of Sigur...* She was delirious. *As the Gods left this world, so too do I...*

She woke several times in a daze, feeling herself being carried, the sound of hooves and wooden wheels grinding dirt. She heard voices talking over her as she lay. Agonizing pain bit into her spine, shooting through her bones. Blissfully, darkness visited her once again.

AS THE ORANGE SUN streamed through a window above, Selene blinked her eyes open. Her vision swam. She moved her eyes with purpose, as though she had to get used to the movement again. A man in a grey robe with a blood-spattered leather apron looked back at her. The room had walls of stone and was chilly, despite the sunlight. She went to sit up, but only one arm did the job and so she fell on her left side. She gasped.

No... Gods be good... She reached over with her other arm and felt only a bandaged stump. Eyes widened in denial. She screamed, again and again, wishing it weren't true. Writhing in panic, loss, mournful sorrow, she felt two hands grip her tightly. The man in grey restrained her. He called for help.

She was inconsolable, tears and screams coming unbidden. It took two grown men to hold her fast to the bed. She kept screaming until her voice went hoarse and choked. Someone forced a white liquid into her mouth. Exhaustion settled over her, and sleep came quickly after.

SELENE HAD FALLEN FROM her horse, she was told. Her left arm was barely attached and had to be amputated. The robed man with the long hair was not an old priest, but a warrior of Sigur, a Golden Sword named Sorenius. He had taken her to a nearby church to be treated, where the doctor was also the priest, Radimir. She blushed as Sorenius came to her in her sickly state. One arm and no good for it. He was beautiful, and she was sure she looked horrible. She certainly felt it.

He had airs of authority, standing straight-backed, with a firm chin and muscular neck. His grey eyes were the only thing dull about him, if that could even be said. Streaks of silver marred his lustrous dark hair tied down the back, with shaved sides. It was an odd style, evocative of a woman's rather than a man's. Still, it did him much favor to attract attention to his sharp, rising cheekbones, a mix of fresh and old scars on them. He wore black; a boiled leather jerkin and black trousers paired with black boots.

"Good to see you're awake," he said quietly. "I was afraid the priest was too generous with the poppy milk."

Selene's throat was hoarse when she spoke. All the screaming, she supposed. "Perhaps he should've been... I might've slept forever."

He sat at the end of her bed. "You know why I saved you? You would've died, the corruption ran so deep."

"Corruption?"

"The wound was infected, that was plain. The priest had to take it up to the shoulder to cut away all the corrupted flesh. That happens when demons attack: corruption takes hold. If you're lucky enough to survive. The strangest thing, though, it was cauterized. I think that was what saved you from bleeding out, allowed you to make it as far as you did on horseback, delirious as you were. My question stands, though. Do you know why I took you to this place?"

"No."

"I saw your strength in your white knuckles clinging to the horse's mane as you fell. The determination in your grazed elbows and skinned knees. The courage in your actions. There is no question that hard steel lies in your heart. The willingness to do what others cannot."

She snorted. He couldn't be serious. She laughed at his stoic look. Clearly, he didn't think it was a joke. "You're not serious! You may as well have left me. What good am I?"

"Everyone has something to offer the world. There is value in all life. It is as Sigur says, 'Each man to their own place'."

Selene took issue. "What about murderers? Thieves?"

"These are but wayward souls, driven to sin by the evil that lies at the root of the world. We can save them, with just punishment."

She sniffed. *Trite answer. But what about...* "Wukodlaks? What value is there in horrible monsters?"

His face darkened. "There is value in their lives."

"How?"

"You wish to bait me? Make me speak something that is not true?" His cold eyes fixed on her. She kept his gaze. She would not cower. He sighed, his face relaxing. "Each one dead brings us closer to the return of the Gods. It was the Great Devil's sin that drove the rift between our world and the Gods. Undoing that sin will heal the rift."

Selene nodded quietly. She didn't know if his words were to be believed, but he certainly seemed to believe them. There was something comforting about them, the certainty with which he spoke. If life was riddled with doubts and fears, this Sorenius had learned how to overcome them.

"Now," he said, getting up. "Time for supper, I think."

THE NEXT WEEK, SORENIUS had gone out, recruiting as he did. Selene was bent low, sweeping the floor with a short-handled broom. It was hard with one arm, exhausting to use the same hand to sweep, keep her hair from falling into her face *and* open the door to sweep the dust outside.

Gods forbid, the wind would blow it back inside. But she was recovering, getting around on her feet now, so she was at least glad for that.

As she swept, she looked upon the various golden figures purposefully placed around the church. Mounted opposite the main doors was a cruciform sword, plated with gold, pointing to the sky. Prongs of brass wreathed its base, symbolizing light piercing darkness. In a small alcove to the side was the icon of a woman engulfed in flame—a messenger of the Gods burned at the stake by non-believers. On a plinth by the altar was a golden lantern that would remain unlit until Sigur's return to the world.

The church of Sigur was a haven for believers, all believers of His word. A safe place for kings, peasants, merchants, vagabonds, outlaws all—as long as they believed. Each one of them served Him in their own way, as Sorenius said.

Folk arrived from the local village for midday prayers. She hid. No one should've seen her like this. She recognized the headman and his family, as well as the smith, the butcher, the baker, and even the shepherd with his stinking sheepskin garments. Her disappearance and the attack at the house would set tongues wagging. It was only a matter of time before people found out.

The priest led them in Gebet, in prayer. His sermons echoed off the stone walls, the vaulted ceiling, in High Istryan, the language of their forebears.

"Sigur harden our hearts against the unwilling, the coward, the selfish, those who pursue self-interest and power above all. I say in the name of the martyrs and the Conqueror, the blood, and the spirit. Father be with us."

As he finished, the congregation sang. Selene's mood lifted as the sweet, somber tones entered her ears. They sang of the strength of Diana, of Orphea, of Martea. Hallowed women that gave their lives for Sigur.

After an hour or so—Selene lost track of time—they finished. She hummed along to the tune. *Mm-m. Mmm. Mm-m. Mm. Mm-m. Orphea found her strength that day...* The congregation filed out the door as the priest caught her eye. He came over to her hiding place and smiled, telling her that Sorenius would soon return. She smiled and nodded, but wondered why he thought it was her business.

She went to her room, unsure what to do now she'd finished her chores. The chores were her condition: not that the priest had asked for payment in swept floors, but they were her own condition, a repayment for all he'd done for her. It was hard work, though, and she was glad it was now over with.

She sat on the bed. Her room was small. There was no gilding on the walls, not like her bedroom at home. No eye-waveringly complex patterns in plaster. No private privies here—she shared hers with the priest and Sorenius. Only a bed big enough for one, and a sturdy, functional dresser in the corner, behind the door.

A glint of something there caught her eye. She groaned as she got to her feet, feeling more exhausted than she had before she sat down. She pulled back the door. It was a dull silver plate, fallen off the counter. Clicking her tongue, she imagined how long it had been sitting there, without a soul to see it. She lifted the plate, and caught herself in the reflection.

Nothing but a stump for a shoulder. She screwed up her face. She had hoped it had been a terrible dream, but now that she saw it for herself... tears couldn't but fall. She sobbed quietly. *Why didn't I have the courage? I should've... I should've fought back. Grabbed the letter knife he kept on his desk instead of hiding like a coward. Maybe Mama would still be alive.*

Her ears pricked up as she overheard a conversation through the door. She wiped her eyes. "The girl is young and spirited. She seems to be recovering well," Radimir's voice came muffled through the thick wood.

"Good," Sorenius replied. "Her guardian is dead. I examined the corpse myself. The blacksmith killed him with a blade he was beating into shape, fortunate that it was still hot, igniting the demon's fur. Unfortunate though that before the demon died, it cut the blacksmith's belly open. And Sigur be true, when the blade fell on her arm, it must've done what you said, sealing the wound closed."

"Hm. What will you do with her, Inquisitor?" *Inquisitor?* She knew the stories. The name spoke to their purpose. They searched out evil. And the man that had raised her... she bit her lip. Had he really died back there, in the yard? It must've been true. Maybe... maybe she could go home. *No. There's nothing for me back there. Only her stiff body in that horrible, angry place. Tristain is in Badonnia. Perhaps I could go there. But would I even make it? And... I'd have to tell him that his father was a monster, who had slain his mother...*

A long pause drew out before Sorenius replied, "Test her. She may prove herself in time."

THE NEXT DAY, SORENIUS came to her as she milked the goats in the little paddock behind the church. He held a broom in his hand. Wind whistled through the valley, rustling the maples nearby. The goats were used to being milked. It took a bit to get the hang of it, hampered as she was. Eventually, though, she found an extra hand was superfluous. Maybe to stop them fussing, but once they were settled, they let her take as much milk from them as she needed.

"Don't tell him I told you," Sorenius greeted, waving the end of the broom around. "But Father Radimir feels guilty about letting you do things around here."

She kept milking. The farmer's wives told her how to do it—Greta, she thought her name was. *Gods, that was years ago.* She smiled as she remembered. *Mother took me to see them—she would never let me forget we depend on their work for our livelihood.* "It is as I told him. I won't let myself become a burden. I want to earn my place here."

He crossed his arms. "And your place in the world?"

She stopped, giving him a confused look. "You speak very cryptically sometimes."

A smile flashed across his lips. Her cheeks flushed. "Hazard of my profession. What I mean to say is, what do you want from life?"

"I still don't understand."

"I mean what I say. What do you *want*?" She didn't answer right away. She wasn't really sure. Marriage, family, children; all things were destined for her, her father and mother made that clear, but now? *Sorenius is right... What do I want?*

"I suppose I don't know," she said.

He seemed pleased with the answer, nodding. "Come with me."

"But the goats—"

"They'll live."

They went to the foot of a maple tree where leaves were yellowing at the ends. Autumn was coming soon, it seemed. He handed her the broom.

"What's this for?"

"I want you to strike me," he replied, stone-faced as ever.

"Strike you?" *Attack a goddamn inquisitor! What's he thinking?*

"Do it."

Selene hesitated, holding the balance awkwardly with one hand. She had never held a weapon beyond a beltknife to slaughter chickens, and the servants mostly performed that unpleasant task back home. She braced the broom against her side, and lunged forward with the end. Sorenius flashed a devilish grin. He easily stepped aside, catching the end of the broom with his hand. He yanked, pulling her off-balance. A trip and a fall later, she was face down in the dirt.

She groaned, rolling onto her back. "Was that fun for you?"

Sorenius helped her to her feet. "Come now, it's just a bit of dirt."

She brushed the dust off her robe. "So, how was my test?"

Sorenius tilted his head slightly. "Oh, you were listening?" He smiled. "Yes, well. You could be faster, but bracing your weapon was very smart. Adapt your weapon to balance your strengths and weaknesses."

"Did me a whole lot of good."

He handed the broom back to her. "Again."

They sparred for a while.

"Again! Faster! Move your feet! Not like that! You'll trip like that. Shift your weight! Pivot on light feet!"

She ended up on the ground time and time again. It was exhausting, and sweaty, and dirty. Her face was caked in dirt by the time they finished. She wondered how many different ways he could flip her onto her back, then dropped that line of thinking before it went too far.

Selene panted, leaning on the broom handle for support. Her sides, her back, everything hurt. It was probably the most physically grueling thing she'd done for years. A top ten for her whole life.

She groaned in frustration. "There's no way. You're too quick. And I'm too useless."

"Yes," he replied, smugness dripping from his words. She could punch him in the face. If she could bloody touch him. "You keep saying that, but you keep getting back up."

"Piss off."

"Sigur says, 'The strong must defend the weak and the innocent.' You are the furthest thing from weak—"

"And the furthest thing from innocent?"

He smiled wryly. "Let me finish. You're *strong*, in spirit, in heart, where it really counts."

"Truly?" she asked, laughing. Sorenius didn't laugh. "Then why can't I do what matters? What use am I with... *this*?"

"You ask yourself. Ask yourself what you truly want."

What I truly want? A betrothal to a knight... a life of having children... a life sequestered away in some bleak place in some backcountry... like Mother...

She pictured the horrible teeth of her guardian father's closing around her head, tearing it free from her shoulders. She thought of Tristain's mother—the woman who raised her—and Tomas the blacksmith, and wondered how many mothers and blacksmiths and other folk the demons snuffed out every day. Her knuckles went white as she clenched her fist around the broom handle. *What chance do I have though? They're monsters, butchers, capable of horrible things. And what am I? Stupid. Nothing. I know nothing of killing.*

No. This man could show her.

"I want to kill demons," she said with finality. "Tell me how."

4

PRAYER

WHEN THE SHADOWS OF afternoon were long and dark and the clouds swelled with the threat of rain, the Grey Citadel erupted in front of Selene, grasped by the southernmost end of a jut of stone and sand, surrounded on three sides by the sea. The stronghold was the centuries-old home of the Order of the Golden Sword in Osbergia, encircled from the north by the capital, Ostelar. At the cliff's base, the water had worn its way into the rock, forming a sheltered cove visible from their approach to the city from the east.

Ostelar and the Citadel were two months from Invereid, and Selene had spent most of that time fairly quiet. The road was tough, but bearable. Sorenius had been enjoyable company—silent and sullen as he always was. They'd trained on the road. Her missing arm had given her no trouble, and no infection had come back. The priest Radimir did his work well.

Sorenius hitched their horse at the citadel stables, and they made the ascent to the top of the hill. It was hard going. The ground sloped upwards, with outbuildings from the bottom to the inner gates at the top, where the Citadel itself sat. The trapezoidal Citadel keep in bleak, grey stone dominated the landscape. Manned with hundreds of guards, the curtain walls were well-maintained, with bolt-loops and murder holes staring ominously like eyes back at her.

As they walked up the hill, she noted two types of people: black-leather-clads, wearing severe looks and blades at their belts; and demure grey-, black-, or white-robes going about their duties. The black-clad fighters trained in the open square at the bottom of the hill. Sorenius told her of them: arbiters fought unusually, their fighting style fit for taking down large beasts than fighting men. One came crashing down near them, having leapt from a high place. She heard the instructors barking orders; "Left! Up! Hold! Dive! Leap! Half-turn! Pirouette!" It was all very confusing, but Sorenius said that was the point. Arbiters worked in pairs or trios—after quick and unpredictable moves distracted the beast, the real threat would dive in from a suitable height, latching onto the creature's back, plunging a blade into the relatively thin-skinned neck. They practiced by using each other as springboards, launching onto targets of her height and once more.

"Their fur is a sort-of-armor, you see," he said. "Steel can hardly get through, and only properly through the neck. But coat your blade or arrow in poison? Even a slight prick will kill them."

Concocting venoms and poisons were what the grey-robed notaries did, and abundantly. The stench of strong chemicals fashioned by alchemists and apothecaries filled the air, spells and prayers chanted over them to double their effectiveness. A basket *hissed* at her as she passed, and she flinched.

"They milk the adders inside for their deadly venom," Sorenius told.

Once at the top of the hill, she turned. It took her breath away. Though the sky was grey, she could see the entire city. Split by the Alba and Tibor rivers, the city straddled the narrow strip of land down the middle, while in the center, the immense Osterline Hill conquered her eye, a full mile in diameter, the grand duke's ancient White Palace on top. The Inner Ring surrounded the hill, cradling the Noble and Merchant districts, and the Upper Market. Beyond that was the Outer Ring, containing Lower Market and the Slums, which bled west into the port, and the harbor beyond that, to the bay. Beyond the walls and the rivers on either side, were shantytowns known as the Outskirts. After that, the flat wetlands of the Alba and Tiber river valleys for miles around, and the small trading town of Dver north of that.

She felt the inquisitor's hand gently pull her beyond the curtain wall and into the bailey.

"Come with me," a woman said once inside, donned in bone-white cloak and stern face.

Sorenius bade her farewell. "You must do this alone," he said. "The rector will tell you where you need to go."

Selene followed her through giant iron doors into the ground floor of the citadel. Striding along the tiled floor, Selene's eye drew upwards to the vast, arched ceiling and complex patterns in mosaic and gold snaking across the lime-washed dome, telling the history of the world and Sigur's eternal struggle against the Great Devil. She realized the citadel's exterior belied its true purpose. Truthfully, it was a cathedral. The altar ahead of her held a large golden statue in a forceful pose, Sigur himself, the God of Light, Death, Strength, and Justice. Priests, both men and women, carted around books, prayed at the altar or icons of martyrs, or simply chatted.

Further inside, dense smoke from incense sticks enveloped Selene, and she hurried along before she lost the woman in the haze. The low light inside didn't help matters, but Selene found her way eventually.

The woman turned before reaching a stairwell. "You'll need this," she said, handing her a set of black robes procured from a nearby stand. "There will be a room for convalescence and quiet to your left when you reach the bottom of the steps. Take your clothes off and leave them there. Change into these robes and proceed down the hall when you are ready."

Selene nodded and descended the steps. The stone spiral was narrow, so she had to watch her step. Now underground, the only light came from candelabras mounted to the wall. They dripped with years of melted wax, mounds of pale stalactites from silver cradles. The candles flickered in the darkness, casting orange light on the stone walls.

Ahead of her extended rows of closed doors on either side. She looked to her left and found the door in question. She pushed it open. A young woman in the same dark robes Selene held kneeled down by an icon on the wall, her palms flat on her knees. The icon portrayed Sigur brandishing a golden sword banishing the darkness, similar enough to the rest of them. After shutting the door softly, Selene placed her robes on the floor, undressing. It was a little strange, having someone in the room as she stripped, but the girl seemed to pay very little mind, not turning from the icon for a single moment. *She probably didn't even hear me come in.*

Selene swept her black hair behind her ears as she unbuckled her vest. She went down to a sackcloth shirt and breeches, a gift from Radimir after having left home without clothing or much of anything. She threw the robes over the top. Taking a deep breath, she steeled herself for what was coming, or rather, what she wasn't sure was coming.

"Are you going to ask the Father for His help?" the girl's soft voice came as Selene touched the doorpull. Selene turned, cocking her head as the girl stared. She was about the same age as Selene, with cropped red hair that sat just below her ears, framing pointed ruddy eyebrows and a sharp chin. Her eyes seemed odd, like they didn't match. "I am told the training is brutal. I'm praying to Sigur for His help. Pray with me."

"Alright," Selene replied, not knowing where she might start. She barely attended the Gebet, and never knew the prayers by heart. In fact, she was never very religious at all. She wished Radimir had taught her at least a few, or she'd at least had an ear peeled when he held the services. *What have I found myself in?* she wondered.

She kneeled next to the red-headed girl and closed her eyes. The woman softly spoke, "Mighty Father, your humble servants beseech You. Give us the strength to overcome the trials that wait for the power is Your Name. One day, we shall return what is owed, freeing this world from evil's grasp."

"So, it shall be." Selene recalled how the prayers were supposed to end, at least.

The girl opened her eyes and smiled at Selene. She *did* have mismatched eyes, one half-grey, half-blue, while the other was all blue. A wicked, curved scar ran across her cheek, running from shortly below her mismatched eye across to her ear. Selene tried not to stare.

"I'm Leona. From the Fork."

"Selene," she replied. "Invereid."

"Nice to meet you, Selene from Invereid. You don't know the prayers, do you? 'So, it shall be' is out of date. Now, it is said, 'so, in light'." *Dammit. I knew I should've paid attention when Radimir had Gebet those months ago.*

Selene chuckled, playing with her hair. "No, I... I don't know them."

Leona chuckled too. "That's alright, I'll teach you soon enough." Selene's stomach grumbled loudly. Leona laughed as Selene blushed. "It's alright. I think they'll serve supper soon."

They got up, and Selene felt a little better. Maybe the prayers had something to them, after all.

Leona told her where they were going, a training gallery at the end of the entrance hall at the bottom of the stairs, passing the closed doors. As they approached, steel rang out and the clanging of shields and the twanging of bowstrings. The hall opened up, and before her stood many in black robes, recruits like her. They were of all ages, both men and women, though the oldest was probably just shy of middle age. They practiced with knives, swords, crossbows, shields; at slow, controlled paces. Columns dotted the room, one every ten paces, ringed with burning candles in silver cradles, while grates in the ceiling above let sunlight in. She wondered how the geography worked. They must've been below the courtyard above, outside of the keep.

The woman in the white robes announced for them all to gather at the entrance. To Selene's right was a young, scrawny, dark-skinned man, while Leona had her left. The dark-skinned man was probably from Vallonia, a kingdom on the southern tip of the continent, below the Three Republics.

"Before we start," the woman declared, "let us give thanks to the God of Light for our lives, our health, and our strength. Let Him penetrate the darkness, and may Godsreturn speed our salvation."

"So, in light," they all replied. Leona glanced at Selene and smiled.

"Good. I am the Rector Palia. For those of you who are new: in the halls of this hallowed ground, I am second only to Sigur himself. I will tell you this only once, so listen well. When you address me, call me Rector, or Teacher. If you address me by chosen name, it will not end well for you. Understand?"

The novices murmured their agreement. The rector stiffened, saying, "Yes, Rector."

"Yes, Rector," they repeated.

"Good. Now, those of you who are new will each be assigned an instructor in groups of six. This instructor will assess your abilities and determine how best to train you."

"Yes, Rector."

"Yes, Rector," Selene said, finding herself a bit out of step. Maybe it was the long ride, those long months of sitting in a saddle from dawn till dusk. The dark-skinned man glanced at her, screwing up his brows. Selene arched an eyebrow. *What's his problem?*

They broke up into groups, and Selene found herself with the dark-skinned Vallonian man; a tall, broad-faced man with a barrel-chest and square limbs; a soldier-type who looked like he could wrestle a bear; another soldier-type that was leaner but still quite strong-looking, and an olive-skinned man with a bushy black beard. She compared the two, and the lanky one was definitely darker. Maybe he was from further south, from across the ocean in Saburria.

"They'll make you shave that off 'fore too long," the broad-faced one said. The olive-skinned black-beard shrugged in response. Selene wondered if the two soldier-types had training—military of some sort. Perhaps they knew how the campaign in Badonnia fared. Tristain was yet gone only a few months, but news was hard to come by.

They stood at the end of the hall, in one of the back corners. Around them sat training targets made of wood and stuffed clothing, made to look like men. They were mounted on tallow-slick slides that Selene tested a little out of curiosity. With each hit, it seemed they would rotate so that the trainee would have to be prepared for a counterattack.

Their setup was a common theme across the gallery: each group was given their own training area with their own targets. Though for safety's sake, Selene supposed, all the archery targets were at one end, placed along the wall.

Their trainer walked up to them. Selene grinned. He met her gaze briefly. *So much for doing it on my own.*

"I am Instructor Sorenius," he said. "I understand that I am to take over from your old instructor. I will dispense with the formalities and get down to it. I do not care what you were before you arrived here. When you descended those steps, you broke all ties with those above, their caprices, and their wickedness. The Order of the Golden Sword is all that you will know. For those of you that are new, we are your family now." She'd heard it from him before, but Selene couldn't think of anything better.

"You, raven-hair." He pointed. Selene stiffened. "Step forward." He fetched a knife and handed it to her, taking a length of chain for himself, winding it around his forearm. "Attack me."

Selene knew this one. She lunged forward. The man easily stepped aside, catching her outstretched arm with the chain, winding around, and biting in. She yelped, not expecting it. He yanked, tearing the knife from her grasp.

She groaned, feeling the muscles ache underneath. The instructor sighed as he unwound the chain. It was painful, but she swore to herself she would not cry.

"Again," he said, this time handing her a spear, taking a sword for himself. She rubbed her arm. *What's he doing?* "Perhaps you are more comfortable with range?"

She stood off with him, out of range of his sword, she hoped. Her spear was long, and she cradled the shaft under her arm, as she practiced. The wood was polished, cool to the touch. She swept it from side to side, keeping him at bay. He sprang forward, faster than she could blink. He easily swept past her guard. She had no chance. She frantically tried to block, but he swept the spear aside with one hand. Holding the point of his blade to her neck, his eyes flashed with disappointment. The look said, *have you learned nothing?* She wilted, letting the spear fall to the ground. The dark-skinned Saburrian let out a chuckle and the trainer flashed with fury at him. He quickly shut up.

"Taking it out on the novices, Instructor," the rector said. "I see. On the heels of a successful hunt, too. Mayhap you're still agitated?" *A successful hunt?* She could only recall one night when he'd disappeared, returning in the morning. *Had it been then?*

"Assessing her skills, Rector, in fact." Sorenius spoke matter-of-factly. "Of which she has none."

Selene sighed deeply, chewing her lip. She felt tears bud in the corners of her eyes.

"Inquisitor, you are here to train them, not to break them down. If I wanted that done, I would let the torturers have them."

The man looked determined to respond, but simply nodded. "Very well, Rector. You four. Pair off, sword and shield each. I gather you have some training, brown-hair?" The thick-limbed one nodded. "Good, take them through drills of blows and blocking. Remember, keep moving. A stationary Sword is a dead Sword. And you two." He pointed to Selene and the other soldier-type. "Start with throwing knives. Go to the targets and tell the keeper there that your instructor has sent you."

The targets were a long row of densely packed haystacks with an abundance of crossbows, short-limbed training bows and long war-bows. There was a crate full of knives as well, which Selene took a handful of, gingerly, making sure not to cut herself. They were all shapes and sizes, but had the same general form of small finger-long handles, and razor-sharp two-sided blades. They were for throwing rather than close fighting.

The soldier-type went first, missing wildly, his clumsy fingers fumbling with the small handled knives. Selene went next, landing hers.

"Nice shot," he said. Selene smiled, feeling slightly better about that dressing-down from before. She put the aloof, arrogant inquisitor from her mind.

She took a second, then lined up another shot. It landed with a soft thump very near to the center.

The soldier-type whistled in admiration. "You're good. I'm Ruprecht, by the way."

"Selene," she replied, tucking a bit of stray hair behind her ear. Ruprecht was kind-faced, with short-cropped brown hair drawn to a widow's peak above his eyebrows.

"Not like that," the inquisitor told as he walked up. Selene wilted. "You think that in the heat of combat, someone is just going to wait for you to hit them with a knife, while you line up your throw?" She shook her head. "That's right. Toss them as fast as you can. At least one of them is bound to hit. Aim for here." He pointed to his chest, drawing a box around his torso.

I'd aim for there, with a crossbow, she thought angrily.

"Like this." He flicked his wrist, without turning head, three times in quick succession. All three knives landed square in the center. Selene stared, not knowing if she would ever become that skilled.

Sorenius nodded and left. Infuriated by his cold regard, she huffed and turned away. Ruprecht tried again, missing again. Two recruits next to them chuckled, and he grew frustrated. "Maybe I should just do something else," he said. "I'm no good."

Selene sighed, before trying the trick she saw the instructor do. She threw the knife forward, underarm, spinning it counterclockwise. *Thump.* She blinked in surprise. It wasn't dead on, but it was close enough.

Ruprecht laughed softly. "That prick's got nothing on you!" She turned as the other novices approached.

Leona was grinning. "Supper," she said.

THEY SAT AT LONG tables in the dining hall, in the annex, outside the keep but still inside the curtain wall. It was late afternoon now, and orange sunlight filtered through the lead-light windows. Selene gorged herself on the delicious soup and crusty rolls on offer. The journey to the citadel had been long, and Sorenius was loath to stop unless they had to. They had often ridden all day. There'd been little choice as she rode with him on the front of the saddle. She had laughed when he brought it up, believing passers by would think they were lovers on a ride. Those concerns had soon vanished as he suggested she could walk instead if she wanted to. His warm manner and his frosty regard switched places often. She could never figure out his moods.

Selene stopped raising her spoon to her mouth. The others watched with mild bemusement.

"You know we have to wait for the rector, right?" Leona whispered. Selene looked up. No one else was eating. She put her spoon down gingerly, wiping her mouth. The rector strode into the room. The woman eyed Selene carefully, then announced the start of pre-supper prayers.

"Join me, please," she said, closing her eyes and tilting her head down. They all did the same. Their voices in unison, they prayed to Sigur for the food in front of them, and for strength in their coming trials.

"So, in light," they finished.

"Now, you can eat," Leona whispered. Selene didn't wait. She dived into the soup again, a pleasant blend of potato and leeks. She bit a piece off the heel of bread. It was all very unladylike, she was sure, but damn it, she hadn't eaten for nearly two days. She was in the middle of a bite when Ruprecht asked her where she came from.

"You heard the inquisitor," Leona said. "We have to forget our past when we come here."

"Oh, come on," he replied. "We have to get to know each other, at least."

Selene coughed, indigestion rising in her chest. "I'm from Invereid."

Ebberich grinned. "Me too. Small bloody world, isn't it? What's your favorite thing about the city? Mine's the river."

Selene nodded. She liked the river, and on the rare occasions she would ever leave the estate, it was to visit Invereid. Not that she could ever see the river up close, out of her sedan—no, there was never enough time between parlor visits and dress fittings. Her guardian father would never allow her to see the city on her terms, and her governess followed this order to the letter. He would never babysit her, of course, it was always the governess. A small part of her was sad that she'd never see her friends again—the mayor's two daughters and the nice tailor's assistant.

"You don't talk much, do you?" said Ruprecht, bringing his spoon up to his mouth and giving it a blow.

"She's probably a bit slow," Salim said. Osbergian was clearly his second language, though he had no trouble with fluency and wordplay.

"Don't be a prick, Salim. It's her first day—she's probably still fresh from the road."

Raul slurped his soup loudly, the brown liquid filtering through his beard. "You'd never hear that from a Vallonian," he said in his strong accent. They turned their heads.

"What's that?" Ebberich replied.

"Nothing," he replied, getting up from the table. He left a half-eaten bowl, walking out of the dining hall.

"Speaking of someone who doesn't say much…"

Supper finished as Solni dipped below the horizon. The twin Gods in the sky did their dance, and now it was Luni's turn. She came out, her bright form for all to see. It was time for Vespers, when novitiates would go to places of quiet reflection and pray. After that, it was bed.

Leona took Selene to a small chapel attached to the annex. The chapel held a few kneeling posts, and there were some black-robed novices there already. The icon hung over the altar was a shimmering form of a sword piercing dark clouds above, held aloft by a woman, Sofiya, the famed martyr and defender of the Godcity against the Great Devil's armies. Her voluminous, golden hair billowed in the wind and her eyes flashed with lustrous fury.

Leona bowed her head as she entered the chapel. Selene did the same, following her lead. She led them in prayers, and they went off to bed.

T HE DINING HALL BUZZED with excitement. Novitiates talked excitedly, turning their heads to the entrance each time someone walked in, as they did to Selene. She felt embarrassed, as if she'd done something to deserve their looks, but they looked away just as quickly.

"What's going on?   " Selene asked as she joined the group at the table. Leona smiled as she sat down.

Ruprecht tore at the heel of bread with great effort, like an animal. "They're-mm... each week-mmh, novitiates who are near their rites have a skirmish. It's called *Velitore.* That's what everyone's worked up about. By Sigur, this has to be more stale than usual."

"Yeah," Ebberich said. "It's about the only exciting thing that happens around here. It's a bit of fun, and everyone gets into it. They fight a wukodlak. If they live, they get to be confirmed."

"*What?*" Selene's jaw gaped. "They—We have to fight a wukodlak?"

"Uh... yeah? That's what Swords do. Why do you seem surprised?"

"I just..."

"How long have you two been here for?" Leona said, rubbing her chin.

"About six weeks," Ruprecht said.

"Three and a bit," Ebberich said. "Yeah, both of us haven't been here that long."

"Alright, novitiates," the rector said from the entrance. Everyone turned their heads, and the room went deathly silent. "Come with me."

She led them to the entrance hall underground, and further down, through one of the locked doors. The corridor was packed, a snaking line of black robes jostling for position, to be the first through the doors. They went through yet another set of doors and the line fanned out. Selene found herself looking upon a, well... arena, it was as simple as that. A pit of sand, about thirty strides wide, lay in the center, forty feet below them. A wide, heavy iron door sat at the back of the pit, driven by a set of pulleys and chains that disappeared into loops set in the stone wall. A short railing encircled the pit, itself flanked by cascading tiers of stone benches. A set of stairs proceeded down to a sturdy iron gate, access to the pit. The gate was shut tight.

Orange light from a large brazier hung from the ceiling flooded the stands, and the pit below, while daylight from a grate in the ground above shone through. The air smelled slightly of sweat and blood.

Selene took a seat next to the others as the stream of black robes contin-ued. Eventually, everyone was inside, and the grate above was snapped shut, creating a red and moody ambiance. A black-haired man in extravagant white and red robes walked to the edge of the pit. The novitiates clapped their hands and cheered. He threw his hands into the air in a welcoming gesture. Cheers and shouts died down, as did the chatter.

"That's Lord Inquisitor Rotersand," Ebberich whispered, seeing the look on Selene's face. "And that's where the fighters'll come out." He pointed to the iron gate at the bottom of the stairs. "And there..." He pointed to the huge iron door. "That's where the beast'll come through."

"Please," the lord inquisitor announced. "Please, be seated. I appreciate your enthusiasm, and there is much to be enthusiastic about. But first, let us bow our heads and give our thanks to the Lord Sigur." They prayed, asking for strength in the great trials to come. "We have a special gift for you, today. This won't be our usual *Velitore*. Our inquisitor in the ascendant, Sorenius, delivered not one, but two of our mortal enemies upon our doorstep. Bring them forward!" *Delivered?* Sorenius hunted not one, but *two* wukodlaks when he'd been with her?

Grinding gears and chains signalled the door open. Selene had no time to think about it. A team of men in grey cloaks filed out, pulling something behind them. Behind the heavy iron door, a wooden platform appeared. Selene gasped, joined by many others. Gasps and screams of terror, laced with excitement.

Two enormous man-wolves, one a dark brown, the other a russet red colour, were wheeled out. Men in dark robes pulled the platform to the centre. Thick steel chains around the wukodlaks' thick necks bound them to the mobile platform. They had brawny limbs, chests that were slabs of muscle, wolf-like faces, and wild eyes and broad snouts that curled steamy breath. Deadly sharp teeth jutted from their mouths. Their snarling faces turned Selene pale. A menacing intent stood behind their bright red pupils. They would tear apart every person in the room given the chance. Her breath was short and sharp. She felt pains in her chest. Bile burned the back of her throat. *Gods... I'd almost forgotten what a thing it was...* Leona placed her hand on her leg. Selene turned, tearing her eyes away from the demons. *It'll be okay,* said the look Leona gave her. Somehow, she thought it would.

The lord inquisitor cleared his throat, calling for silence. The arena went quiet, until the only sound was the soft growling of the two man-demons at the center. "But this is not all," he said. "We have a hypocrite for you. A baron, who passes judgments of the law, and yet steals from the people, and debauches himself with wenches!" The crowd hissed and booed. The baron was dragged out, swearing and shrieking at the sight of the two monstrous creatures in the center. His disheveled outfit would have been nice, once, but now it was ripped and torn. Chains strained and rattled as the creatures smelled the man's fear. They yearned to be freed. And then the chains snapped, sending the guards scrambling. The iron door clattered shut just as they made it inside. The wukodlaks seemed like they didn't quite know what to do, but it wasn't long until their gazes turned to the baron. They licked their chops.

The man screamed, trying desperately to scramble up the smooth walls of the pit. Raul jumped up, watching with a grin on his face. And he wasn't alone. Though most of the crowd watched with a mixture of curiosity and horror, there were more than a few who became giddy at the events unfolding in front of them.

The baron's face was a cocktail of fear and outrage. It twisted into a terrified grimace as he realized his fate. His fingernails scraped, bloodied and broken, against the cut-stone. It was a waste. The walls had been ground smooth. There were no handholds there, or anywhere.

The demons leapt on him, eyes wild with hunger. The tan one wrapped his giant hands around the magistrate's head. The russet one latched onto his legs. They tore at him like dogs, shaking his body violently. Selene had to turn away. His sharp, wet screams sent shivers up her spine.

The tan one took to his now beheaded and bloodied torso, digging around. The russet one challenged the other one with a growl, seemingly appalled that it didn't get a look in to the carcass. The tan one responded by taking the baron's body to the other end of the pit. The russet stood on its hind legs, arching up until it was its full height, over seven feet. It charged, claws forward. The tan was skewered. It let out a clipped roar as the russet lifted it into the air. Cheers erupted from the crowd, watching with excitement as the devils tore each other apart. Selene held her hand over her mouth in horror.

A man in white signaled for the fight to come to an end. A ring of arbiters took up position at the top of the pit, shooting crossbow bolts into the creatures. They both fell, hitting the sand with a thump. The fight was over—the baron's lay in a scattered, bloody mush, while the creatures had collapsed in two huge, furry heaps.

Selene's thoughts were a blur, racing as she walked to her evening prayers. She didn't realize until long after that a drop of blood had landed on her cheek.

5

BETRAYAL

LEON HEAVED, PUSHING THE mass of bodies off his frame. Sweaty, hot air filled his lungs and throat. His shoulders strained at the weight – there could've been dozens on top of him for all he knew. The world was dark. A pauldron shifted, sending a gush of water into his face. He spluttered, groaning. At last, he pulled his face free, and threw his visor up, taking a cool, fresh breath for the first time in minutes. The first rays of dawn fell on his face. *At least it's stopped raining.*

He looked around. Carnage unfolded in front of him. Not anything he wasn't used to. He'd seen a man stretched and quartered by horses; heads on spikes along a palisade; faces contorted into more expressions than a skilled actor. One thing was new, though. Never before had he seen so many limbs unattached, so many bodies unrecognizable as human. He pushed it out of his mind.

He unclasped his dented helmet, feeling blood run down his cheek. A Badonnian had smacked him in the head with a hammer, he remembered now. He dragged himself free and checked for injuries. His back ached, his head pounded, and he was pretty sure he had a dislocated wrist. Sigur, he needed a drink. He reached for his flask, but it was gone. He frowned. Plate-covered boots thumping on the muddy ground, he checked each of his company for signs of life. Both Triburg brothers lay in bloody heaps, a spear sticking from one, open stomach on the other. Both had shit themselves. That was something Leon noticed; no matter where you were from, no matter what kind of life you lived – all men smelled the same when they died. He found a flask still attached to their belt, and uncorked the cap.

"Ah, just water," he growled, and threw it away.

He moved on, kneeling next to the corporal, Caen. The man had a bloom of dried blood on the side of his face. He checked the blood; dried. Leon brought his ear close to his mouth. Shallow, soft breaths. Leon gave him a hard smack on the chest.

Caen gasped, thrust awake. He clutched at his head. "Aghhh, can't you let me have some fuckin' sleep?"

Leon swore in Hillard, "*Sal'brath.*" Fuck, the corporal was an idiot sometimes. "We have to move."

Caen groaned as Leon helped him to his feet. "I think I got stabbed."

"Relax, it's not deep. Find any survivors, if you can."

"Right."

They began checking men for breath. Each one they came to were quiet, chests silent and still. Disappointment grew. Leon felt a vein on his forehead pulse. Heat rose in his chest. It happened again—he'd let the whole lot of them down.

Leon was glad for the scruffy-haired corporal from the Spear. He didn't think he could handle it if he woke up alone. Through them all though he never saw one face in particular.

"You seen my squire anywhere?"

"Over here," Caen replied, then he vomited into a bush at his feet. Leon walked over. Lifting aside a branch, the smell hit him first. The smell of blood and death, hanging heavy in the air. It was distilled here. The sight nearly brought last night's ale onto the ground.

"*Ugh,*" the corporal said, wiping his lip. "I can't say I've seen something like that before."

Tristain lay in a circle of bodies... no, bits... around his prone form. The man was immaculate, aside from his clothes. The lad was bare-chested, his mail and shirt discarded in pieces, like the figures around him. Heads, stomachs, intestines... scraps, scattered all around. *I thought I must have hit my head... but, here it is... Sigur's fucking balls.*

Leon walked up to the squire. He tapped him with his foot cautiously. "Think he's dead?"

"*They* sure are," Caen replied, waving his sword around.

Tristain shot his eyes open. Caen swore in surprise. The squire sat bolt upright, gasping, like he was choking for air. He glanced around, seemingly unaware of what happened to him. "What? What... happened..." He then turned and vomited. Leon tried to imagine the white bits in the spew weren't what he thought they were. They weren't bones—human bones.

He kneeled down. "Are you injured, lad?"

"I don't think so," Tristain said, voice flat. His eyes were looking past Leon's own. Staring. "What..."

"Listen... I don't know what happened here, but we need to move. It won't be long before the Badonnians realize their patrol went missing. Let's go. We'll come back to bury the dead, preferably with an entire regiment."

Leon picked his helmet back up. As he did, he caught a flash of scared innkeep from behind a curtain. *They're not on our side, are they...*

As they found their horses, he heard the sound of hooves behind. Leon snorted softly. *I was wondering when they would show up...*

"Sir Vorland." It was the general's steward. He sat clean and proper, on a fucking pony. His black hair was brushed back with that slick oil. *Slick, like a fucking snake.*

"I'm sorry, sir," Gida said from next to him.

"Seize him," the steward yelled.

Three men-at-arms wearing the general's colors snatched at him. He ripped his arm away, breaking another's nose with his fist. He bellowed as they threw him to the ground, writhing in anger, swearing in every language he could think of with such profanity it would make a sailor blush. Mud entered his eyes and mouth as the soldiers shoved him against the ground.

"You've been charged with dereliction of duty, knight," the steward sneered rather than spoke. Nothing seemed to make him happier than Leon's face pressed against the mud. The bastard had always had a problem with Leon, and he was hardly the only one—Leon was a lowborn, knighted, but still the son of a poor farmer.

"For drunkenness leading to the deaths of soldiers. Seize the squire and the corporal as well. I wish to speak with them."

"On whose authority," the corporal shouted, drawing his blade.

Leon spat mud out of his mouth. "Stow your blade, Corporal," he yelled. *No one else is dying on my account.*

The steward grinned. "The general's authority."

TRISTAIN'S SHACKLES CHAFED HIS wrists and ankles. The cage was stark, only a hard mat of straw to lay upon, and that was shared with three others. Their privy, if you could call it that, was a bucket that backed up against the jailor's quarters. They were afforded no privacy, of course. There was something satisfying about defacing their captor's lodgings, even if was only a small deed. Caen sat across from him, joined by two deserters headed for the noose. Tristain wasn't quite sure where he was headed. Caen said he'd like to go back to the Spear one day, see his daughter grow up.

Tristain had laughed. "You've a daughter?"

"What's so funny about it?" Caen had replied, folding his arms, awkwardly with the chains around his wrists. He was serious.

"Nothing, it's just... you're not much older than me."

Caen grunted. "Yeah, well. It's nothing I planned. It was the miller's daughter. A little dance under the miller's nose, we had. Then she was with babe. So, I took off for the war, I was no father. But a while back I was told she had a daughter. Thought I might go one day. See what I spawned into the world."

"She's like to be a witch," a deserter had said. "Witches and cravens is what come from lone mothers."

"Really? So, we know what your childhood was like."

Tristain chuckled. "What's her name?"

"Vera."

"Interesting name. Any meaning?"

"It's Hillard. Means mercy."

"Mercy..."

Caen hung his face low after a moment. It wasn't sullen, but thoughtful. *He might not say it clear, but it's obvious. He thinks he'll never see his daughter again. I wonder if I'll ever see Selene again.*

The two deserters stood. "Right, here's to Vera," one of them said, placing his fist on his chest in salute. It was a little ridiculous, if sincere.

The other folded his hands one of the other. "May Ginevra bless her with long life." It was about the only invocation the craven would know. He'd likely never seen the inside of a church his entire life. "We're headed to the rope. Gods know we need some fucking mercy, right now."

IT WAS THEIR THIRD night inside the cage, and Solni had long set. The deserters were right. They needed mercy, and they had it swiftly, through a long drop with a knotted rope, having broken their necks instead of choking. It had been a mercy, if there was any left in the world.

The jailor kept watch, torch in hand, yawning. A group of drunk men-at-arms jeered at the prisoners as they passed. Catching their tongues, they went quiet as a group of men in grey cloaks walked past. One of the greycloaks caught Tristain's eye, and asked the jailor a question, keeping his eye on Tristain while he spoke. Their voices were too distant, too quiet to hear, but it was clear what they were asking: to speak to the prisoners. *What do a few priests want?* The jailor nodded, and they came over.

"Sigur's blessings upon you, good men," the greycloak who caught Tristain's eye before said. He seemed to be their leader, or at least the one who spoke for them all. "I'm afraid we bring troubling news."

"Aye, and who you supposed t'be?" Caen said, leaning on the bars.

"We are servants of the Holy Order of the Golden Sword. We have uncovered a field of mangled bodies, and evidence of devilry and corruption. You two wouldn't know anything about that?"

Tristain was about to open his mouth when Caen shot him a look and Tristain felt a chill move up his spine.

"Aye, Swords," Caen replied. "We know not of any devilry or corruption. T'was just a fierce battle. But we spoke to the general already. Talk to the duchess, you'll hear right."

The greycloak seemed to think through Caen's words, but simply said, "Very well. We'll speak to the general."

As they walked off, Tristain leaned back against the bars, quiet, consumed by thoughts of that night outside alehouse. Flashes of faces in pale terror. Blood, flesh... The taste of copper on his tongue, as real as the air he breathed.

Tristain felt Caen shake his arm. "Hey, squire," he said. "You can't dwell on what happened. It happened. And it won't be the last time."

Tristain wiggled a finger in the mud. "It might be the last time. We don't know what the general wants from us. And what do these priests want?" Caen went silent.

After a short while, he crossed his arms, chuckling to himself. "I don't know if I should thank you or curse you."

"For what?"

"You killed the bastard about to bring an axe down on my head. Still not clear if that was a blessing or a curse."

"Hm. I guess we'll find out."

"Psst," a voice came. Tristain turned. In the darkness, he spotted the scruffy servant boy's face.

"Nikkel," he said, shuffling over.

"Had to see it for myself," the boy said, leaning on the bars. "I thought you were dead."

"No such luck. Any news about Sir Vorland?"

The boy grimaced. "They have him caged in the parade ground. The steward's given the men free reign to pelt him with food. It ain't right. Slimy Republican bastard."

"He eats well, then," Caen cut in.

Nikkel laughed. "I suppose he does."

Tristain took something out of his pocket. It was a letter, addressed to Selene. "Listen. I have a feeling this might be the last chance I have to do this." *If at all.* "Take this to my father's ward, in the Oncierran estate outside Invereid."

"How-"

"Find my horse."

"You're kiddin'. I don't know how to ride that beast."

"He likes apples. Be careful—he bites if he's hungry. Water him when he starts to tire, and stick to the roads. He gets a little jittery on unsteady ground. My father'll give you lodging for returning my horse home, and for the letter. He might even have work for you."

"What do you think's going to happen?"

Who knows, but I have to get a letter to her. "Will you do it?"

The boy sighed. "All right. Your father better have work for me, though."

"I'm sure he will. The tenants are always looking for more hands."

"Oncierran," a gruff voice said, approaching.

"Go, Nikkel." The boy ran off, letter tucked into his shirt. Tristain muttered a quick prayer to Ginevra for his safety. *You'd better take good care of my horse.*

"Oncierran lad," the voice came again. Tristain turned. A torch fell upon him. His eyes adjusted as the cage door opened. "The general wants you." It was a guard in the general's colors. They lifted him to his feet, unlocking his shackles.

T RISTAIN FELT THE GENERAL'S anger in the bunch of her shoulders, the clench of her jaw, in spite of her silence. She waved her hand for Galeaz, her steward, to speak.

"Squire," he said, standing rigid. "You've been called here to give an account of the events outside the abode known as The Ox's Balls, on the night two falls past, and the circumstances that led to the deaths of twenty-five men-at-arms."

"We travelled up the north road from the southern forest, patrolling, as instructed," the squire replied. "We were making our way—"

"Get to the point, boy, where we lost twenty-five good men for no reason," the general interrupted.

"There... there's very little to say, my Lady. We were ambushed outside the Ox."

"Was that all," the steward said. "Sir Vorland made an unscheduled stop, did he not? And he drank himself into a stupor?"

"I will not lie, my lord. The patrol was tiring. A quick drink was all that was needed, and a warm bath, that we had."

"It was more than a few drinks, wasn't it?"

Tristain stiffened. "It... was no more than three." *Seven.*

"And then?"

"We were leaving the Ox, and a storm deadened our hearing until the Badonnians were on us. A group—"

"A group of knights, yes. We spoke to the lieutenant already. She wisely suggested that the convoy keep moving, stay off the roads."

"That she did."

"Is there nothing else?" The general had pursed her lips hard enough they started to turn white around the edges. *She cannot say it to my face, but she wishes to rid herself of the knight. The question is why?*

Tristain sighed inwardly. *Perhaps... perhaps it would be easier if Leon was out of the way. He knows what I am. Maybe he deserves it. A lowborn knight, and a drunk. His hens are finally coming home to roost.*

Heat rose to his cheeks. *Am I truly capable of that? So much for loyalty. Besides, their blood is on my hands as much as it is his.*

"I... I suggested we stay," he said. The general sat up in her chair. "It was foolish of me. The lieutenant was right. We should've avoided the roads." *Maybe things would've been different.* The taste of blood filled his mouth. Screams filled his ears.

"Your honesty is commendable," Lady Adolar replied. "But not actionable. Your knight should've known better."

"He should hang," Galeaz said.

"And you should watch your tongue, Republican. Sir Vorland is a knight of the realm."

"An incompetent fool and a drunk."

The general sighed. "What is the feeling amongst his men?"

"The lieutenant has voiced her concerns. Some of the men are displeased, but none so far have been insubordinate. They accept that Vorland has failed in his duties."

"The other knights?"

"Sigibund and Clearwater are of the opinion that only the emperor can sanction the disenfranchisement. Vredevoort suggested dragging him behind a horse."

"He would." She rubbed her temples. "My mind feels heavy at the moment. If you'll excuse us, squire."

"General—"

"You'll be assigned to Vredevoort's regiment for now," the steward said. "Report to Sergeant Dengeld." Tristain bowed. *I'm not dead. Was it really this easy? But... now I have nothing. My knight is disgraced, and his shame will turn to contempt for me. I have no hope of becoming a knight, now.*

Now outside, he chewed his lip in frustration. He felt like punching something. The greycloaks watched him. He felt their eyes on his back.

"What!" he screamed, turning to face them. "Sigur be praised, what do you want?"

They flinched, all but the leader. A sinister grin spread across his face. Tristain felt the hairs on his neck rise. Tristain cleared his throat and quickly excused himself.

As he walked back to his tent, he wondered what the next few days would hold for him – a new regiment, no one he knew. A new captain: Vredevoort the Grim. He knew the stories about the harsh, violent man. And these troubling greycloaks, asking altogether too many questions about what happened that night.

Breathing a sigh as he flopped down on his mat, he wondered if the ordeal of the past few days was finally over, or if his ordeals had only just begun. Certainly, something snagged in the back of his mind. He didn't feel in complete control of himself. His skin felt slippery, as if he could shed it at any moment and become something terrible. The passage in the *Histories* flashed in his mind. *Demon... Devil... Shapeshifter.* Unease settled in and a shiver went down his spine.

6

KNOWLEDGE

S ELENE PRACTICED WITH A blunt-loaded, one-hand-operated crossbow sometime the next week, after that ordeal with the dissected
werewolf and the Lord Inquisitor. It was easy to lose track of time. She
was either training, praying, or sleeping, during what little sleep she could
actually find. Her nights were filled with nightmares. They weren't of
the demons in the arena, no. She hadn't thought on that since the day it
happened. The terrible dreams involved her guardian mother and father in
some way or another. Still, the day-to-day kept her busy, kept her sane. She
thrived. She felt good, filled with purpose.

"I figure you're highborn," Ebberich had said to her yesterday during
a break in morning training. She laughed it off. *How could he know? No.
Relax, Selene. You're probably not the only highborn in the ranks of the
Order...* "Yeah. It's your fingers. No calluses."

"What are you talking about, I have calluses," she replied, waving her
hand.

"Nuh. Those little nubby things aren't bloody calluses." He held up his
palms. They were wrinkled, rough, the lines scored with dirt that looked
as though they'd never come out, no matter how much he cleaned them.
"These are the hands of a lowborn. Not to mention you've got perfect
skin."

"I'll take that as a compliment," she said, laughing.

"Ah, Sigur. We should get back to it."

"No, come on. Any more compliments? Or am I going to have to tease them out of you?" He flushed red. She laughed, taking it as a sign of victory. "Come, let's spar."

Sorenius barked commands as he watched. "Higher! Half-turn! Pirouette! No, not like that! Pivot on your front leg! Fast! You have to be quick, keep moving! A stationary Sword is a dead Sword! Good! Right, time for training with poisons!"

They finished after another few hours. She was exhausted, but greatly pleased with herself and how things were going. Her lack of ability hadn't held her back, and she was grateful to Sorenius for showing her how to fight on her own terms, with her own strengths. Though he still seemed disaffected with her, for some reason. He avoided her gaze as he left the training hall.

She had to confront him. She saw her opportunity as he leaned on the curtain wall, watching the novitiates run around doing their chores.

She strode up to him. "What in the emperor's sixth concubine was that?" He had a blank look on his face. "You know what the hell I'm talking about. That first day, it was like you forgot you knew me. What, I fulfilled my purpose, filled your quota of recruits, and that was it? Nice to meet you, all the best?"

"I—"

"And you knew you could beat me—there was no need to show it off for your compatriots. Beating up a cripple... where do you get off?"

"A *cripple*—"

"And bloody hell, those months where we didn't stop for nothing more than a few short hours... I didn't complain, not once. Not even when I *had* to stop because my arse was raw, my insides felt like they were turned inside out, and below my waist was a fucking nightmare. We rode, and rode, and I grew weaker and weaker. I cried myself to sleep most nights. You never *once* asked me how I was. Never *once* asked me why I wanted to stop more often, and getting you to stop so we could just sleep was like pulling fucking teeth. What was the goddamn hurry?"

"I had to—"

"I had a bleed on the third night, you know that? I had to steal a poor fucking woman's hat to clean it up. And despite all that, I kept going. You bloody well forgot I was a damn *woman*? I came with *nothing*. You're lucky it wasn't the first time it had happened. I knew what to do, thank Sigur."

Sorenius found it hard to answer that one, flapping his mouth. "Shit," was all he said, eventually. "I'm sorry."

"Alright."

"And are you now—"

"Taken care of."

"Good. Alright... I'm deeply sorry. I truly am. But... if you're asking me to take it easier on you—"

"I'm not. I'm just asking for a bit of understanding, and a drop of fucking kindness for a change."

"Alright, I'll try. I will. I swear to Sigur."

"Good."

They sat down by the wall, sitting in silence for a while, watching the sky turn orange as the sun set. Sorenius started to laugh. "*The emperor's sixth concubine...*"

Selene laughed too. "I don't know. It's what came to mind. Hey, when did you find those demons? Two, no less."

He sighed. "That was why we had to hurry. Don't give me that look. I said I was sorry. It won't happen again. Anyway, it was reported that of one of them was at a charcoal-burner's camp, out by the Spear."

"So, when we headed east on the smallroad instead of the emperor's road..."

"That's right."

"And when you disappeared that night?"

"Yes. Turns out there were two."

"And you're okay?"

"It was a tough fight; I'll give them that. The lord inquisitor wanted them alive, which made it even harder, of course. It's much easier to just kill them."

"How did you make it out?"

"The trick is not to get hit."

She blew her lips. "Yeah, right. Poisoned bolt?"

He chuckled, confirming that she would never know for sure, but how else could he have done it? They sat in silence for a while longer until it was time for supper.

"NOVITIATE," RECTOR PALIA SAID during supper. Selene jerked upright at the greeting, nearly dropping her spoon. "I would ask you to come with me."

"Yes, Rector," Selene replied, followed her through the hall. They walked out of the annex into the garden, soft grass under her shoes. The sound of cicadas filled the air. The small little garden was outside of the annex, both on the same plateau that the keep stood. Pollen drifted past, kicked up by a gentle breeze. A small flowering birch tree sat in the center, directly in front of a mound of rocks, upon which sat a plaque that memorialized all the previous lord inquisitors.

"I hope Inquisitor Sorenius hasn't been too hard on you," the rector said. "He can be a bit intense."

Selene shook her head profusely. "No, no, not at all."

The rector smiled. "Good. I would like you to come with me tonight. The Lord Inquisitor is having a ceremony, invitation only. I would like you to have a look in. If you want to, of course."

She had never felt more a part of something than now. *Invited to a special ceremony!* "Of course, Rector."

"Excellent. I will meet you when Solni has departed."

\#

Selene stood in the now dark garden, playing with her hair. It was nervous tic, one she had from childhood. The garden took on a different hue after dark, and with no moon tonight, everything was black. She had a candle, but that had long gone out in the wind. The warming days stirred up strong winds at night. Squalls howled coming up the black cape, while unknown things rustled in the privet nearby. On the curtain wall, she saw torch fire flapping around. At least the guards were still there. She took a deep breath, settling her nerves. *It's just a simple ceremony... what's the worst that could happen?*

"Novitiate." Selene nearly jumped out of her skin. The voice came from a cloaked figure by the edge of the garden. *How long has she been there?* "Come with me."

She followed the rector. "Any reason you're walking around in the dark?" she asked, hoping to lighten the mood. The rector didn't answer.

They went down the stairs to the underground hallway. The woman reached for a key hanging around her neck. The mechanism clunked as they entered one of the locked, mysterious doors that she walked past every day. Selene had almost forgotten they were there in the day-to-day. She followed the rector inside.

Rector Palia turned to face her. "Novitiate, I would swear you to complete secrecy. You are to repeat nothing of what you see here, to anyone." Selene nodded, twisting her hair. Her heart fluttered with mixture of anxiety and excitement. They came to another door.

The door creaked open, revealing a chanting man in fine robes in a circular room with cut stone walls. He wore a gilded mask, chanting over a waist-high table, lifting a burning thurible into the air, filling the room with a slightly sweet, woody smoke. He was chanting in the language of their forebears, High Istryan. Selene recognised a little of it, but the resonance was so strong, and the syllables so drawn out, it sounded nearly nonsensical. A brazier burned next to him, an iron poking rod in the fire. Three others were watching, a woman in white robes—another high-ranking vestal like the rector—and two men in black, novitiates. Selene didn't recognize their faces. The rector locked the door behind her and led Selene further into the circular room.

She gawped. A tan-colored demon lay flat on the table, its abdomen cut open. The skin was peeled back, revealing a ribcage and organs inside. The cuts weren't sharp, rather... melted, somehow. It smelled like a strange mixture of rotting meat and alchemy. Selene tasted bile in her throat. She swallowed hard, trying to keep it down, sensing the gravity of the situation she found herself in. *Because normally I would puke,* she thought.

The robed man stopped chanting. A grave silence took its place, like the weight of anticipation pressed the voice from their lungs. He placed the thurible on a metal stand gently, taking absolute care not to disturb the quiet. He turned, facing his observers, and brought one hand to the mask, lifting it off slowly.

Behind, the Lord Inquisitor's deep green eyes bored into Selene's soul. His face was gaunt, and his shoulders narrow. Selene found him hard to look at directly.

"Welcome," he said, every syllable smooth and broad. "I am very glad you are here. Glory be unto Sigur."

Selene joined the room in a bow. "Glory be unto Him."

"You novitiates may consider yourselves very particular and exceptional after this night. You are privy to a ceremony that only a select few take part in. Here, so to better understand the enemy we fight; we dissect, we examine, we coldly separate our emotions from objective reality. That objective reality is that we are weak, and they are strong. But it is not hopeless. They are not unstoppable."

He reached for a knife, waving it back and forth as he spoke. "Before us we see the demon as he truly is. If you kill one, he reveals his true form. That form is mighty and fearsome at first glance, but becomes nothing more than the reflection of their damned souls upon a second look. Demon skin. A material that resembles animal skin, with fur, pores, layers of dermis and epidermis that would all seem familiar. Except for one thing." He jammed the knife down into the beast's forearm. *Bang.* Selene jumped.

The knife barely entered the skin. It toppled over, clattering on the floor.

"Nearly impenetrable. The back of the neck, under the mane," he lifted the thick brown hairs of the beast's neck, "is the thinnest part, but even then, a strong thrust only enters a scant inch. Enough to sever the spinal column, certainly, so we are lucky in that instance. But a cut? Sheer stupidity. However." A vial of green liquid appeared his hand. "Acid does the trick."

He poured it on the beast's wrist. The nasty mixture reacted immediately, bubbling, popping, sinking slowly into the flesh. It gave off foul, black vapours. A novitiate brought a hand to her mouth, retching. Selene watched with fascination.

"As does fire." Searing flesh and igniting fur, the scarred man swept the brand across the beast's arm, filling the air with an awful smell. Selene covered her nose and mouth, groaning. He tamped down the fire with a wet cloth, putting it out. "Now you see, the devil is not so mighty or fearsome as he appears.

"Of course, its interior is just as fragile as ours." He picked up another knife, with a thin, tapered blade, and placed his hands inside the chest cavity. The long seconds he was inside drew out. Selene expected the demon to wake any moment. But it didn't. He jerked his hand three times. The liver pulled free. He placed the organ, three times larger than it should have been, onto a set of scales.

"Novitiate," he said to Selene, wiping his hands on a rag. "Weigh this for me."

Selene stepped forward. Next to the scales lay a collection of assorted weights, iron masses ranging several pounds to a few ounces. Stacking them up, the scales balanced at eleven pounds.

"How is this possible?" Selene said quietly, the sheer size of it leering at her. It was bigger than her head. Up close, the pathetic creature before her, like this, splayed out—while disgusting—meant nothing more to her than a rotting corpse. She reached out, running her hand along the creature's furry foot, goosepimples shooting up her arms, imagining it might wake up at any moment. But it didn't, and nothing happened. It was dead.

"Nothing to be afraid of," she spoke quietly.

A novitiate puked all over the floor. They turned, the smell turning the rest of them green. Another one lost their stomach. Selene wasn't affected, thankfully.

"Right. This process requires the strongest stomachs, I suppose. Rectors, please escort the novitiates from the room. I must dispose of the body."

S ELENE LAY ON THE floor of the sleeping hall, with the rest of the novitiates, tossing and turning. Her dreams haunted her. She had dreamt of her childhood friend Mikhail. His body laid broken on the battlefield. His voice echoed, taunting her, calling her a coward, telling her she should've saved his mother.

She sighed, getting up. There was no sense laying on her bed-mat hoping that sleep might free her from her thoughts when sleep brought the nightmares. She wandered the annex. The dining hall directly below the sleeping quarters was empty so late at night, of course, while her candle flickered, casting long shadows across the stone. The darkness outside the window was stark, ominous.

She stifled a yawn as she walked in the hall. Light came from the small chapel ahead, the martyr Brigida's. Leona was there, her short red hair twirling as she turned her head. Selene smiled as she walked in, and the girl smiled back. Selene kneeled next to her on cushions on the stone floor. Leona muttered a short prayer, and whispered, "Why are you up so late?"

"I couldn't sleep." Selene's voice was hushed. "Too much on my mind. And you?"

"Same. We should pray. Perhaps we can ask the Lightfather to still your racing thoughts." Leona took Selene's hands and placed them in her own. "Father of All. Still my friend's mind, and bring her the strength she needs."

"So, in light." Selene released her hand, but Leona held onto it.

"I feel I can trust you," she whispered.

Selene blinked. "I barely know you, Leona."

"I know, but... it feels as though we have a kindred bond. I never really had a family of my own, and I think you feel the same way."

Selene nodded. "I had family, but... we were never really close. They left me to the Count of Invereid's care when I was very young. I had no one, except for my ward's son, Tristain." Warmth spread inside her chest as she remembered their games in the grounds, chasing each other with dandelions, trying not to get the flowers on their clothes.

Leona pointed to her mismatched eye. "See this? It made me stand out from birth. One night, my brothers tried to cut it out with a hot knife, believing it would make me better. I'll never forget that smell, as long as I live."

"I'm sorry."

Selene felt Leona's hand tighten. "That's alright," the red-headed girl replied with a smile. "That's why I'm here, for a second chance, to make something of myself."

Selene smiled brightly and Leona smiled back. That was enough, and together they prayed to the God of Strength and Justice.

THE NEXT DAY, SPARROWS circled around Sorenius's head as he explained the proper use of traps to ensnare, harm, and kill a demon. They were just outside the city, in the narrow estuary between the Tibor and Alba rivers. The air was cold and damp, and the muddy grass covered with morning dew. Trees around them yellowed with the coming arrival of autumn.

He held up a mechanical-looking device; two metal loops attached to a spring-weighted pad. "Your basic snare. Press the arms down one at a time, and unhook the catch. Place it where you think the demon might come from, and it cover with some heath. Alternatively, place a ring of these around your camp or hiding spot, so you won't be caught by surprise. Just remember where you left them!" The novitiates chuckled. "Another thing, tying a chime to one of the arms can be useful—when it goes off, you'll know the demon was caught. Though his roars should give it away well enough.

"Next is the poison oak. Be very careful handling this one. The thorns are extremely sharp." He lifted a supple green branch into the air, a bramble of thorns on the end of it. "And they're covered in a sap that'll kill you in minutes unless you have the antidote. For a demon in human form, it'll do the same. For a demon in their true form, it'll cause them intense pain and disorientation. Using a sapling allows you to use its suppleness—tie them to a tree, or just off a path, where the demon is likely to pass, and pull the thorny end back, binding it to the tripwire using a slipknot." He demonstrated by putting one end of the branch under his foot and pulling back hard. "Pressure on the tripwire causes the slipknot to undo, releasing the tension in the branch, causing it to—" the branch flicked back to position with a snap "—come back to position. Next, we have a simple trigger catch on a crossbow, pre-loaded with a bolt with your favorite toxin. Make sure to aim this one a little in front of the tripwire—demons move fast enough that they could be meters away from the shot before it goes off."

"What happened to a simple blade in the gullet?" Ruprecht asked. "If I knew it was going to be this complicated…"

Sorenius scratched his face. "Well, you try it. Try to put your simple blade in my gullet."

"No—"

"Come, then, try it." Ruprecht stepped forward gingerly, drawing his beltknife. He lunged. Sorenius swiftly disarmed him, kicking his legs out from under him. Ruprecht groaned. "Get up."

Ruprecht slowly got to his feet.

"How do you expect to get a blade into a beast that moves faster than you; is ten times stronger than you are; has armor for skin; when you can't even get the best of me?"

The others laughed.

"I wouldn't be laughing." Sorenius cut them off. "Us humans are pathetic by comparison. And if you're close enough to be able to stab them, you're already dead. Right, we'll go on to scents and camouflage, and why you might want to cover yourself in mud and animal dung. Fresh meat is your best friend, and a bit of straw and spare clothes can also be useful…"

7

SACRILEGE

ONTHS LATER, SELENE HEARD Ebberich's unmistakably loud voice coming from the dining hall.

"We must celebrate!" he yelled.

Selene smiled as she walked in, wearing two sets of robes for the cold wintry day ahead. The hall was a bustling, noisy place, just before supper, and today was no exception.

"What's happened," she asked.

"Both Salim and Ruprecht are being confirmed, can you believe it?" he replied. "I never thought these two idiots would be before me." They all laughed.

"You have to give them a break, Ebberich," Salim said. "They don't know what it's like to be a blockhead like you, so much slower than the rest of us."

Selene laughed and Salim caught her eye. He smiled. She remembered when he came around. It was a good day—she had disarmed him, somehow, and managed to kick him in the genitals. Accidentally, of course, in a way that it most certainly wasn't. He fumed, ready to grab a weapon and do her in, but then he collapsed, laughing as he clutched his groin in pain. After that, he opened up a little, and it had only been getting better since.

Raul was a different matter. She dreaded seeing the Vallonian's face. Ever since the demons in the arena, a look in his eye had developed. A look that held ill will. Thankfully for her, he had been unwell the last few days, and been confined to the infirmary.

"Each of our times will each come," Leona said. "What name will you choose, do you think? I would choose... Rufia, after Sigur's confidant, or maybe Linaria, so it's not too different."

"Oh, Linaria's good," Ruprecht replied. "Pincushioned with arrows for not renouncing her faith, yeah, that's good. Myself, I would pick maybe... Georgius."

Leona quivered. "Ooh, the great slayer of demons! Fearsome warrior, you are." Salim blew his lips in a fart. Ruprecht socked him in the arm and laughed.

"What about you, Salim," Selene asked.

"Oh, me? Haven't really thought about it." He shrugged. "Yourself?"

Selene scratched the back of her head. "I'm not too sure either. I don't really know too much about the martyrs, if I'm honest."

"Well," Leona began. "There's Aella, Sigur's wife. She killed herself instead of letting herself be captured by the Great Devil. Then there's Sofiya, the mighty warrior who held Sigur's golden city for thirty days and thirty nights with just a handful of men. Or Domitice, who was renowned the world over for her skill with a bow, until she was raped and butchered by the Devil and his minions."

Selene chuckled softly. "They all sound a bit grim. Isn't there a martyr who died peacefully in her bed?"

They all laughed.

"That would preclude the 'martyr' bit, Selene," Ebberich said.

"No." Leona raised a finger. "There was one. Diana."

Ruprecht raised an eyebrow. "Diana? She's a martyr?"

"What did she do?" Selene asked.

"She foretold the coming of the Age of Disarray," Leona said. "When men would be free from the yoke of the Gods, and would rise and spread over the earth. She died peacefully in her bed. And yes, some scriptures say she's a martyr, since she was pursued to the ends of the Continent for her prophecy."

Ebberich touched Selene's forearm. "Well, there you go. We'll be saying hello to Warden Diana in no time."

Selene nodded, smiling. Inside though, she wondered if she would be alright with changing her name. Her mother gave her the name Selene, after all. It was the only thing she had left of her old life.

S ELENE CRADLED THE BACK of her head in her hand. The five of them slept on the uncomfortable wood of the sleeping hall, like all the other novitiates. She felt dogtired, but couldn't, or wouldn't, go back to sleep. Sleep was a luxury these days, between early-morning prayers and recurring nightmares, but still, she was awake. She began to think back, think of her guardian mother. She had no memories of her real mother, after all. Her perfume—lavender, the scent of the Goddess of Fertility, Eme. She found the plant in the preceptor's garden, and memories came flooding back. The sweet sound of her singing voice, the word games they played, the times spent in the estate's garden, picking flowers. Her guardian father scolded her for getting dirt on her shoes, she remembered. She wondered if she had been married, would her guardian mother have come with her? Or had Tristain succeeded in his plan to gain employment as a household guard? What happened to her guardian mother was awful, but not the fault of anyone but her horrible husband. The images of that horrible day flashed into her mind again. The bloody face of her guardian mother's dead body, life snuffed by her demon father.

Selene heard shuffling next to her. It was Ebberich, facing her. "What's on your mind?   " he whispered. The others snored softly around them, dead to the world. The training was gruelling, and the wake-up early, so they slept soundly.

Selene looked at the beams above. The ceiling creaked in the cold wind outside. "My mother."

Ebberich smiled and nodded. "I'm the same, sometimes. I remember the touch of her hand, stroking my hair as I drift off to sleep. Then I wake, and forget it again."

She rolled over to face him, propping up on an elbow. "She was a singer."

"Oh, like a minstrel?"

"No, nothing like that. She sang to me and my ward's sons, sang us off to sleep. Her voice was indescribable, like it belonged to a time before men."

"Sounds lovely. Mine was a clothier. Nothing special, just made linens with a loom."

"But she meant a lot to you."

Ebberich smiled. "Yeah."

Selene leaned back, feeling sleep attack her. She stifled a yawn. "Do you know much about Salim?"

"I don't know. Why?"

"I don't think he likes me very much."

"He's just a surly bastard. Don't let it get to you. He probably wouldn't want me telling you this, but he was a slave, not that long ago. He thinks he has something to prove. He doesn't, of course, but he's too stubborn to realize that. I mean, he's being confirmed ahead of all of us except Ruprecht, for Sigur's sake."

"A slave?"

"Yeah... he's from Saburria, a place far across the ocean."

"Saburria? I thought he might be from Vallonia."

"Me too, at first. But then he told me he was taken as a boy, sailed across the ocean and sold to some noble in Ostelar."

"How did he end up here?"

"His master was a demon, from what I can gather. He won't tell me exactly, but I figure that's what happened. Swords raided his master's house, killed the master, and rounded up all his servants. Salim ended up being recruited out of that." Selene nodded. *A slave...* She yawned again. They said goodnight. She truly felt exhausted, and sleep came almost as soon as she closed her eyes.

"A GAIN," INSTRUCTOR SORENIUS TOLD Selene. She lunged for his chest with her dagger. He snatched for her arm. Avoiding his grasp, she did a quick half-pirouette, bringing the blade around. He caught her wrist, but only just. The point was an inch from his eye. The others let out astonished laughs, but her victory was short-lived. He kicked her knee, sending her to the floor. It came rushing up and she braced, landing with a soft grunt. The impact on cold stone hurt her body. But she was getting used to pain. Pain reminded her she was still alive, after everything.

"Better." Sorenius helped Selene to her feet. "But you leave your back wide open. It would serve you better to do a full turn. You can still thrust into the eye from that position, just adjust your wrist angle." He showed her what to do and she nodded.

"Alright, next, Novitiate Ebberich. You've been getting better with the axe. I want to see how you fare. Pair up with Novitiate Selene. You two, spar as well." Salim was getting ready for his confirmation and *Velitore* they'd been told, and Raul was reassigned to a group one short of a pair.

"Yes, Inquisitor," they replied.

Selene took up a stance, shifting her weight so she became light on her feet. Ebberich followed suit, wielding a bearded axe in one hand and a shield in another. She eyed the sharpened steel. The novitiates trained with sharp weapons, of course, and injuries were commonplace. Luckily, neither her nor any of her friends had been injured beyond a few cuts and bruises, unlike some others.

Ebberich came for her, slowly at first. He swung in an arc, testing his range. She stepped out of the way. He swung again, this time faster. She pirouetted, getting around his guard. She pressed her dagger against his neck. He laughed in surprise, and they reset.

Ebberich adjusted his grip. "Alright... I won't hold back."

"Good."

His eyes glinted in the candlelight. He lunged forward, sweeping fast. She jumped back, then rebounded while he brought his axe around. He put his shield up, catching her body on it. He stumbled. She quickly brought her dagger under his chin. He laughed again, a goofy laugh that made Selene's chest flutter. *He's... cute.*

"You're too good with that blade," he said. "Six months and you're already better than the rest of us."

Selene scratched the back of her head, stifling a yawn. "Come on, Ebberich. Be serious, I'm not that good. Nothing compared to Sorenius." Ebberich laughed, handing her his axe. She looked at him as if he was mad. "What's this?"

"Consider it a handicap." He reached for another axe as she put her dagger away. The heft and bulk were all wrong to her—she much preferred the swiftness of a dagger or a sword. Still, she took a stance. Ebberich came for her again, but without a shield arm, she had to dodge. He turned his axe mid-strike. The axe came within a hair's breadth as she leapt back. Ebberich blinked, apologising profusely. She laughed.

"Well, it's not surprising that I've got you with the axe," he said.

She smiled, stretching her neck and shoulders. "Come on, again."

Ebberich smirked. He swept forward. She expected it this time, and performed her own little trick. She feinted, coaxing his shield forward. As it did, she flipped her axe down and hooked it under. She yanked, opening him up. She kicked savagely with her left foot, right into his solar plexus. His eyes bulged and he dropped to the floor with a wheeze.

The others gave bewildered looks. "Where in Sigur's name did you learn that," Ruprecht said, laughing.

Sorenius scowled. "Watch your tongue, Novitiate."

"Sorry, Inquisitor."

They went back to training, another two grueling hours before a break for lunch. The arbiter caught her outside the dining hall.

"Novitiate," he said. "I would like to talk with you about something."

Selene smiled. "What is it?"

"Not here."

They went behind the annex, next to the curtain wall.

"Novitiate," he said. "Your training is progressing well, much faster than I would have ever expected. Rector Palia tells me that you are learning the prayers, and I have seen that you are active at all the Gebet, chanting and joining prayers. Tell me, does your past still weigh on your mind?"

Selene smiled slightly, thinking it over. Still, the dreams of Tristain haunted her sleep, his broken body a threat, yelling horrible things until she woke streaming with sweat. "Yes."

The arbiter nodded. "And you wish to speed through training? I would tell you that there is no such thing, Novitiate. You are confirmed when you are ready, no sooner."

Selene looked down, chuckling softly. "Please don't mistake me, Sorenius. I am grateful for the Order, and the opportunity to prove myself. I am trying to right a wrong done to me. If it wasn't for them... for you, I might have died all those months ago."

"Hm. I realize vengeance is important to you... but I wonder if you place your personal concerns above the Order, and the good of all people, themselves. You say you are trying to right a wrong—what of all the wrongs in the world that you could right, as a Golden Sword? Do you feel any concern for the people done wrong?"

Selene felt her breath catch. "If I have transgressed in some way, Inquisitor, I apologize."

"Do not worry, Novitiate. It was just a simple question. Meet me in the annex's garden, after Vespers. There is something important we must do. Now, let's go, we have more training before supper."

Selene nodded, and they left for the training hall again.

T HE MOON WAS BRIGHT that night. Luni hung high in the sky, her full face towards Selene. Solni had long completed his journey. It was a warm night, too, and Selene ruffled her robe, aerating her sweaty body. It was nearly the summer solstice, and the celebration of Sigur's Day. More people than usual wandered the grounds in the warm night air, chatting, singing, chanting. Ebberich and Leona rounded the corner.

Selene blinked. "What are you two doing here?"

"The arbiter asked us to be here," Leona replied. "And you?" Selene nodded.

"Bit strange, no?" Ruprecht's voice came from behind. Selene's heart was in her throat. She recalled that night with the Lord Inquisitor, reminded of it in more ways than one.

"Novitiates, good," Sorenius said, arriving not long after Ruprecht. "Come with me."

They followed him into the keep, down the steps. He unlocked one of the doors. This one was new, neither leading to the arena nor to the circular room with the table.

He led them down a long corridor. There were many closed doors on either side, loud voices coming from behind some of them. None of them dared ask what they were, or where he was taking them.

"Here," he said, stopping to unlock a door. The bolt clicked. Unoiled hinges squeaked. Selene's jaw dropped. A dark-skinned man, naked down to his breeches, sat there in a chair. Salim. His hands and legs were bound, tied to the frame of the chair. The inquisitor closed the door behind them. Off to the side was Rector Palia, her stern face eyeing up the young pack.

"What is this?" Ebberich shouted.

"This," the rector spat. "Is a punishment."

Selene raised her eyebrows. "For what?"

"Novitiate Salim has been shirking his duties. It has also been raised that he does not hold the Lightfather in his heart. However, it is also an opportunity. I would have had you four punished for failing to report the novitiate's behaviour, but the inquisitor here promised me that you would prove yourselves."

"Prove ourselves?"

"Yes. Extracting information is an important part of your duty and service as a Golden Sword. Extract from the novitiate the reasons for his transgressions, and you will be rewarded." Selene stepped forward. Salim trembled.

"Selene, you can't be serious," Ebberich yelled. "That's Salim, our friend!"

"Novitiate, calm yourself, or you will be removed."

Selene stepped closer to the slave from Saburria, pursing her lips. She would not fail herself again by avoiding the hard things.

"Why, Salim?" she asked. He didn't answer, turning away from her. "Why?" The other novitiates watched, frozen. She turned to the rector. The woman was unreadable. She turned back to Salim. "The Order has given you everything, just as it has all of us. Why turn your back on them?"

"You have no idea, do you," he yelled. "I had nothing. I will always have nothing. It doesn't scare me to go back." They fell silent. The inquisitor took a dagger from his belt. Selene's eyes narrowed. Salim wriggled in the chair, groaning, as the blade glinted in the candlelight.

Sorenius held it out for her. "You must learn, Selene. I have faith in you."

She sighed softly, taking the dagger.

Leona placed a hand on her back. "Do it. You have to. Sigur tests our faith, but we must be strong."

Ebberich pleaded with her. "Please, Selene! Don't do it!"

"Get him out," Rector Palia said. "Now!" Ruprecht and Leona jerked, taking Ebberich by the arms and pulling him from the room.

"No, you can't!"

"Inquisitor. Make sure that novitiate knows the consequences for disobedience." He nodded, leaving the room. The door squeaked shut. Selene was alone with the rector and Salim. She felt alone, and that was a strange feeling. Not long after she'd come to the Order, the constant day-to-day, the dogtired feeling she was left with at the end of each day kept her mind off things, mostly. She was too busy to feel alone. But not now.

Tristain. The name flashed in her mind. It hurt her to think of it.

She palmed the handle of the weapon. It was smooth, made of ivory, and fit her palm nicely. The blade was well-weighted and nimble. "Why did you do it, Salim?"

"I don't have to answer you, you northern bitch." She narrowed her eyes. She flicked her wrist, drawing blood from his cheek. He recoiled. "Fuck you! Pox and shit on you! Goddamn one-arm freak!"

That was it. She'd heard enough. Hatred boiled inside of her. Salim became the target of all the wrongs that had ever been done to her. It felt good to stoke the fire. She darted the dagger across again, cutting his shoulder. Another cut, and another, and another, quick slashes in succession. She lost count. The man howled in pain, begging for her to stop. He blubbered like a child. It only made her angrier. Then the adrenaline wore off.

"Enough! Please!" he screamed.

Selene stopped. She blinked, seeing the destruction she wrought. She pressed her fist to her mouth, suppressing a scream. The man's torso was covered in small cuts, dripping with dark blood in the low light. She swallowed hard, blinking back tears.

"I'll tell you," he said, trembling. "Okay, I'll tell you, just stop... I can't do it anymore. I can't pretend I'm a loyal servant or whatever horseshit they try to shove down our throats, not anymore. Look at us! This is what they do to us! Our enemies are monsters, but they're making us into monsters to fight them. That doesn't make us better. It makes us worse!" His eyes burned with anger.

"Lies," Rector Palia snapped. "We took you in, we took you *all* in. You were rejected, cast aside by your families, by society. By all those with hate in their hearts. We expected nothing in return but your devotion, and your loyalty. Finish this, Selene."

Salim clenched his jaw, closing his eyes.

"We cannot brook traitors here, not in the heart of our halls... *kill him,* Novitiate!"

Selene's eyes stung with sadness. She swallowed.

Salim blinked open his eyes, looking mournful.

"If you don't do it, you'll join him in hell yourself!"

"Please, Selene," he begged. "At least make it quick." Her hands trembled. Her breath came hot and fast. Then a memory. A memory of her mother, singing as she did in the parlor room, so long ago. Selene never tried cultivating any talent for it, her father would never allow such fripperies. But her mother was renowned for her voice.

Oh, gentle breeze,
I feel you on my cheek,
You pass by me so gently,
And I miss you so sweetly.
Oh, gentle lover,
I feel you on my cheek,
I pass by you so gently,
And I let you go, so sweetly.

A tear ran down her face, and she rammed the blade home.

8

CONFIRMATION

S ELENE SAT IN THE contemplation room below the church, the first
room she'd ever come to in the Citadel, thinking about her guardian
mother. The room was one of the few places in the Citadel for privacy. Many outright forgot about it, praying in the many nicer places for
prayer—the gardens above, or the chapels in the annex. She didn't know if
she could face everyone after what she'd done. What would they say when
they found out she'd killed Salim?

A knock came at the door. It opened, the hinges creaking slowly. The
red-headed girl with the mismatched eye stuck her head around the corner.
"Selene," Leona said gingerly. "How are you doing?"

"I'm... I'm okay," she said, biting her lip slightly. *I'm not... not really.*
Images of Salim's crying, pained face stayed on her eyes like a stain from
looking at a bright light for too long.

Leona walked inside, closing the door behind her. "We want you to
know we don't hate you for what you did. Salim was a friend, but so are
you."

"He's dead, Leona."

The girl went silent. Then she sighed. "I'm sorry."

"Don't be sorry."

"No, I was the one who told them about him."

Selene gasped, flaring her nostrils. "You *what?*"

"I didn't know it would come to this! I thought they might just whip him, or make him say a thousand prayers, or something like that. Not *kill* him."

"I can't believe you would do that!"

"It's not like he didn't have it coming, though... I mean, I know it sounds harsh, but if the Lightfather truly wasn't in his heart, surely, he deserved *some* punishment."

Selene exhaled. She felt queasy.

"No... no..." she muttered, holding her head in her hands. Leona came up to her, placing a hand on her shoulder.

Selene flinched. "Get away from me."

"No, I'm here for you."

"No, Leona. I... I can't do this, not anymore." Salim was her friend. What business was it of Leona's that he might not have held Sigur in his heart? Gods knew she didn't, not all the time.

"What do you mean?"

"It's that dead part of your eye, like a dead part of your soul."

Leona blinked, tears dripping down her cheek. She breathed hard, her lips trembling. "You can't mean that..."

She wilted, shrinking as Selene got to her feet. "I do."

"Not you, too..."

A well of anger, deep inside Selene, sprang forth. Her voice grew loud, quaking her chest. "I hope Sigur *never* forgives you for what you've done. I hope you go to the deepest depths of hell and dwell there *forever.*"

Leona went pale. "No... no..."

"Yes. I hope you wander alone until the day the Gods return, and *never* find salvation, *never* find peace for what you've done, and then Sigur himself strikes you down."

Leona squeaked, running from the room.

Selene strode to the door, her breath quick and her jaw clenched. She sighed, swearing under her breath as she watched the horrible girl run off crying.

S ELENE WAITED IN THE hall underground for Inquisitor Sorenius to arrive. It was daytime above, just after waking. It was the time for her rites, her confirmation, and the inquisitor was her sponsor. Three others were there, waiting for their own sponsors. She had a rope net over her shoulder. Her idea: the net would restrain the creature, so they'd have an easier time of killing it. She smiled as she caught the eye of one of her fellow *Velitore* fighters, a woman with blonde hair. They each had their own weapons—two with big crossbows, another with a spear.

She wasn't sure of the woman's name. She hadn't had many friends in this place, hardly knew anyone. It seemed strange, that she felt at home, but barely knew a face among them. *Ah...* Ebberich, Ruprecht... Leona. They were her only friends left in this entire place. They ate together, prayed together, slept alongside each other in the sleeping hall. They talked over meals, passing the time with stories of their pasts, despite Sorenius telling them to renounce them.

Ebberich was the son of a corn farmer and a clothier, and had been training to join the army before he threw in the with Order, thinking it was better to kill wukodlaks than men. He found his way to the citadel after an arbiter came through town and hunted a local manwolf.

Ruprecht was the fifth son of the Baron of Triburg, with no hope of inheriting land or titles. He was a guardsman in Triburg until the town was attacked by a demon. He was nearly killed along with two dozen of his fellow guardsmen until they were saved by a passing Sword. It was then he decided to join them, and fight back.

Leona was the youngest of five, with four brothers. Cursed and disowned for her eye, she was neglected and abused. She turned to Sigur in moments of despair, and joined the Order as soon as she could make the journey. Selene thought perhaps she had been too harsh on her—knowing how similar their childhoods were made her sympathetic—but she still hated her for what she did to Salim.

And Salim, the slave from Saburria, who would never see his homeland ever again.

She whimpered involuntarily, bringing a hand to her mouth. A twisted face. Stiff pain in her hand—steel glancing off bone. Glassy, brown eyes. A soft exhale. Selene swallowed, forcing tears back.

"Novitiate," Inquisitor Sorenius said, bringing her back. "Are you prepared?" Selene nodded firmly.

The door opened. They were led out as the Lord Inquisitor announced their presence. The crowd looked on, some with nasty looks, some eager looks, and yet others with fear. They were led downstairs, a notary unlocking the iron gate. She glanced behind. A small hole was made in the wall behind the notary, covered with an iron grate. The hole led somewhere dark and cramped—only the first two feet were lit by the brazier above. It wasn't locked, but it did seem out of place.

The Lord Inquisitor seemed to speak in a different language, even though he didn't. Selene had her focus on the vast door ahead of her, walking onto the sand. The gate locked behind them. Four novitiates. It was expected that at least one would die. She would make sure it wasn't her.

The huge door rattled to life, chains pulling it open. It was black inside, the prison beyond shrouded in darkness. A demon would be let out of its cell, free to wander the halls until it smelled the blood and fear in the arena. Smelling that enticing cocktail, it would come running.

The crowd went silent. Selene's heart pounded in her ears. She went over her weapons again in her head. *Two acid flasks. One dagger tipped with poison oak sap. A hand crossbow and ten bolts, all tipped with adder venom. The net—*

A vicious roar interrupted her thoughts. Selene smelled something acrid. She looked down. The man next to her had piss running down his leg onto the sand. She threw her head forward again. *No distractions. Focus.*

The roar came again, this time louder. Heavy footfalls. Grunting, louder and louder. A manwolf burst into the light. It ran straight at them, bent low for the charge. Selene dived to the side, sending sand into the air. The one with the spear moved in. His weapon was bat aside, and he followed, tumbling onto the ground. Crossbows twanged. The beast dodged.

She unhooked her crossbow, throwing her net to the ground. The beast was too far away for the net to be useful, anyway. She lined up her shot and pulled the trigger. The mechanism snapped open and the bolt whistled through the air. The beast moved unnaturally fast and spun away. It turned its cruel eyes on her. Down on all fours, it leapt at her. Too fast. It knocked the wind out of her. She coughed, hitting the sand. Looming over her, it stared, angry.

It yelped, recoiling in pain. A spear planted in its neck. Blood gushed onto Selene's robe.

She scrambled to safety. The others circled. She remembered the net.

With a victorious screech, she looped it over its enormous head and shoulders. The beast growled in frustration and tried to snap at her. She jumped back and with a shaking hand, tried to reload her crossbow, placing the stock against her belly. The demon hooked an arm into the ropes, and pressed down. *Snap-pop.* The ropes unraveled, tearing open. *Snap!* Selene stumbled back.

Her hand rattled. She fumbled the bolt. *Come on!*

The beast broke free. Lashing out, it caught the spearman's arm. Bones crunched. The novitiate screamed in pain. The creature yanked the spear free. With the other hand, he ripped the novitiate's throat out. He died as he hit the ground.

Selene backed up even further. The beast cast the net aside, going after one of the others. It landed nearby.

A net is useless against something so strong! But all I need is one moment!

She could use the others as bait. *Better they die than all of us, and this monster survive.* The woman circled closer to Selene, keeping at a distance to the beast, trying to reload her crossbow.

The woman grunted in surprise as Selene brought her legs out from under her. Wrapping the ropes of the severed net around, making her entangled. She cursed at Selene, eyes wide with fear.

Selene quickly loaded her crossbow with a fresh bolt. The beast danced around the sand, catching the other one on his own. The man let out a clipped yelp as a clawed fist punched into his chest, spraying blood across the sand.

The beast turned. Its quarry was waiting. *How kind of them, he must be thinking.* If the beast thought at all.

Selene backed up slowly, knowing that moving quickly would only attract its attention. *Dumb, predator animals.* It snorted. Sand kicked up behind it as it bound forward. It came after the entangled one, as Selene expected. It leaped, pouncing on its terrified prey.

Selene threw the acid flask. It smashed against the beast's face. It howled, reeling. Droplets sprayed all over the novitiate beneath. She screamed as her chest and face started to melt. The pain must've been unimaginable.

The beast recoiled, stumbling, grabbing at its smoking face. Half of it was destroyed. Selene unhooked her crossbow. Her hand was steady. The string twanged and hit its mark. Straight into the beast's gullet. The poison made short work of it. It stumbled, grasping at its throat, before making a choked, gurgling noise and collapsing on top of its prey. The woman's screams were silenced.

The crowd roared as the Lord Inquisitor took up his podium again, calling for quiet. His voice was a blur. Selene groaned as she pushed aside the beast, exhausted, hoping the woman was still alive. She wasn't. The beast had crushed her body when it fell.

Selene sat down on the sand. Everything was a blur. Sorenius came down to congratulate her, helping her to her feet. She was led up the stairs as the bodies in the arena were taken to the hole at the bottom of the stairs. Its purpose became clear now. It was a corpse chute, and probably emptied out into the sea at the foot of the cliff.

"Sponsor," Lord Inquisitor Rotersand spoke in the dark room just off the training hall, the one used for the dissection. Selene was still stunned, disoriented. She couldn't stop thinking about the woman's screams. *It was you or her, Selene. Stop thinking. Make yourself present. This is your moment.*

"Do you lay your blessing upon this novitiate," the Lord Inquisitor said, "knowing that she commits her life, body, and eternal soul to the Lightfather himself?"

"I do," he replied.

Selene stepped forward.

The high inquisitor brought his arms high into the air. "Speak the words, Novitiate Hunter."

"I pledge my heart and soul, my body and being," she spoke, willing her mind to be quiet. The death of that woman was avoidable—*but this is the service that Sigur requires of me.* "My mind and spirit, my life, and my eternal soul and service, to the great Sigur, the Lightfather, the Father of All. I pledge to seek out evil and vanquish it. I pledge to bring justice to injustices. I pledge to forgo all pleasures of the flesh, all vices of wine and ale and all others, so that I may better serve Him. I pledge to commit my all to the destruction of the Great Devil, and his agents in this world, and the next."

"Step forth, Diana, Warden of Justice, and drink the blood of your enemies."

Rotersand held out a goblet filled with a thick, dark liquid. The blood of a demon. She took the goblet in both hands and drank deeply. It tasted of copper and was still warm. She coughed as she withdrew it from her lips.

"Know that from this day forth, you will always have a home in any church of Sigur. Seek shelter in His walls should you ever need it, and He will protect you from any harm. And know that when you die, you will join Him in Hell, to fight in glorious battle."

Warden Diana bowed her head. The Lord Inquisitor went on, giving the other novitiates a slightly different ceremony. Each one in turn approached the altar in the center, saying similar words to her, but with variations as they were all notaries, and did not fight in the *Velitore*. She was the only one who survived the trial.

As the ceremony ended, Sorenius came up to her. "Deepest congratulations, Warden Diana," he said, bowing his head slightly.

"I would almost say you're happy," she replied.

"Of course. Why wouldn't I be?"

"It happens all the time, doesn't it?"

"Yes, but that doesn't mean I'm not happy to see it happen. And besides, were you told?"

"Told of what?"

"I'm to be your mentor, to travel with you as a pair. As mentor and apprentice."

Diana chuckled softly. "Good. I just hope you know a few tunes to sing so I don't get bored."

"Careful, Diana, I am still your superior." They shared a laugh. "Come, I'll take you to the armory. This'll be the most exciting part, I hope."

A dazzling array of weaponry and armor sat before her. Ranging from small one-handed crossbows hung on the wall, all the way to giant metal arbalests, veritable siege engines, weighing many hundreds of pounds. Dozens of racked blades, from the smallest knife to the largest two-hander. On a small shelf sat a collection of vials, all labelled—poisons, acids, and poultices in equal amounts. In the corner were a selection of pressure traps and snares.

Diana chose a nimble looking dagger, a foot in length. Its ball-shaped pommel was embossed with a design of Sigur's sword. She then took up a nice hand-crossbow, made with an ebony oak-cored stock, and metal arms. It was much more pleasing to the eye than the chipped and damaged training bows, though her last one had served its purpose well, and she would miss it. She thanked the old girl as she placed it aside. She tucked a dozen spare bolts into her beltpouch, along with a couple of acid flasks to replenish her supply.

A rack of black armor caught her eye. Leather jerkin, trousers, and thick leather tassets over the thighs. The left arm was sewn over, reinforced with a curved pauldron of steel, stamped with a maker's mark of a blooming rose seen from above. She grinned.

The inquisitor nodded. "Made, just for you."

She raced off, changing behind a screen. Sorenius turned his back, giving her some modesty. Though she might not have minded had he wanted a peek. *Pleasures of the flesh are forbidden... doesn't mean I can't imagine things...* His neck curved and graceful, but strong with muscle. His jaw, slender but handsome. Those leather trousers that hugged his body. *I'm only imagining...*

She stepped out, fine, tooled-leather boots echoing on the stone. "How do I look?"

"Take a look for yourself." He pointed to a mirror in the back corner. She stepped over.

It was the first time she had seen her own face in months. It was nearly blemish-free, and her nose had matured slightly, becoming higher in the bridge and slightly longer. She remarked to herself that it looked better, paired with soft red lips and a gently pointed chin. Black made her skin shine; her long, thick raven hair sitting past her shoulders, wavy and tousled. Her body was strong, her legs long and her stomach taut. Her dark green eyes like a pine forest stared back at her. She smiled wistfully. She never thought she could be prouder of herself in that moment.

"Stunning," she muttered, turning to see her whole outfit. It was form-fitting, but fearsome. Both the jacket and trousers were lined with interlocking metal plates, but they were still quite breathable and light.

Sorenius caught her eye in the mirror, then turned away, pretending to be looking at something else. Diana chuckled inside. "We leave tomorrow," he said, fingering the handle of a greatsword idly. "For a village in the Hag's Arm. And now that you're going to be my apprentice, call me Soren."

She turned, surprised. "Oh." *I should see the others before I go.* "Can I say goodbye—"

A scream came from the annex. She frowned, drawing her dagger. Sorenius drew his own weapon.

They rushed over, joining a throng of people crowding around the chapel with the icon of Brigida. They moved people aside, pushing to the front. She saw what they were all looking at, and froze.

Diana exhaled. She sunk to the floor, numb.

VOLUME TWO

The duty of heavy cavalry at the attack is to shock, disconcert, and shake the enemy's morale. To this end, they should prepare themselves with heavy arms, lances, and long axes. The second line and the footmen should always prepare themselves to cut off the enemy infantry their escape. In doing so, the premonitory general will surround and envelop the enemy, if they are so able. If the enemy have their own cavalry, it is the duty of fast-moving skirmishers and light-armored riders to harangue and distract the charge. The general may also employ fortifications or entrenchments to prevent the charge.

Entrenchment, however, is to be considered as a last option only. Either the entrenchment is too extensive to be defended properly, or the enemy may just avoid it entirely, finding a place at the rear to strike. One pre-eminent example comes to mind. The army of Duchess Else Adolar had invested themselves inside the walls of the city of Rennes, relying on a series of trenches in front of the walls to slow and harass their enemy. As the Duchess was preoccupied in an exchange with the Emperor's Lionguard, Prince Reynard of Annaltia noticed that their camp was unprotected, and open to attack. Soon, the Duchess was fighting on two fronts, and was defeated forthwith.

— *Institutum Militaris,* or *Emperor Franz II Osterlin's Instructions for His Generals.*

9

THE BLACKSMITH

WARDEN DIANA STOPPED ASTRIDE her horse on a hilltop overlooking the valley of the Hag's Arm. The northern reaches of the Alba river were fordable, nothing more than a few lazy streams coming from the South Hills. Up here, it was nothing like the enormous river mouth that emptied into the Bay of Empires. Pine forests extended in all directions, untouched by logging and farms. Apart from a tin mine in the distance, there was very little sign of civilization at all. She had no idea Osbergia went out this far. *How does the archduke get his taxes all the way out here?* Soren didn't know either. They travelled together as a pair, making their way east.

They had been on the road for a couple of weeks now, on horseback. Diana thought she would have to get used to travelling like that. No parlor rooms or goose down quilts ever again. Despite that, she had fallen in love with these lands, with the way the sun fell lazily behind the horizon, and of a morning, the air filled with the scent of wildflowers.

It was late summer, and the nights were warm enough that she could sleep under the stars, and they did so often. More than once she imagined climbing under Soren's blanket. Physical relationships were forbidden by the codes, but who would know this far out? He was handsome, well-muscled, and intense. And they were close. But maybe he was a bit too intense. Too focused on being a good Sword to share himself with her. Even after being with him all this time, she still didn't know where he was from, or his past before he became a Sword. Once, she tried asking him about his past.

"We must remain professional," he had told her. "I don't ask you about your life, and I would expect you to do the same."

Her horse nickered   softly, and she ran her hand over her neck. She was a beautiful mare, dark brown dappled with white. Fourteen hands tall, she was on the smaller side for a horse. Diana admired the beast's eyes—deep pools of coal tar that spoke to her intelligence. The warden had taken to her immediately. She hadn't picked a name yet.

"Soren, how 'bout that," she whispered. The horse blew a refusal. "Or... hm, what about Eda." Diana nodded. The name seemed right. It took a place next to her heart, and she smiled. The horse swayed its head up and down, like an agreement. "Alright, Eda, it is."

"Are you talking to your horse?" the inquisitor asked, laughing.

"Yes, what of it?"

He shrugged. "Nothing. Just strange, seeing as the beast couldn't possibly understand you."

"Ignore him," she said.

Eda blew her lips.

The road soon changed from forest trail to well-trodden gravel and forests gave way to fields. The stink of mud and sheep filled Diana's nose. The road was enclosed by wooden fences in various states of repair, perhaps at one point in time meant to keep livestock in.

Over the next rise, the village was in sight. They rode into the little community of Kuhurt. The mud-sheep smell concentrated more here, bringing a tear to the warden's eye. A thick-set, brown-haired man in a loose-necked linen shirt and a blackened leather apron walked up to them, hammer in hand.

"Who in Sigur's name are you," he said in a Hillman accent. The man was overweight, but his forearms and shoulders bulged with the work of many years pounding away at an anvil. He wore an angry scowl. *Distrustful of strangers in his village.* Based on the looks of some others, he wasn't in the minority.

Both of them dismounted and Soren spoke, "Good man, we are servants of the Most Holy Order of the Golden Sword. We mean you no harm."

"Holy Order?"

"What's that," a man with a milky eye asked. He leaned on a walking stick and had a flock of sheep at his side.

"Order," Sorenius said. "Of the—"

"What?" the sheep herd yelled.

"T—"

"Huh?" He cupped a hand to his ear. "Can't 'ere 'im."

"Aethelen," the blacksmith shouted. "Get after your flock. *Sal'brath.* They're off again!" The man with the walking stick glanced around, swearing as the sheep ran off down the road, taking after them.

"I 'ave 'eard of the Order," the smith said. "Though I can't say you're welcome 'ere. We've 'erd stories that you put whole villages to the torch."

"Good man, we are on the hunt for subversives. Those who would cause harm to good folk like yourselves."

"Subversives? Like robbers 'n such?"

"And others of the like." Soren liked not to reveal their true purpose, as he described, since shapeshifters hid in plain sight. Any one of Kuhurt's folk could be a devil.

"Ah! Why ya' not say so?" He plopped his hammer into the pouch on the front of his apron, and grabbed the inquisitor by the shoulders, huge grin on his face. "Us good folk are just wary of strangers, 'at's all. We're all friendly 'ere. Apologies, we're had some trouble of late, with some robbers 'anging around in the woods." He let go of Soren. The inquisitor was left mildly annoyed, frowning.

"Robbers?" Diana said.

"Aye, young lass. They're out in the forest. Been 'avin' bonfires an' keepin' us up of a night with wild shoutin'. They 'aven't been seen near the village, everyone says, but I'm sure they come 'ere, when we're all asleep, creepin' into our 'omes. That's probably what 'appened to the poor miller's boy."

"Miller's boy?"

"Aye, and no lie, it was a right mess. The poor lad was strung up by his feet down by the river, danglin' from a tree. Looked like 'e'd been nibbled at by a bear or summin'. The miller's still distraught about it. We 'ad to cut the poor lad down. We don't 'ave proof the strangers took 'im, but who else wouldn't done it? We've sent word to the lord but we've not 'eard anythin' back."

Townsfolk started to gather around. One of them was a woman with a long red dress—a kirtle. The dress had a low neckline, and her bust was covered by a loose shift that billowed up from underneath. The woman wore a white wimple on her head to keep the sun off.

The smith greeted her. "This is my wife, Joseline. I'm Baltash."

"Inquisitor Sorenius," he said.

"Pleasure, I'm Se—" She interrupted herself. Soren glanced at her. "Warden Diana."

"Pleased to meet you, kind folk," Joseline said. "So, do you drink ale, mead... barley tea?" Her voice was warm, inviting. Diana was reminded of a mother's voice.

"Oh, barley tea, please," she replied. Alcohol was strictly forbidden by the codes. She figured it was because they just didn't like fun. Soren replied with a curt shake of his head.

"Very well, three barley teas."

The smith stopped himself. "Why are yeh's still out here? Come on, let's get out of the sun."

They took the two Swords inside. Their house was small, but homely. Little touches of a hard-working family that took pride in their vocation were here and there. Intricate, looping bronze-work on the front door. A pewter goblet on a mantlepiece over the hearth, their dedication to the goddess Ginevra. Small bronze swords made for children to whack each other with.

Joseline brought out three finely decorated bronze cups and a small jug. Designs in twists of blue and green and yellow were painted on them.

"Oh, these are very nice," Diana said.

Joseline looked down at the cups and smiled earnestly. "Oh, thank you. My son Toldash painted them."

The inquisitor glanced at her. He thought she was too unserious for the work, but this way suited her just fine. *Soren can have his gruff mannerisms and stern looks, but a bit of charm can go a long way.*

The inquisitor queried for more detail about the miller's boy. "Oh, terrible thing, that. He was always so lovely," Joseline said as she poured the amber-colored tea from the jug. Warm wisps of steam rose from the cup.

"You heard them stories that the priests tell, 'a those devils that hide as men?" Baltash said.

"Yes, the wukodlaks," Soren said. Diana took a sip of tea. The taste was nutty, and a bit bitter. She felt the warm liquid slide down her throat easily. It was pleasant after a long ride, if nothing else.

"Yeah, them. I think it's one 'a them that done it. Those strangers are probably all them."

"It's possible."

The husband and wife looked at each other. "So, they're real? I was just guessin'."

"They are certainly very real."

"And you 'unt 'em?"

"We do."

"Maybe you should go ask after them strangers then. Be careful about it though, if they're monsters, you might get hurt."

Two young boys came roaring into the doorway, one chasing the other with a little pewter knight in hand.

"Ayeee, stop there, young lads," Joseline called. The boys stopped dead in their tracks. "Come, meet our guests."

"Hello there, little ones," Diana said. The two boys had little button noses, big eyes, and long eyelashes. They were positively the cutest thing she had ever seen.

The boys looked at each other. "Wow, you're really pretty," one of them said.

She grinned. "Thank you, you're too kind."

Baltash introduced the two. "My little boys, Caldash and Toldash. They're learning how to be smiths, like their father, and his father before him. Aren't you, boys?"

They answered at the same time, "Yes, da."

"Well, they're adorable," Diana said.

The inquisitor snorted.

"Thank you, lady," Caldash said, the younger of the two.

"Thanks, pretty lady," said Toldash.

"How old are you?" Diana said.

"Seven," Toldash replied.

"Five," Caldash replied. Diana chuckled. *They're very cute.*

"Now, run along," Joseline said, pushing them out the door. Soren got up, seemingly having his fill of family time, and waved at Diana to join him.

"Thank you for your hospitality," he said. "But we must continue our search. We'll take our leave."

Diana bowed her head. "Thank you, kind folk. The tea was lovely." They seemed properly surprised that a pretty stranger was so friendly to them.

"You're very welcome, lass," the blacksmith said. The couple waved the Swords off as they left.

"**I** DON'T SEE THE problem, Inquisitor," Diana argued. They rode to the camp in the forest, the one the blacksmith had told them about. "Being friendly to folk goes much further than being rude."

Soren waved his arms. "I'm not rude, I'm-"

"A jackass?"

"No, I'm objective, Warden. Being objective allows me to do my work effectively."

They rode staggered to the place in the forest where the strangers made camp. Late Solni drifted lazily through the trees along the trail.

"Sigur's Lantern," Diana swore. "Objective, meaning you only have to care about yourself."

Soren's forehead creased. He eyed her sharply for the curse. "You'll see, forming attachments as a Golden Sword is a terrible idea. You of all people should know this."

There was a flash in her mind. An unmoving, mismatched eye. "No, I won't let that happen," she said, trying to focus on something else. "I won't be that selfish person who uses others and only cares about themselves."

Soren waved his hand vigorously. "Shhh!"

Diana shook at the reins. Eda protested at the sudden movement.

"No, I won't be quiet," she yelled. "You were the one who brought it up!"

The inquisitor scowled at her. "Be quiet! I see something."

He pointed to a figure in the distance, leaning against a tree. She squinted hoping to glean something from the distant shape. "They're dead," Soren said.

"What?"

"Shhh! Keep your voice down. I think we're being watched."

Diana gulped. "What should we do?"

"We get off the horses and send them back to the village. No sense in them being in the way."

"Alright."

Diana gave Eda a hard smack on the rear as Soren did to Sullen, Diana's name for his horse, a grey gelding. She thought the resemblance was fitting, of the name, and its rider. The horses would find their way back to the village or would stop for tasty rushes along the trail. Either way, they were out of the way in case they were attacked. Horses panicked terribly at the sight of devils, and the Order had not managed to breed the fear out of them yet. The idea was that horses were sensitive to the evil exuding from them.

That makes two of us, Eda.

"Quiet. Pretend nothing is wrong and I'll see if I can spot our watcher," Soren whispered.

They walked along the trail towards the body in the distance. Solni fell below the horizon, long shadows falling across the trail. Diana's hand rested on the dagger's handle, arm coiled and ready. As they drew closer, she could see the carnage as it lay bare. The body was a woman's, no older than Diana herself. Her torso had been torn wide open. Fresh blood was sprayed across the ground. More bodies lie further on as well, much in the same state. Diana's stomach churned. *This could only have been in the last hour or so... the devil's probably still here.*

Bile stung the back of her throat. She swallowed hard, forcing herself to be still and quiet. Luni turned her back on them tonight, and darkness was setting in.

"There!" Soren unhooked his crossbow and ran ahead of her.

She lost him quickly in the darkness. Black shapes blurred past, flitting between the trees. Diana drew her dagger. She whipped around, trying to track the shapes, her dagger extended.

Boof! Brown fur filled her vision. She hit the ground with a thud. Groaning, she turned over. A huge brown manwolf with a thick mane towered over her. Its monstrously large teeth bared at her as it snarled. She stared, and it stared at her. She moved to defend herself, but she could sense something behind the eyes. *Is it scared?* The demon stood still.

The expected attack didn't come. All it was doing was breathing, chest like a man's but three times as large, heaving in and out. It let out a yelp, shot with a bolt. Diana held her dagger out, bracing for the attack. The demon had other ideas. It leapt away, whimpering as it tore through the brush and out of sight.

Thank Sigur. Soren came running. "Are you alright?" he said.

Diana brushed herself off, her breath returning to normal. "Yes." She shuddered. "It just stood there, staring at me."

"Maybe it likes playing with its food."

"Come, we'd better catch up with it."

"No need. Its heart will give out soon." She raised her eyebrows, giving him a smack on the shoulder. He'd poisoned the bolt.

"What if you'd hit *me* with it!"

"I wouldn't have. Let's go find it."

They headed off the forest trail, finding snapped branches and snagged fur. Sure enough, they came to a heavy-set man writhing in the dirt. His clothes were tattered, and he was coughing up blood. He moaned, "My children..."

Diana blinked in disbelief. "This devil has children?"

Soren nodded. "It's likely he would have used them against us, had we attacked back in the village."

"What do you mean?"

He kneeled down and yanked the bolt out. The monster groaned, writhing in pain. "You don't recognise him? He's the blacksmith."

It took her a second. His rotund frame. Brown hair. Thick arms, uneven from working a hammer in one hand.

"*Sigur, it is!* Gods, he seemed so friendly though!" The man struggled for breath. Diana felt for the man for a second before suppressing that thought. *He's a beast. He ripped apart those poor people back there.*

"Wukodlaks would use our own sense of kindness and humanity against us. That's why we must hunt them." The blacksmith fell still, and croaked his last. Diana still couldn't believe it. *He really was a monster all along. Maybe it was wrong of me not to become detached.* Soren got up and placed the quarrel back into his pouch, wiping it clean of the blacksmith's blood.

"Come. Let's go," he said.

10

THE ASSAULT

THE HORNED RAM BATTERED the gate as anxiety charged the air. Wood splintered. Strings twanged, arrows whistled. Broadheads planted in the ram's rawhide skin and wood frame, unable to hit the drivers beneath. Soon enough, the archers gave up. Tristain shuffled his feet in a muddy dugout, thirty feet from the gates, arming sword and heater shield in hand. His shield was a spare, clumsily painted with Sir Vredevoort's colours—a red bear on a green field.

It had been two weeks since he'd left the general's quarters and joined Vredevoort's regiment, under a gruff sergeant named Dengeld. They were all gruff. It came with the territory. When you knew no more than a few of your men would survive in any given battle, which could be the next day or the next, or even that same afternoon, it was hard to get attached. Vredevoort's regiment had the highest casualty rate of any.

Tristain had laid low, not attracted attention. The greycloaks hadn't shown themselves since that horrific night, but still he kept his head down, keeping to his tent between drills and chores. Not getting to know anyone. Eventually, the ram was completed, and the catapults measured up for distance. The general declared it was time to take Rennes, and the night outside the alehouse became the last thing on Tristain's mind.

Two men down from him, someone dropped silently, an arrow through their chest. The gap was quickly filled. A whistle. An arrow landed in front of him. He blinked. Mismatched feathers—one from a raven, another from a goose. The shaft was nicked. He raised his shield, protecting his face. His open-faced pot-helmet would provide very little protection if he was hit in the face. Over the rim, he spotted the gate crashing open. A mighty cheer came up around him.

Vredevoort the Grim led the charge, all steel and plate. Enormous longsword in hand, he bellowed as he charged. Tristain clambered up over the chest-high trench, arrows planting themselves all around him. Shields up. Swords and spears ready. Boots thumping on the ground. Yells and shouts around him. The drivers moved the wooden beast back, out of the path of the charging line. Tristain felt the world melt away. All that stood in front of him was their enemy, red and blue acorns. Their terrified faces.

Until pitch started flying. Horrible screams rippled the air. Heat from the boiled tar hit him, nearly knocking him off his feet. Torches descended upon them. Fire roiled in waves through dozens of them. Tristain's skin sizzled. Luckily the pitch itself hadn't hit him, but it still burned. Alongside him, men were turned into bright candles.

He pushed forward, pushing the stone down in his gut. Tristain stabbed what he could. A boy dropped. He was younger than Tristain. The man next to him stabbed back. Tristain put his shield up, feeling the point glance off. Tristain lashed out, slicing his foe's face through a gap in a helmet. Another took their place, bringing their axe down on Tristain's still-extended sword arm. He gasped. Someone leapt in, turning the blow aside with their shield. They brought their sword around and through, chopping and chopping, using their sword more like an axe.

"Feel the fucking terror in the air!" the man cried.

Cries and shrieks reinforced his battle cry. Another Badonnian fell as Tristain's sword opened up his neck. Blood jetted out of the wound. An axe planted in his shield, jarring his arm. His attacker cried out. The axe was stuck. He cried out again as Tristain planted steel in his belly. His face contorted in pain as he coughed blood onto Tristain's face.

Tristain turned to face another, yelling in fury. A sickening crunch rang out as his opponent's helmet caved in from a hammer. At Tristain's rear, someone caught a spear in their guts. They were pressed in, and troops on both sides fell as the tide went back and forth.

He felt his cheek open, recoiling. He grunted in anger, bringing his sword to bear again. A shove, a grab for his shield. Tristain ripped the shield away, slashing wildly. There was no room for finesse. Stab, stab, stab. Stab until they stop moving. Deep inside, he wished he had a spear. But swords were weapons for knights—and knights in training. It was a matter of pride and tradition. Who was he to say no to tradition?

The battle went on for Gods knew how long. Exhaustion came for Tristain, until he couldn't lift his shield anymore. He felt the battle open up behind him. He stumbled back. Breathing came shallow and quick. This wasn't his first battle, but it was his first with so many casualties on either side. Despite their months of isolation, starvation and disease, the Badonnians were still putting up a fierce fight.

A discordant horn blew from behind. He turned. Hundreds of knights in black plate streamed in from the north. He glimpsed a red flag with a black lion *rampant*. The arms were not familiar, though red and black meant they were Annaltian. Annaltia, their northern brethren. *Are they here to help us?*

The Annaltians formed a wedge. Tristain admired their discipline and their tactical genius. A wedge now would destroy what remained of the Badonnian line.

The knights charged into their rear. The Osbergian rear. Tristain gawped. Frantic shouts rang out as panic set in. Tristain's countrymen were taken by complete surprise. White hot pain shot up through Tristain's chest. He twisted his face as he turned back. A spear shaft stuck from his breast. It planted deep in his sternum, nicking a rib.

His skin prickled with fury. *Oh, Gods.* The crush around him slowed. His stomach lurched. His vision narrowed. He thanked Ginevra the change was less painful, this time.

L EON HEARD SHOUTING. HE came to the edge of the cage, kicking a bit of cabbage out of the way. Panicked cries echoed as camp followers and injured men ran, those that could. A mighty roar in the distance, but still loud enough to be heard. *Huh?* A flaming arrow whacked into the dirt nearby. *Fuck.* A knight in black plate galloped past. What was happening? There weren't no Annaltians here. *Shit.* He kicked over his slop bucket, sending foul smelling brown over the ground.

"*Hey!*" he smacked the bucket on the bars. It made a clanging noise. "Someone get me out!"

The fire from the arrow started to spread, igniting dry straw on the ground. Even though it had rained two weeks past, it had been dry ever since. The ground was waiting to go up—a few hours of wet that long ago wasn't enough to stop that. Leon banged furiously.

"*Someone get me the fuck out!*"

I T WAS A BLOOD haze around the demon. The air was thick with violence. He raged, thrashed, destroyed. Friend and foe alike fell to his claws, horns, teeth, strength. The battle thinned out on both sides as they were felled by the black beast. Those who weren't killed, ran.

The air vibrated with a sudden eruption. A head-sized boulder, thrown by great engine, brought down a tower above. The side crumbled, filling the air with a cloud of dust. The black beast felt something strike the side of his head, and his world went black.

C AEN LIFTED A ROCK off a boy from the Twentieth. The poor lad had a mangled leg beneath, tibia poking from flesh. The boy went stiff, falling silent. Caen looked down. Short, white feathers prodded from his chest. *Shit.* Caen threw his shield up.

A bolt chunked into the wood. He flinched as the narrow bolthead poked through. It was only a thin layer of dyed cloth covering a layer of ash wood, after all. The dust cloud resolved, and he'd lost sight of the beast. He thanked Sigur for that.

Now he had a new problem, in the form of twenty crossbowmen in black and red, fresh to the fight. He stepped back, hiding behind his shield. One bolt. Another. He cried out, bolt stabbing into his arm. He jumped behind a fallen pillar and breathed again, yanking the bolt out. Vredevoort in his steel came clambering into sight, bloody and limping. He was surrounded by dead of all colors. He raised his sword.

Behind his helm, he bellowed, *"For Osber—"*

He was cut off by a bolt through his leg plate. He howled, pushing onward regardless. Two more bolts. The Grim dropped to his knees, and the third one finished him. Caen looked up. Vultures circled above, patiently waiting for their meal. *Piss off. I'm not fucking dead, yet.*

The wall cracked open from another boulder. Somehow, the siege engines were still firing. Caen coughed, dust rippling over him. *Now, you idiot!* He ran for it, diving over the rubble.

The dust settled, and Caen found himself inside the walls of Rennes. *Now what?*

T RISTAIN'S HEAD POUNDED AS he awoke in the dust covered street. His helmet was gone, and his armor was in pieces. Groaning, he rolled over. Slowly, it came back to him. He'd been knocked out when the tower fell. He crawled, getting to his feet. The gate was blocked by rubble. With no other choice, he went the other way. *Maybe I can find a postern gate. Get out there.*

"Monster!"

Tristain looked around. An Osbergian had his sword pointed at him, trembling. Tristain's heart sank. He'd seen him transform.

"Die, devil!" The soldier swung his blade.

Tristain leapt back. He patted his side. No weapon. *Shit.* He tripped, letting out a grunt as he landed.

"Sigur, give me strength," his attacker yelled as he raised his blade.

Tristain closed his eyes. This was it. Maybe it was what he deserved.

He heard a cry and something warm spattered his face. He opened a single eye, unsure whether he would see his death barreling down on him. The soldier gasped, clutching at his chest. Steel flashed, and the man dropped.

Caen came into sight behind. "I think Leon would have my head if I let you die," he said, pulling Tristain to his feet.

"Caen? What in Ginevra's name are you doing here?"

"What does it look like, squire? Making us even. C'mon. We need to go." Tristain dragged his heels. Caen turned. "What are you doing?"

Tristain felt an overwhelming ache in his chest as his lip quivered. "Why? Why do you care? I'm a monster."

"Look... I'm no priest, and I'm not here to pass any judgment. But right now, it's only a matter of time before the Renneans, Annaltians or, Gods forbid, fuckin' Sigur comes for us. We need to go."

"Go where?"

"The army's done for. Ginevra knows why, but the Annaltians are tearing us to shreds. Both Waters and the Grim're dead. I wouldn't 've believed it, had I not seen it myself."

"Gods... The general?"

"Probably dining with Sigur already. Let's fucking go."

Tristain pushed down his fear and followed Caen. They clambered over the rubble, following a line of fleeing Rennean peasants out of the city.

"Down!" Caen dropped prone into long weeds. Tristain followed. A group of black-armored horsemen rode through, carving their way through the peasants. A flash of blades, and their screams went silent. Tristain felt his breath hot against the weedy ground. He wondered how much blood would water these wildflowers. *They might even develop a taste for it.*

Caen lifted his head and moved it on a swivel. "Let's go."

The camp was soon within spitting distance. Fortunately, the Annaltians were so preoccupied with butchering the assault force that they largely left deserters alone. *Imagine if Father could see me now. Running like a coward.*

They rounded a building. Tristain's feet ached—it was then he realized that his transformation had torn his boots to shreds. He ran on bare feet, cut up by the gravel and dry ground. "I need to find some boots. Where in the Gods' name are we going?"

"I was hoping you might know," Caen yelled back.

I can't go back. Not to how things were. Home. Back to Father.

Tristain came to a halt just as a squad of spearman in black and red passed.

"Hide," Tristain hissed. They hid behind a wall.

"*Attack!*" the head of the squad led a charge into the parade ground in front of them. Screams and shouts came over the wall.

Tristain breathed hard. He and the corporal looked at each other shamefully. Creeping along the wall, the battle grew louder. Hitting the ground from the around the corner, a servant fell all bloody. Tristain held his breath as a spear came down. The shaft twisted in his guts, and the servant stopped moving.

The clash grew quiet, and they crept along further. Rounding the corner, death unfolded before them. It was a massacre. The camp followers that remained were mostly servants with tools. The few men-at-arms that had remained behind—to guard the camp from a counterattack by the Badonnians—had been slain. The spearmen disappeared behind a barrack, marching back towards the parade ground.

Tristain swallowed hard, leaning down. Sheathing his sword, Caen came to his side, rifling through their pouches. Tristain blinked, watching Caen as he took two pieces of silver, placing them in his own beltpouch.

"You gonna' stand there staring, or you gonna' help," the corporal said. "We need coin if we're gonna eat. Gotta survive. Not like they need it, not anymore."

Tristain looked over the dead. Something felt wrong. "Are we to be cursed?"

"Sigur strike me down if there's something wrong with it." Nothing happened. "See?"

Tristain sighed. Ten coins they found in total. Enough for a few tavern meals. *I need a weapon, too.* He found a sword that had a few nicks but was otherwise well-balanced and sharp, and a pair of worn boots, but they did the job and fit well.

"Good," Caen said. "Let's go."

They ran for the stables, hoping one or two horses would still be there. Even a pony would've been enough to get them to the nearest village. They'd be stuck in Badonnia, but anywhere was better than this field of death.

Tristain heard a shout in Annaltian. He looked behind. Smoke rose above a line of tents, toward the parade ground. *They're burning everything to the ground.* An arrow hit the ground to the side of them.

"Run!"

They bolted. Tristain turned. A black rider kicked up dust behind him, hot on their tails. The enormous destrier under the rider bared down on them. An alleyway opened up between a row of buildings. They ducked down it. Caen threw open an armory door and they headed inside. Chest and legs aching, Tristain leaned against the wall as Caen shut the door.

"Quiet," Caen hissed. They were silent, the sound of their breath the only noise. Then came the brief sound of hooves clattering on dirt. Tristain willed his breath quiet. He slid his sword from its scabbard, as Caen did. The door creaked open. Heavy clanks of plate foretold the rider's entrance.

"You can't hide," he said. Caen swung his weapon, hoping to catch the Annaltian off-guard. Grunting, their pursuer caught the blade in his lobstershell gauntlet. He smashed Caen in the face with his other. They wrestled when Tristain drove his sword through a gap at the back of his knee. Yelling, the knight fell forward in a crash of metal. Tristain found the gap between his breastplate and arm-plate and drove the point in, cutting through the mail and jacket. The knight grunted, twitched. Blood leaked from beneath his breastplate.

Caen chuckled slightly, wiping blood from his mouth. "Thanks. Eme's tits. Bastard should know better than to turn his back."

Tristain eyed the blood dripping through the floorboards. "That's a knight. I just killed a knight."

"No shit."

"I'm a deserter, too. And a demon. How many men have I killed already?"

"Maybe they'll tell you his name when they're hanging you for it."

"Hmph. Don't know about you, but I don't plan on sticking around for that."

"Me either." Caen stuck his head out the doorway. "Let's go."

Tristain spied the knight's blade, a longsword with a ring pommel. Set in the center of the gilt cross-guard was a polished sapphire. He eyed it enviously. He drew it from its scabbard. It was well balanced, perfectly weighted. *Stealing from the dead, now? You've pilfered a bit of silver. What's a sword?*

He stepped outside, ring-pommeled sword in hand, duty arming sword tucked into his belt. The knight's giant destrier waited where he'd left it. Shouts came from elsewhere, and he could hear the sounds of battle inside the camp. Someone was fighting back.

"Let's see..." He walked up to the beast. The horse whinnied, clearly expecting another master. Tristain brushed his hand. *It's not biting or bucking, so that's a good sign.*

"*Get them!*" someone bellowed. Tristain turned his head. The twenty spearmen in black came rushing at them.

"Get on!" He climbed on the horse, taking the reins with one hand. He pulled Caen into the saddle. The beast whinnied in protest, but after some cajoling, took off.

They sped along, flitting between buildings. It was nothing like his other horse. This was a beast bred for war, and he had to fight to keep it under control. Eventually, they neared the edge of camp. Tristain heard fighting. He turned his head for a quick look.

Behind them, beside a barrack that was now an inferno, they saw a pale, red-bearded man in sackcloth fighting off a group of axemen. It was Sir Vorland. The two swore audibly.

The copse outside the camp and freedom beyond opened out to them. Only screams and fires lay behind them. The horse pulled, wanting to run, be free of this place. No one was chasing them. They could ride away, and no one would follow them. *No. No more running.*

"We have to help him," Tristain said.

"What are you fucking waiting for," Caen replied. "Permission?"

Tristain dug his heels in, wheeling the destrier around. The horse kicked up dust as it took off.

The Annaltians were taken by surprise. The sapphire-set blade flashed as Tristain charged, yelling. An axeman was knocked down by the destrier. He sliced a hand off. Another swing severed a neck. Tristain slashed wildly. Caen jumped off, cutting away with his own blade.

Leon blinked in surprise. He snatched an axe off the ground, jumping into the fray.

Fending his attackers off, Tristain felt the horse lift, rearing and kicking. He held on for dear life. *Shit.* An axe came down on his leg. He blocked it, coming around and planting his sword through his foe's face. The last one fell as Leon cut him down.

Tristain caught his breath, his legs, arms, shoulders burning from exertion. Leon panted, helping Caen to his feet. "Nice sword," he said. "Nice horse."

Tristain nodded, climbing down from the horse. Leon laughed, throwing his arms around him. "Good to see you, lad." Tristain groaned. The knight with melons for biceps squeezed the ever-loving life out of him.

Tristain stumbled as he released him. "And you, Sir. I'm sorry we couldn't stop the general."

"Ah, forget it. Sigur's blessings that we're all uninjured. Now... I'm done with this place."

They found their way to the stables. Only a sumpter and a shabby pony remained.

"Sir—" Tristain held the destrier's reins to his knight.

"No, squire. You've earned it."

Out they rode, smoke clouds blowing along their path to the Pass. Tristain looked back. Rennes was aflame. A stream of black dots rode through the camp. Men were cut down where they stood. He swallowed. They were the few that remained, a long way from home. *Has the world gone insane?* He supposed it had. A living myth, inside him. A civil war. The Annaltians served no master but themselves—Rennes burned under their torch as well. Perhaps it was the same disease inside Tristain, turning these men into monsters.

"Tristain," Leon said, pulling him back. "Come. The leviathan awaits, and then home."

II

THE HERBALIST

EVERGIA, THE NAME FOR the ancient kingdom in the southeast of Osbergia, was long forgotten by everyone except priests and historians. Avercarn was built on the ruins of their capital, Evarn. The kingdom haunted the land with its memories, dotting the landscape with a ruined pillar here, a crumbling foundation there. Evergia had ceased existing for centuries, long before the arrival of the Conqueror, Istryan, and the consequent flood of migration wiping the place from the face of the earth.

An important figure from the Age of Light, Confessor Torfinn, gave his life to defend Evarn. The city was conquered by the Great Devil's forces, and the kingdom was scattered to the wind. Torfinn's bones were considered holy, and were interred at the preceptory on the road north from Avercarn. Soren, Diana, and the preceptory's priests prayed at the foot of the martyr's stone casket, behind closed doors.

A month had passed since her hunt of the demon in the Hag's Arm. They'd not been back to the citadel since they left for Kuhurt, while the war in Badonnia was in full swing. Rennes lay under siege, and news was hard to come by. The day before, they'd encountered one of the local lord's patrols, men in red and silver, bristling with lances and hammers. They surrounded them, eyeing them warily until they noticed the inquisitorial badge on Soren's cloak.

"Apologies, lord," the captain had said. "Been too many bandits on the road, lately. Ever since the knights pissed off with their levies, brigands and thieves think empty fields and homes sit ripe for takin'."

Diana had to ask. "How goes the war?"

"Poorly, mistress. There was a battle between there and the Pass, many kinsmen died." She knew the place. It was called the Giant's Footfalls, after the strange rock depressions in the area, shaped like giant footprints. It was a barren place and would not offer much cover for an advancing army, and too many places for enemies to hide ambushes.

"Too many," the man said. "Maric here lost his uncle an' brother. That damn lady Duchess. Ain't right, a woman leading a host. Nothin' a woman good for other than motherin' and whorin'. No offence, mistress."

"Thank you, Captain," Diana replied. "Now, I'll remind you that we are duty bound to the law of Sigur, not to the laws of men. Are we to be detained?"

"Ah! Beggin' your pardons, mistress. Alright, men, let's speed out of these holy warriors' way."

They did, and let the Swords continue on their travels. She didn't have to remind herself that there were a multitude of reasons she'd joined the Order. That women could excel and face no impedance to doing so was just one of them.

Diana exited the church after the prayers had finished, leaning against a wall. Soren had stayed to talk with the preceptor. She tapped her fingers on her side, passing the time watching a honeysucker flit around the branches of a yellowing birch in the middle of the garden. The preceptory was small, just a church, a stable for their few mules, and a dorm for the priests to sleep and eat, and a high stone wall separating the place from the impure world outside. There was no training hall though; no recruits headed for the crucible. A pair of priests in black robes nodded at her as they walked past, speaking softly. She could pick out the words *beast* and *Badonnia* among other ones, like *corruption in the ranks*. She found herself wondering if the

Order had spies in the army—rooting out devils before they rotted it from within. Maybe the devils were to blame—why they'd lost their fight in the Footfalls.

Diana walked over to the stables to check on Eda. She was in the stables with Sullen, both taken care of by the half-blind but attentive groomsman. The mules had been moved outside to the yard.

"Greetin's, Warden," the man said, his wrinkled jowls wobbling as he spoke. He was stooped, hunched over by a third. He was brushing Eda with a stiff wooden comb, humming as he did so. The mare was enjoying herself, leaning into the brushing. Diana was glad. The horse had been through a lot. She had been near frightened to death on the last hunt.

Soren received a letter from the Lord Inquisitor telling them of a group of village folk just south of the Vinpa river in Annaltia, who'd captured a demon. He was the local tax collector. Diana had laughed, thinking it was a jest, until they arrived, and the beast leaped for Diana on her horse.

She had dodged, leaping off Eda. The beast clipped her as he soared over her head, and they landed together in a tangled pile, rolling off the road into a ditch. The creature growled, snarling as the disgusting creatures did. Its mistake.

Her venom-coated dagger already in hand, she stabbed it three times, lightning quick. The adder venom took its ice-cold grip quickly. The creature writhed in pain, raising its great clawed hand, to no effect. The hand came down with no more force than a soft thump. The beast slumped, collapsing on top of her. It died, then it was nothing but an unclothed man with a sizable paunch and two chins. Soren had a devilish smile on his face as he shoved the fat, naked tax collector off.

"Not how I imagined that going," she had joked.

Soren had just shaken his head. "I know better than to make a comment about something like that."

The village folk should've known better. There was no holding a devil without thick chains, and even then, it wasn't guaranteed if they were sufficiently riled. The only safe demon was a dead demon. The tax collector had escaped, slaughtering his captors in his flight. Even the children hadn't been spared.

Diana ran her hand across Eda's neck. The horse snorted in appreciation. She walked back into the yard as the door to the church opened. Soren walked out with the preceptor. The women were a Gods-send. Back in the citadel, any number of helpful philters; for pains, sores or bruises they would provide, no questions asked.

Diana smiled as the two approached. "Mother Cecilia," the inquisitor introduced, "Warden Diana, my apprentice. Mother Cecilia is the preceptor here."

The woman bowed her head. She was in her twilight years, like the groomsman, with a crooked back and her ghost-white hair tucked under her veil; white linen to match her robes. "Pleased to meet you."

Diana bowed her head in return. "Likewise, Preceptor."

"You know the lands we stand on? You know of the ancient kingdom of Evergia?"

"I can't say that I do, not much."

"It was a place of gold, and milk, and honey. No one ever went hungry, and it was said that men lived into old, old age, just as healthy as they were when they were young. But the Great Devil saw to that—growing jealous of Evergia's wealth and utopian ideals. So, he wiped the place from the Continent."

"I see."

"That's why we fight." The preceptor placed a hand on Diana's right arm. "I see you've had something taken from you, forever, as well."

She looked down. "Yes." *But I fight, so that no one else may suffer the same fate.*

"Someone 'elp, for Sigur's sake," someone yelled from over the wall. Diana glanced at Soren. The three of them strode to the gate, joining a few priests.

"What's so urgent," one of the priests snapped. A group of peasants flooded into the preceptory as the gates were opened.

"Sigur's Blade," the preceptor said, sighing loudly. "We've heard these ones before."

"You're the Order, right?" one of the peasants asked. "We saw the hunters on the road. We're—"

"What is the meaning of this?" Soren said.

"Forgive us, Lord, but we've come to plead on behalf a' our eternal souls!"

"They're convinced a wukodlak lives on the outskirts of their village," the preceptor said. "I've had a look, Inquisitor, and I believe it to be nonsense."

"No nonsense where the agents of evil are concerned," Soren answered. "We'll see into this matter." Diana agreed.

THE WOMAN'S COTTAGE WAS far outside the village. Their investigation had proved to be a tale of two women in one. Some described her with horns, giant teeth, and a vicious glint in her eye, snatching babies and cursing men to impotence. Others described her as a quite normal woman, blessed with the gift of healing, with no husband or children, and in her middle age, but that could also be deceptive, as the monsters were known to hide their true nature.

Nestled by a brook and a small overgrown orchard, her house was a typical homestead of the region, with a main house and a shed, a hen house, and an herb garden, all fenced off by low stone walls. Wild goats wandered placidly in the orchard, munching on the apples that hung low enough from the unkempt trees, bulging with fruit. Hens pecked at the crumbs and seeds discarded by the goats. It really was hard to believe that anyone other than a quite normal peasant woman lived here, if perhaps a bit further out than was usual.

The fowl clattered madly at their approach. Soon enough, a short, sun-darkened woman appeared in the doorway. Her madder-dyed kirtle came down to her ankles, and wine-colored hair speckled with grey poked out messily from beneath her wimple. Diana dismounted Eda, utilizing one hand and the stirrups at her saddle. The mare pulled ahead, tearing a juicy-looking bulrush next to the stone wall.

Soren climbed down from Sullen. "Good woman," he said. "Sigur lay his blessings on you."

"And you," she said, eyeing the blades at their belts. "Is this about the Master? I told you before, the rash will only go away if he treats it every day. The lazy bas—" She stopped herself, tipping her head back slightly. "No, you're Order, aren't you? Been said you were on the road. What're you doing here?"

"Good woman, the ground is cold through our boots. We'd much rather discuss the reason for our visit inside."

She relaxed her face. "I'd prefer you keep your weapons outside, but I've no reason to refuse ye'." They headed inside, stepping carefully through the woman's garden. She passed under the lintel with no trouble. Both Swords had to duck their heads. Inside, the cottage was surprisingly well-lit for its location in a glade. Paned windows and dormers opened up the space. The woman headed behind a curtain to the kitchen, sending the fragrant smell of herbs into the main room.

"Expecting guests?" Sorenius asked.

"Nay," she answered. "Just me-self. Forgive me if you were looking for a five-course meal."

A woman of the land, Diana thought she might fit right in between the tenants of her old guardians' estate.

"Don't mind us, we're not hungry," Diana said. They'd eaten at the preceptory, though taking food from a suspected she-wolf would've been suicidal. Who knew if she'd poison their food?

Diana looked around. On the woman's shelves were a few curios—a small doll made of wool, clothed like a child; a letter knife; and a necklace made of silver, hung with a pendant. She popped it open. A portrait of a young girl lay inside. She showed Soren, then put it back.

The woman pulled back the curtain, platter set with steaming, thinly sliced potatoes topped with cream of goat milk. She set them down at the table and urged them to take a seat.

"So," she said. "Why have the Order of the Golden Sword found themselves in my house?"

"Forgive us, good woman," Diana said. "We heard rumors of your—"

"My devilry and my heresy," she interrupted. "I assume?"

"Yes."

"I wouldn't think such trifles would concern the Order; great arbiters of truth that you are."

Soren grunted. "Normally, yes, if we were to investigate every frippery, pockmark, or wayward spouse under the influence of the Great Devil, we would find ourselves with no time to deal with serious matters."

"What are serious matters, then?"

"When half the village is convinced that you're hiding pointy ears under your veil," Diana said, "and a mouth lined with fangs the size of fingers, and as sharp as razors. Yet, the other half seems to sing your praises. Those ones seem to think you're the next coming of Ginevra herself."

"I make potions and poultices from time to time, sell them to womenfolk, mostly. One that'll settle your guts, one that'll do the opposite. Don't drink my tea if you value your bowels."

"Hm. I suppose you could answer a few of our questions, then?"

"And what if I said no?"

"I suspect you know what comes next."

"I do. What did you do to your arm, Sword?"

Diana wouldn't be deterred. "What's your name?"

"Lorena-Maria Ulgart."

"Lorena-Maria? Are you Republican?"

"Alanian, yes. On my mother's side. She came here to be with her love, my father, oh... sixty-two years ago. My memory is a bit fuzzy these days, but that's the right of it."

"Right. Married? Children?"

"None. Been alone my entire life, the way I like it."

"No children? Who will look after this place when you die?"

"No one, I suspect. Let the forest grow over it, I won't mind." *Acerbic, and tight-lipped, too.*

"Let me move on. Why did you think we were here for a 'Master', before?"

The woman sighed deeply. "Oh... I shouldn't have opened my mouth. You're not with the baron, are you?"

Diana shook her head. "Most certainly not. The Order answers only to Sigur himself."

"Right. The baron has himself rather a problem with a rash... in his nether regions. His wife won't touch him until he rids himself of it. Doctors tried and failed, so he came to me. I guess one of the folk here had spread the word that I had remedies for all sorts. That was an afternoon, let me tell you. The man was so nervous I thought he might shit himself on the chair. I inspected the man's horn, and between you and me, I think the surgeon'd tried leeches or something... it was angry, red, like a new-born." Soren shifted uncomfortably in his chair. "I gave him a paste of wolf's bane and ground willow bark to ease the swelling and itching. It's probably Night Pox, so there's no cure, but it'll go away in time. They came here... oh, two days past, to say it's not working. I say the only way that's like to happen is if he's not putting on every day, the lazy bastard. I've seen more than my share of it in the menfolk, so I know what I'm doing. Anyway,

I been sworn to name him the Master to all his servants. I thought that's what you two were, 'fore I realised."

"I see. I gather we won't have this information confirmed?" Soren asked.

Lorena-Maria shrugged. "Likely not. Sorry."

"And where did you learn to make these medicaments?" Diana said. "I understand that the academies do not take women, one of the few doors that are closed to us."

"If you think there's only a few doors that are closed to us women, you're sadly mistaken, child." She paused. "My mother taught me, just like her mother before her."

Diana turned. Wild clucking came from the garden, raising the alarm. Something was out the front. She went to the window. A crowd of peasants had assembled outside the garden. They stood in silence, but their faces were frozen in anticipation. *Don't get any closer now. It's dangerous.* Diana turned back. She noticed the woman's eyes flash for an instant to the pendant on the shelf. She tensed up. It went silent, anxiety charging the air.

"Hm," Diana said, narrowing her eyebrows. "There's one thing that's bothering me. See, I think you're lying to us about not having children."

Lorena-Maria laughed. "What are you talking about? I don't have children."

Soren leaned forward in his chair. "There's something you're not telling us, isn't there?"

"I have no idea what you're talking about."

"I think you know where this is going. Either you answer our questions truthfully, or we'll be forced to use other measures."

"Ain't answered 'em nothing but truthfully."

Soren got to his feet without a word. He walked over to the hearth. Embers smoldered quietly. He chanted a prayer to Sigur, closing his eyes.

"*Lightfather,*" he said loudly. "Fire given by your name, I purge you by the holy God. Bathe us now in the light of purification for the salvation of all faithful. Let every unclean spirit be commanded by Him who is to come to judge the living and the dead and the world by fire."

Diana saw Soren's hand flick almost imperceptibly towards the flame, tossing some sort of powder on it. The blaze erupted in yellow, filling the room with a slight metallic smell. Golden light bathed the room. It died down, returning to its regular orange color, but it burned stronger than it had before.

"Step forward, Healer. Prove your innocence in the pyre."

The woman gulped. "You can't be serious."

"Prove your innocence. No more than a hand's worth. If your skin blisters but does not catch fire, we will know your purity."

She sighed. Coming over, she said, "If I pass your test, will you leave?"

"Without hesitation."

Soren pulled up a chair. Lorena sat down, waving her hand over the fire. Sorenius took hold of her wrist, pulling her into the flames. She yelped. The heat licked her skin. Her flesh turned red and angry. She groaned. Diana saw a flash of something in her eyes, but it disappeared as soon it arrived. The woman started to scream. The peasants outside raised their voices in alarm. Lorena gasped in surprise, covering her mouth with her free hand.

Diana ripped her hand aside. Teeth, as long as fingers.

Soren leapt to his feet. The herbalist dived, grasping the side of the dining table. She flipped it with a grunt. Hot potatoes and cream sprayed into the air. The table crashed into the Swords, thrown with surprising strength. Diana groaned as she hit the floor.

A growling noise filled the air. A flash of dark red fur, the same color as the woman's hair. It tore past them, hurtling through the door. The peasants yelled in surprise. Sorenius helped Diana to her feet. They burst outside. *Twang-thunk.* The beast gasped, half-woman, half-demon falling to the floor.

The peasants cried fury. As the woman died, venom-covered bolt in her chest, the townsfolk pelted her with stones. Soren squeezed her shoulder for a job well done. The trap had been Diana's suggestion, and only a last resort. She was just glad the peasants didn't trigger the trap themselves. Rigging up the twine had to happen under the cover of darkness – and Diana counted herself lucky that the woman's garden didn't look tended to, giving her plenty of dense bush to hide a crossbow in, and less of chance that she would accidentally trigger the trap prematurely.

The village folk looked satisfied that Lorena was dead, and stopped throwing rocks. Diana played with her hair idly. It seemed that the peasants were all too ready to turn brutally against a woman who'd lived there for years, as a long-standing pillar of their community. But Diana understood. It *was* betrayal. She had lied for so long. The people of the village had a bright future ahead of them.

"Let's go," she said to Sorenius.

He nodded. "I trust these people can take care of a pyre by themselves. Her body is to be salted and burned, and her ashes are to be taken to the preceptory to be disposed of. Yes?"

The folk nodded solemnly.

12

THE FOOTFALLS

TRISTAIN, LEON, AND CAEN ran their horses ragged. They rode far as they could manage, through the night and another day. It seemed like they'd outridden any pursuers. As night gripped them, Tristain's head spun. He slowed. The world flipped until the sky became the ground, and his mouth filled with dirt. As his head pounded, he realized he hadn't eaten for nearly two whole days.

The destrier snorted, grumpy at the constant riding. He found a tasty shoot of ryegrass and was content. He was soon joined by the sumpter and the pony. Tristain was helped to his feet. A fire was made, and Leon sat him down. Tristain felt cold and beyond hungry. The fire helped.

"I don't think I ever thanked you, lad," Leon said. Tristain blinked lazily, his vision blurry. He made a vague sound of agreement. The corporal handed him a heel of bread. He didn't have a bag or a pouch. Tristain didn't want to know where it came from.

"Here, *Althann*," the knight said. "Eat."

Slowly, things became normal again, as he ate. He didn't feel so faint. "What was that, Sir?"

"Don't think I forgot how you two saved my life," Leon replied. "Charging in like that was reckless, but still..."

"Don't forget it when you're back in the halls of good grace," Caen said.

Leon chuckled. "I don't see that happening anytime soon. The general will have almost certainly made my disgrace known; written a letter to the emperor to have my investiture rescinded. And even if she hasn't, people talk. Nothing sets a court aflame more than a scandal."

They went quiet. Tristain took another bite of bread and broke the silence. "What will you do?"

"I'm not sure yet. I suppose I'll leave it to the Gods for now. What about you, lad? What will *you* do?"

"I... I don't know. I don't even know what to make of it all. I'm a monster... some evil writhes inside, waiting to get out."

"Well," Caen said. "Do you *feel* evil?"

"I feel cold, despite the fire," Tristain said, hugging himself. Caen chuckled. "But no. I feel uncertain, and not quite like myself, but not evil. My stomach turns at the thought of what I've done."

Leon leaned forward; his eyes cast in bright orange from the fire. "You remember what happened?"

"Not quite. I remember... I think I died. I felt impossibly cold, then a bonfire light up beneath me. The pain was... I can't describe. One part, I remember distinctly." Tristain held up his hand. "Claws came shooting out of my fingernails. It felt like I was having them removed with pliers."

Caen shivered. Leon remained as stoic as ever.

"But after... it was like my whole body was filled with spirit, both in strength and feeling. I felt... better than anything. I killed those Badonnians, and I enjoyed it. At the time at least."

Caen laughed. "Those bastards deserved everything they got. I would've loved to 've seen their faces. I bet they didn't expect that."

"Neither did I. I suppose the priests would say I'm cursed."

"Let the priests and their incense-addled heads theorize what in the Gods' name it means. We're alive because of you."

Tristain looked down at his feet. There was a lingering sense of shame about it, stirring deep inside.

"Lad," Leon said. "I can't say I know much about this, but I do know sometimes you can be a gloomy, defeatist prick. You could've killed us too, and you didn't." He took the flask from his belt, giving it a swig.

"I guess that's true. There must be something inside, something holding me back."

"Let's get some rest," Leon said, wiping his mouth. "On the morrow we'll be nearer to the Pass."

"How are we getting through? Isn't it full of... well, full of ours?"

"Yep. That's why you're not Tristain, son of Sebastian, or Caen son of... whoever the hell you're son of. Not Leon Vorland the Strong and his retinue anymore. I'm a farmer, and you're my two sons."

"Fuckin' blessed Ginevra," Caen said. "I've always wanted to know my father."

Tristain snorted with laughter.

"Yeah, and I'll spank you like your father should have," Leon replied, smirk flashing across his lips. "Smart mouth."

"I expect we'll have to leave the destrier behind, too," Tristain said.

"You'd be right," the disgraced knight replied. "That warhorse'll give us away for miles. Even the pony might be a bit much."

Caen grumbled. "Right, so you get the only horse."

In the morning, they sent the destrier and the pony on. Perhaps they would live out their lives in the wild, or maybe they would fall prey to starving hunters or village folk. It was hard to say. Tristain thought of Onyx and Nikkel. He wondered if Nikkel had made it Invereid already, although he only had a week or so on them.

By the time the sun was highest, they came upon a group of peasants driving an oxcart—two-wheeled and high-sided. *Farmers, by the look of them.* It was risky business considering the war raging around them, but determination on their faces made it clear they wouldn't be stopped. Some of the folk noticed their approach.

"Have a care," Leon said. "They might take us for outlaws."

Caen shot him a discourteous look. "We ain't?" he whispered.

Leon stepped forward. He spoke in Badonnian, "*Buojour, sono vri?*" The ploy seemed to work, as the headman turned his head and smiled at their approach. He said something back, and Leon conversed with him. They shared a laugh, and Leon turned his head to the other two and nodded.

"They're going to the Pass," he whispered. "And they'll let us tag along. It's safer in numbers."

"Helps they 'ave food," Caen replied. "Aye?" Leon agreed.

T RISTAIN'S MUSCLES ACHED AS he tried to push the wagon through two peaty grooves, known as a road to the locals of the Footfalls. The Giant's Footfalls was a sparsely vegetated place, and sparsely developed at the best of times. During the war it had been burned, and the trees that dotted the place were blackened. Soft peat under the oxcart's wheels had jammed it in place. Ash from fires. Weeds choked the fields around.

The Footfalls were sparse of most things, most of all people, which had bidden well for their travel to the Pass. Strange craterous formations made the land pockmarked. They looked like footprints of giants, hence the name. Eagles circled above, howling cries echoing across the barren place. To the north were the wall of mountains that was the South Hills—south for an Osbergian—and the Avallano Mountains further south of that.

They gave up as the headman said something in Badonnian. Leon answered, and Tristain wished his tutor taught him the language before he left to join the war. Either way, Tristain soon realized what was happening as they broke off and started preparing a fire. Leon ushered him and Caen on.

"Let's get some firewood," he whispered in Osbergian. He kept his voice low, taking a swig of his flask. "Make ourselves useful."

Tristain nodded and followed.

Caen was close behind. "I thought I was gonna' shit my pants," he said as they moved out of earshot.

"That face you were pulling, Corporal, made me think you were pretty close," Tristain replied. "Let's just hope we make it to the Pass before too long. I can't keep answering their questions with a nod. They'll think I'm mute or something."

Caen nudged his elbow. "Let 'em think you've been mule-kicked in the head. Wouldn't be too far off."

Tristain blew his lips. "Shut up."

"Stop your yammering," Leon grumbled, wiping his face. "Find some fuckin' firewood before I strangle you both."

Tristain scratched his head as he looked for good branches. He wondered what had brought on the knight's bad temper of late.

The headman, thankful for their bundles, offered them all a swig of a wineskin. Tristain took a sip. It was deeply acidic, like strongwine, but worse, and foamed around his lips. He coughed. They laughed.

"Soured milk," the headman said in Osbergian, laughing. Tristain wiped his mouth, flicking his eyes to Leon. Then his eyes went to the longsword hidden under the sumpter's pack. "It's okay. We tell from first day. Clothes—" he said, gesturing to their rags "—not ours."

Tristain glanced around. The headman was right. All the villagers wore similar clothing, cuffed woolen tunics in blues, and very few hoods. They wore box-shaped wool hats instead. The three Osbergians wore what an average Osbergian soldier would under their armor; knee-length woolen tunics in brown and yellow.

The headman held his hand out. Tristain took it. "Roupert. You are?"

"Tristain."

He turned to Leon. "And we know you, *Chevalier*. You are fearsome to kill the King's brother and all his men in such a way."

Caen coughed. "*King's brother!*"

"*Wi*. We call you the Flame. Is okay. The King's brother was a cruel man." He spat on the ground. "He under the mountain now."

Leon crossed his arms. "The Ox's Balls?"

The headman nodded. "You are hero."

Tristain and Caen looked at each other incredulously. Caen laughed. "*Hero—*" Leon flashed Caen a stern look. The corporal shut his mouth.

"You know... we're probably going the wrong way, Sir," Tristain said, smile flicking across his face. "You might be in good stead with the Badonnians."

Leon snorted. "Might be."

"Oh no," Roupert said. "King Broca want your head. He loved his brother."

"So much for that," Caen said, taking another swig of the fermented milk. He inspected the skin. "It's horrible and tastes like cow sweat, but I can't stop drinking it."

"Is too bad. We have lots back home."

Tristain sat down by the fire, warming his fingers. It was colder in the Footfalls, close to the ranges they were. "Was it the war? Why did you run?"

Roupert sat down as well, joined by the others. Tristain caught the eye of a young, brown-yellow haired man and smiled. The young man smiled back. His big hazel eyes held a glint of mischievousness to them. He was all chiseled jaw and high cheekbones, and Tristain felt his heart flutter.

There were eight in total—five others, discounting the head man, his wife, and the blond man. One man wore a fraying straw hat, who looked like he was a few teeth short of a full set, with a pockmarked, sun-damaged face. Accompanying him was a woman who was either his wife or his sister, or perhaps both, as they had the same features, and seemed very close. The fourth was a stocky, weather-beaten man, who could've been a fisherman or sailor, down to the blue woolen cap and pierced ear. A small boy with a matching cap, but in red, travelled with him.

Roupert glanced at his wife, an older woman with greying hair. "This is my wife and son, Marie, and Luka." Luka was the young man with blond hair. "We flee the war, yes, but we try to start a new life. We hear the Empire will take anyone who work hard. Life here is bad. The King is cruel, like his brother. Anybody who say a bad word against him ends up..." He drew a line across his neck, grimacing. He looked at his wife again. "Marie father, he end up like this. The war was just push to make journey. The King's brother was his *chasseur*, his devil. Anyone refuse to pay tax, he is there. Anyone refuse to swear fealty, he there. And..." He made a noise as he drew a line across his neck again. "We owe a great debt, *Chevalier*."

"You owe me nothing," Leon replied. The head man's wife nodded, a small tear gathering at the corner of her eye.

"Thank you," Roupert replied. "Still, anything we can offer, is yours."

"How about a fire and conversation?"

Roupert nodded. They were eight in all, and the three deserters made eleven. He told them of how each of the refugees had been picked up along the way. They'd have to be on the road before long, lest they make a tantalizing target for criminals or slavers. But Tristain would protect them, if it came to it, and he was sure Leon and Caen would, too.

"So, what was it you wanted to be? A father and his sons?" the one with the blue cap said, laughing. He spoke better Osbergian than the others, and definitely wasn't Badonnian by his accent. "Bold claim, that. A damn sore sight if I've seen one—how does a ginger make a strawhead, *and* a blackhead? Your wife rainbow-haired?"

"Sounds like a mummer's jest," Caen replied, laughing.

The blue-hat laughed. "I suppose it does. Well, Ginevra be praised. For the Flame'll get us to the Pass, and then."

"And then, what?" Leon replied, running his hand through his beard.

"I've a debt to settle. You've no doubt heard of the *Arabella*? The fastest ship in the south? No? Anyway, that bastard of a captain Chesterfield marooned us in Ammercy. This is Bean, and I'm Lorrin. We've been trudging through marsh, avoiding both the Badonnians and the Osbergians, on our way back to calmer waters, if you'll excuse my expression."

"Bean is your son?" Tristain asked.

"Nah. He's a stray that hung around long enough for Chesterfield to take him on. Eventually he just became part of the crew." The boy looked at the sailor but didn't say anything. "'e don't speak. We don't know his real name, but he loves beans, so we called him Bean."

"You talk enough, we eat," Roupert's wife said, and no sooner than she had did Tristain find a steaming bowl in his lap. As he chowed down, the sailor started singing a ditty about a woman pregnant with a horse, and her husband's consternation at the birth. Tristain caught Luka's eye again and smiled.

Luni was high in the sky as Tristain lay back on the straw that was his bed under the stars. A gentle breeze blew over his face. It was peaceful. He could almost forget the horrible events that had led him here. A shadow moved across the sky. It was just an eagle making its way home, he imagined. He drifted off to sleep as he imagined he was the eagle, soaring his golden wings over the grey steppes.

TRISTAIN SAW LEON AND Caen lag behind as they crossed a ridge. He looked over the landscape. At first, it wasn't clear what they were looking at. But eventually he spotted bleached bones and tattered cloth. A field of dead men. They'd been left behind, left for the crows and the wolves. Already picked clean, they'd been there for months. With so many dead, he wondered how anyone would've survived. He wondered what it was all for.

Leon was taking a swig from his flask as Tristain walked up. Remembering that they'd both fought in the pitched battle, he kept quiet. The knight sniffed. "I knew we'd pass by here eventually," he said, dejection in his voice. "Doesn't make the wound any less nasty."

Tristain looked at the knight. "Was this...?"

"Yes," he replied. A few moments passed. "I never buried him; you know that? I saw him fall, but when I went back, I couldn't find his body."

Unusually sincere, Caen said, "What would you say to him if he was here?"

Leon sniffed again. "I'd ask for forgiveness, and for dragging him into this stupid war." He let out a great sigh. "A cursed man I am, to outlive my child."

Caen's face grew pained. Tristain thought on Caen's daughter. Eventually, the corporal said, "The Gods have their strange ways."

They let the silence drag out for minutes, until he said, "I think it's best if Eiken didn't see me like this. I'll admit, I've not been the best knight I could've been. I apologize."

Tristain nearly opened his mouth to say something smart, but there was a time and place for jokes, and it wasn't now.

"Anyway," Leon went on. "We should get back to the caravan before they leave us behind." Tristain looked back as they left. He caught the silver of Leon's flask by the edge of the ridge.

A yell came from up the road. They ran, coming around an outcropping. The caravan was being waylaid by thugs. Tristain bolted. He breathed hard, his legs carrying him as fast as they could. He drew his sword as the thugs were within spitting distance. They pinched at the wagon, tossing through the contents. The head man and his wife tried to stop them. The others watched on.

"*Bastards, get!*" he cried. They looked over. One of them yelled in Badonnian, throwing himself on the ground.

"Please! Don't hurt us! We are only hungry!" They were Badonnian, but spoke Osbergian reasonably well. Tristain wondered quickly if he was the only person on the whole Continent that only spoke one language.

"Get back," he warned, waving his sword. They quickly backed off. Tristain felt a hand on his shoulder.

"*Goddess*," Leon said. "What's happened here?"

"Please," the bandit said with ragged breath. "We just want some food." He stepped closer.

"Get back! I'll gut you where you stand," Tristain said, feeling his skin prickle with anger. He wasn't sure why, but his fury needed to free itself from his body. He advanced. Leon gripped his shoulder hard.

"Tristain," he said firmly. "*Sal'brath*. Look at them. Not a weapon among them."

Between quick breaths, Tristain glanced over them. They were half-starved, rags hanging off them, and Leon was right. They had nothing that could even be considered a weapon. But Tristain remembered what his sword instructor, Master Loren, told him.

He found himself yelling. "Fists, knees, elbows... what are those if not weapons? They're hoping we'll let our guards down, and get us when our backs are turned."

"Please," the bandit pleaded again. "We've nothing left."

Caen went to speak. "Just give 'em a scrap—"

"We're not bloody priests, Caen," Tristain snapped. "This isn't a charity."

"Can I offer a solution," Leon said. "Enough food and ale for a day, and be on your way."

"Thank you, sir... we've nothing left, nothing."

Roupert nodded as he handed the men a skin of ale and three heels of bread.

"*Mercee*. Been much kinder than the other imperials we've seen."

Leon's ears pricked up. "Imperials... Osbergians?"

"*Non*, not white, or red, but black like night. They burn from the north. They burn it all."

"They burned us, too," Caen said offhandedly. "Why *are* the Annaltians here?"

"To take advantage, would be my guess," Leon replied.

It was known that the emperor was deeply fond of his six sons, each princes of their own imperial province. Osbergia was the southernmost province, and the largest, with the most fertile land, and borders with the merchant republics of the south. Of course, the sons were much less fond of each other. Annaltia's disruption of their war in Badonnia likely stemmed from some feud between the Archduke and his brother, Prince Reynard.

"Of course..." Tristain felt the lull and started to calm. The prickling under his skin went away.

Caen crossed his arms. "Want to enlighten us?"

"What are brothers if not envious? Gods know I was." He was envious of his brother's looks, his age, the admiration of his father. Until Bann died, slaughtered by brigands on the road. Perhaps that was the reason for his outburst.

"Prince Reynard," Leon said. Reynard ruled in Annaltia. "I don't know much about him. But if the princes are going to war..."

"All the more reason to get through the Pass," Caen said.

"What of these ones?" Tristain said, sheathing his sword, but keeping it close.

The starving peasants looked on with haggard, tired eyes. They were probably simple village folk, their lives destroyed by the war.

"Let them be," Leon replied. The others seemed to agree that was best. "No sense in slaughterin' men down on their luck."

The sailor Lorrin offered a small bit of hope. "Maybe the Annaltians'll give up soon enough—after all, if it's as you say, they'll be at war with Osbergia, and everyone'll forget all about Badonnia. Who knows, maybe they'll need folk to rebuild."

"Thank you, sir, thank you," the leader said. "Gods be with you all. Gods bless your journey."

They parted; the bandits going east, Tristain and the others west.

13

OUTRIDERS

EIGHT OUTRIDERS SILHOUETTED AGAINST the grey sky on a ridge to the north as the wagon rumbled along the rocky road. The ox grumbled as the headman brought him to a stop.

"Who are they?" the boy Bean asked the sailor. He didn't answer, flexing his jaw.

"No sudden movements," Leon replied, resting his hands on the weapons at his belt. Tristain turned his knuckles white as he squeezed his hand around his own weapon. They waited there, unmoving on the ridgeline. *It's them. The hunters. Those greycloaks told them about me.*

Tense minutes passed. Eventually, they moved off, disappearing out of sight.

"Must've thought we were someone else," Caen muttered to himself. Tristain relaxed.

"*Bon.* Let's go," the headman said, sending a lash across the ox's back.

"Stay on your guard," Leon whispered as the ox started moving again. "That won't be the last time we make eye nor ear of those ones."

Lorrin sang a song and they fell into good spirits. At last, the keep came into sight, and the pass beyond that. The leviathan itself stood looming in the distance, so enormous as to be seen from miles away. So enormous and distant, in fact, it was half obscured by mist and fog. A snow-capped peak in the shape of a dragon, it was said to be the bones of an ancient dragon that lived before the time of the Gods, and depending on the legend, made the world. Tristain thought it was just a weirdly shaped mountaintop.

Eventually, they crested a rise, and the keep drew into sight all at once. Banners of the Archduke flew over the walls—a gold bear on red field—as well as banners of the empire; split black-and-red field with gold lion. Pennants in different colors dotted the towers, representing each army that had taken the keep. A man every ten feet on the walls, armed with crossbow, oiled mail, and steel helm. The keep itself was a hundred feet wide, spanning the narrow gap between two slopes. There was no other way across the mountains, at least not one that Tristain knew of. This made the keep a strategic position.

The gate stood open, and the ox lumbered into the bailey, hard-packed ground 'neath its hooves. The dray creaked and swayed as it shambled in, its axles about ready to snap. It was a small wonder it had made it this far, and yet it still had further—the whole ten-mile-long Pass still laid before them.

So long as the deserters kept their faces downcast, and their hoods high, they would avoid scrutiny. They would pass as father and sons, and last they checked, seeking refuge in the empire wasn't forbidden. Of course, as a last resort, they carried swords and axes under their cloaks.

The guards didn't immediately intercept them. At first, they circled the wagon, observing their quarry. Tristain sent a glance over the captain. He had a patch of three silver trees on a black and green field. Invereid's own, but he wasn't immediately familiar. He carried spear and shield, sword at his hip. He looked like he knew how to use them.

"What business have you in Osbergia?" the captain spoke at last.

"Refuge, sir," the headman answered. "We're only simple folk."

"And the wagon?"

"All we have left, sir."

The captain walked around, giving the wagon another look. Tristain felt his cheeks flush as the man lingered on his face.

"You travel in odd company, Badonnian," he said, not taking his eyes off Tristain. "These two look feral—what, there wasn't a single razor amongst any of you? Even a simple knife and some water... though you've not been the strangest to have come through, I suppose. No matter." He clicked his tongue. "Yeah. There's gonna be paperwork, of course. You'll have to wait until it's been returned from the capital."

"The *capital?*" Caen choked out. "That'll take weeks!"

"Months, but needs must. Where're you from, Osbergian?"

"Uh, the Spear, sir. Came to Badonnia to see my cousins, got mixed up in the war."

"Right. Well, there's that small matter—we have to notarize your entry into the empire. Wouldn't want any deserters slipping through the cracks."

"Of course not."

"Naturally... it could be rushed, for a fee."

Caen smiled, expecting the bald-faced suggestion of a bribe. "We have coin."

"Aye... ten a head... three for the women. Seventy-eight silvers," he answered without hesitation. "Aye, two for the lad."

Caen grumbled. "That seems steep." It was steep. Ten silver would buy a week's worth of ale. Forty silver was the price of a well-made sword. No chance a few farmers would have that much between them.

"*Wi*, we have not that much," the headman added.

The captain clicked his tongue. He was about to open his mouth when a white-haired, broad-shouldered woman in plate walked out of the barracks at the other end.

"Hold, Captain," Gida said in her strong northern accent. Tristain laughed. Caen chuckled. Leon folded his arms, seemingly indifferent.

"Ah, here's the commandant," the captain said, leaning on his spear. "She'll sort this business out."

"Lieutenant?" Tristain couldn't believe it. He pulled his hood down.

A smile flicked across her face. "It's Commandant, now." She gripped him by the shoulders and laughed. "I'm glad you're not dead, Squire. And who's that? Is that the corporal?"

"Come 'ere, you big bitch!" Caen threw his arms around her. She laughed, gripping him tightly. The captain and the others seemed positively thrown. She turned to Leon.

Leon kept his distance. The memory of his time in prison, his impending date with a noose was still fresh. They stared at each other tensely. Finally, he said, "You're not dead either, aye?"

She laughed, and so did he. They embraced each other. As they broke apart, she said, "Gods know they tried! It's good that I should run into you three, actually. Who do you travel with?"

"The enemy," Caen said with a smirk. "Good people, it turns out."

"If only we knew," Gida replied. "Before we burned their fields to ash."

The captain made a gesture. "These ones, Commandant, they ain't pay yet."

"Let them go, Captain. Any who aid a Knight of the Empire prove themselves worthy."

"Very well, Sir."

The refugees thanked them profusely. In good spirits, the headman threw his whip over the ox. They yelled goodbye, and Tristain wished them luck. The wagon creaked as it rolled over the uneven ground. *They're gonna need it.* He caught Luka's eye, and felt a sting behind his own. He wondered if he would ever see the man again.

"Commandant," the captain said, gesturing to Caen. "This one said he was visiting cousins in Badonnia. Who are they, really?"

"This is Leon Vorland the Strong, Knight of Ineluss," she replied. "These two are his retinue. The coal-hair is the son of the Count of Invereid, Tristain Oncierran, squire to the noble knight. The straw-hair is Corporal Caen, formerly of the Spear."

"Well met," the captain said, bowing. "I am Vidan Geldchen, of the Geldchens of Ostelar."

"Burghers?" Leon said, scratching at his ever-growing beard. It was touching his chest, now. Vidan nodded. "Heh. Count on a merchant to earn his gold. What's a merchant's son doing on the edge of the world?"

Vidan smirked. He was dark-haired, with complex eyes—brown, with a hint of gold and green. *To match his name, I suppose.* He had thick dark eyebrows and a shadow of stubble on his shaved chin. "Yes, Sir... It's complicated, and a story I won't tell, excepting over an ale that's been bought for me."

Caen laughed. "I think the man needs an ale!"

"Yes," Gida said. "That's a good idea. After duties."

"Yes, Commandant," Caen replied, saluting.

"Back to your duties, Captain," Gida said, slight annoyance passing over her face.

Vidan saluted and disappeared.

"So... Commandant," Caen remarked. "That's quite a step."

"Right," Gida said. "We should talk."

She took them to her office at the top floor of the barracks. It was roomy and had comfy furnishings. Her window overlooked the pass, but was facing the wrong way to spot the leviathan. Tristain wondered what the leviathan looked like up close. Probably just a bunch of big rocks stacked on top of each other, and like nothing at all. The effect was given by observing it from the right distance and perspective. There was something to that, though. Why would it happen to be at just the right angle and distance to look like a dragon? And from both the Osbergian and Badonnian sides? No, that was nonsense. He put it out of his mind.

Gida smiled, genuinely beaming as she sat at her desk. "Gods, it's good to see you. I thought you three were dead, for certain."

"No such luck," Leon replied. "Now, what's happened?"

"With what, sir?"

"You said it was good that you should run into us."

She smirked. "You've always been sharp, sir. I have a request of you three. There would be silver in it, of course."

Tristain cleared his throat. "How much?"

"More'n you've seen in some time, by the look of you." She grinned. "No matter, we have warm baths, and servants that'll clean you up in no time."

Tristain glanced down and silently conceded the point. "What's the job?"

"Vyahtkenese horses."

"Warhorses?" Horses of Vyahtken were native to the eponymous wild lands far to the east. They were stronger, livelier than other breeds, and absolutely fearless. They were perfect for battle, and highly prized for that reason. Tristain knew better than some—Onyx was one, a gift from his mother for his twelfth birthday.

"We need a guard," Gida replied. "Someone to transport them to Avercarn."

Caen's uncertainty was clear from his tone. "Why us? You've a whole keep of men, by the look of it."

"There's simply no one else for the job, Corporal." She was cagey, holding something back.

"They weren't legally obtained, were they?" Leon asked. Gida declined to answer. After a few moments, he said, "What do you need a guard for? We hold the pass from both ends."

"I suppose you've not heard, being on the road."

"Heard what?"

"The roads are dangerous, and war is coming. T—" She stopped herself. Leon leaned forward in his chair. "What is it, Gida?"

"There's talk the Empire is unravelling. Annaltia has attacked Osbergia. Nothing like this has ever happened. The Archduke is scrambling. In fact, I should probably mention that every knight has been called to arms."

Leon sighed. "Brother against brother. This bloody Prince Reynard. What is the meaning of it? Surely, it's not just bald-faced greed."

"I cannot say. But he holds our trade routes to the capital hostage." Gida was right. Annaltia was directly north of Osbergia—and all routes to the capital of the Empire, Istrheim, ran through the province. Trade, taxes—both would be disrupted.

"A lot of people are going to be angry," Tristain said.

"They already are," Gida replied. "We've been spared the worst of it, out here... but there's already shortages, and the Archduke has proposed a new levy to fund the coming war. Already, the lower classes rise up, and some take up arms."

Leon swore. "For Ginevra's sake."

Caen threw himself upright. "Any news of the Spear?"

"Nothing, as yet."

Caen sighed, leaning back, deep in thought.

"So, you see, we need all the men we can spare, here. The Badonnians can't be allowed to just march back into these halls, especially when we fought so hard to take them. Rennes is the least of our concerns, now, but we can at least hold onto what we gained."

"Then let us stay," Tristain said, looking to Leon. The knight sent him a glance. "We can help."

"I understand you want to help, but—"

"You said you need every man you can get."

"True, but... this is, arguably, more important. If we can use these horses to resupply our army, it might mean the difference between victory or defeat."

"It surprises me to hear an Annaltian say that."

"My loyalty is to the Empire, Squire. Not to a single man. I would see the prince in chains for what he's done."

"Forgive me, Gida, I didn't mean anything by it."

"No harm done." She whistled and some servants bundled in with towels and razors. She rose from her chair. She carried herself with strength, a stiff spine. Her eyes held harshness, but there was sadness, too, behind them. Something happened to her during the battle, Tristain was sure. A servant boy led them to a squat building opposite the barracks, filled with steam from natural hot baths, where a bath and a shave were in order.

AT DAWN, THE MEN loaded grain, wine, sacks of flour, and what else they could spare into wagons. The smiths straightened horseshoes, fifty down, and fifty more to go. The head smith's voice was a lash, spurring them to work as fast as they could. The farriers worked as fast as they could as well, shoeing the Vyahtkenese by the dozen.

By mid-morning, Captain Vidan rustled the dozen or so grooms into the muster, who led the hundred or so horses. The beasts were black as pitch, a sea of smooth midnight coats. They stormed, stomping at the ground, kicking up dust, butting up against each other, gnashing their teeth in shows of dominance—to be expected from lively horses bred for war.

Tristain wondered how in Sigur's name they were going to make it through the pass without losing a few to falls or fights. Thankfully, that wasn't his problem. The grooms had that joyless task. Tristain's only job was to protect the convoy on their way to Avercarn.

Tristain secured the chinstrap of the bascinet around his shaved chin. The servant boy handed him a spear and shield, decorated with the Osbergian bear. At his belt, in its scabbard, his sapphire longsword. He reveled in the familiar smell of leather, the weight and feel of oiled steel. The armorer had fitted him with padded jacket, mail and breastplate with spaulders, and the bascinet, of course. Over the breastplate and past his thighs he wore a tabard of Osbergian red, with a sigil of a white eagle stitched to the breast, thanks to one of the men's wives. It was cinched in with a dark leather belt. Nothing fancy, but it offered more protection than a sackcloth shirt. He wondered if it would last, or he would simply tear it at the seams within a week. The memories of that horrible night still haunted his dreams, even if he knew what happened was right.

"Apologies, Sir Strong," the armorer said, bowing his head. "A' know it's no harness an' plate, but I simply had nothing better for you." Leon had much the same as Tristain, the best the keep's armorer could spare.

"No matter," Leon replied. "A good shield turns blows aside just as well as plate."

The armorer chuckled. "Too right." The armorer was in his late fifties, in his twilight years. The wisps of hair on his head were white as snow. He'd come to see them off, as did Gida and a group of soldiers. His upper back was rounded slightly. He had a solid frame, and hard, callused hands. The man had commented on Tristain's blade when he'd visited the armory.

"That's a stately blade," the man had said. "Fit for a prince."

"I suppose so," Tristain had replied. "The Annaltian I took it from didn't seem like a prince, though."

"Princes and traitors seem close company these days. Maybe it's only right that the blade ended up in your hands."

"Why do you say that?"

"I'm near the end of my life, son, but I've still enough wit to tell a good man from the rest."

Tristain had been stung. He'd felt like a coward, a blackguard... deserting his country, his duties... bringing shame to his father, his family name. He expected nothing more than the end of a rope, and yet as he threw his leg into the saddle of his own Vyahtken, he felt like a knight, marching off for empire and glory.

"We'll have to get that ale some other time," the knight said to the captain. "A shame we won't hear the story of the merchant far from home."

"Aye," the captain replied.

The commandant whistled, calling over a groom. Tristain turned. Gida was as striking and beautiful as ever in the haunting white light of the pass, but at the same time, cold and distant.

"No such luck, Captain," she said. "You're going with them. A letter arrived in the night, from Lord Galeaz. You're to deliver the horses to a village ten miles south of Avercarn, Esstadt."

The name slapped Tristain's ears. *The steward? What's he to do with this?*

"Very well, Commandant." He had a slight smile play across his lips, perhaps looking forward to the chance to get away from this frosty place. Tristain knew that he was.

They farewelled their old friend Gida with a few tears and headed through the gates west. The frozen ground beat under the weight of hundreds of hooves, the thundering sound filling Tristain's ears. He wondered if this many horses would shake the weight of the mountain down on top of them. *Don't be ridiculous, Tristain. Thousands marched through the pass on the way to Badonnia. You were with them.*

The pass stretched out before them as the sun reached its zenith. They were headed toward home at last. He wondered if he would see Selene before war called again—and what he would say to her. *Gods, I hope you'll forgive me.*

T RISTAIN TOOK IN A sharp breath. The Dragon's Alley opened out in front of them. The sky-piercing apex of the leviathan was drenched in shafts of light, impaling the snow atop in a bristling, moving line. Then it happened all at once—the clouds above broke like foes before the might of the mountain. The dragon's mouth stood open, drenched in sunlight, ready to swallow the world. Mist grabbed pathetically at the sides of the towering beast, settling for draping its foothills, and the valley below, in a veil of smoky white.

"That's even better than last time," Leon said. The captain, Vidan, whistled his agreement.

They assembled at the edge of a plateau. Below them in the valley, thick grass and virgin forests of conifer and cypress broke only at the bank of a narrow stream that came from higher up the mountain. Glacial flows, now melted, turned rocks in the winter, creating enormous heaps of stones at the foot of the mountain. Gazing ahead, a winding path left the forest behind, passing over talus and grey rock, and up, switching back until finally squeezing through a gap between the mountains, the way out the other side.

The sight was aweing, filling Tristain with an almost sacred quiet, despite the hundreds of hoofbeats. Maybe he'd grown used to them now.

"You know why it's better?" Caen said. "'cause we're going home."

The pass broadened on the other side of the valley, leading through a ravine. Some of the horses grew spooked, but the grooms led them on. Eventually, the pass led into a thick wood, where dry branches fell over the trail. The horses grew wary of the unsteady ground, and so they stopped, and the grooms had to clear the path. It was like this. The Pass was only ten miles long, but they moved at a glacial speed, making sure none of the horses didn't get separated from the group.

"Can't they just beat on 'em until they move?" Caen wondered out loud.

"You try and beat on a hundred destriers, corporal. They'll beat on you, most likely," Leon replied.

Before long, the path was cleared, and the pass opened out again. Eventually, the keep on the other side drew into sight, the back of its walls much less guarded than its front would've been. The sentries waved their hands in greeting as the sun started to set. *All things considered... not a bad day's work.*

Tristain sat with his knight and the others as the smell of chargrilled lamb filled the air. The commandant of the western keep, a hefty soldier known as Gerold Milkwine, for his ability to drink wine like it was milk, welcomed them with open arms. He offered them all the meat they could eat, and more than enough ale and wine to wash it down. Tristain suggested the best cuts should go to the grooms.

"They worked harder than any of the rest of us," he said, unbuckling his armor. They cheered him half-heartedly—not ungrateful, but exhausted. The Vyahtkens had been corralled in a hastily constructed pen, now resting for the night. "How they managed to do it without losing a single one, only Sigur knows."

The commandant passed it along, and the cooks brought the grooms the king's cuts; the shank, the legs, the shoulder. Caen sung a ditty as servants brought the ale out.

There once was a Countess from Delph,
Whose breasts sat as high as a shelf,
So only the tall, could see them at all,
And the Count had to take care of himself.

The men laughed, cheering with their tankards, splashing beer on the dirt. Milkwine joined in, telling his own ditty.

Tristain noticed Leon hadn't taken one. "No ale, Sir?"

Leon smiled, but didn't respond. Tristain saw his eyes turn glassy, orange reflection off the fire. *What's going on with him?*

"Oi, here," Caen said, thrusting a second ale into Vidan's waiting hand. "It may not be bought, but you've an ale. Tell us: what's a merchant's son doing out here?"

Vidan took a sip. The froth sat on his upper lip as he spoke. "Our family's cousins of the rich Geldchens, you see. Same grandfather, but my father didn't inherit his father's talent for business, or anything really. My father was a gambler. Unlike my grandfather, he had some deluded idea in his head that money could be made through luck or chance. He would go down to the port every Lunsday and put money on cock-fighting. You can guess how that went. When I came of age, my father had already lost the house, and was in a large amount of debt to some important people."

As the night grew on, the grooms faded away, going to bed. Milkwine belched and said goodnight, and Caen and Leon went to bed as well. Tristain couldn't sleep—his thoughts fixed on Selene—so it was just Vidan and himself left by the fire.

"So, where do you go from here?" Vidan swirled the wine in his cup and sipped.

The fire popped a shower of sparks, its last breath before the darkness of the night would descend on them. Tristain shivered. "Once we get to Avercarn, it's back home to Invereid."

Vidan's dark, serious eyes passed over him. "Are you cold?"

"A little."

The captain gave the ground next to him a little pat. "You could come here, and we could keep each other warm."

Tristain blushed. The idea of being so close to another man was intriguing, and he'd wanted to do the same to Luka on that night in the Giant's Footfalls, but his parents had been there. "I'll get more wood."

"Oh, come on. I don't bite." He laughed. "Unless you want me to."

Swallowing, Tristain got up and walked over. He crouched down, and Vidan made room next to him. The ground was cold, but Vidan's body radiated warmth. Tristain soon stopped shivering.

"What's waiting for you in Invereid?"

"My mother and sister... well, she's not quite a sister, but she's close enough. She's my father's ward."

"Your father's ward?" Vidan's breath was warm and boozy on Tristain's neck.

"Yes."

"You don't talk much, do you?"

Tristain turned. He didn't like this line of questioning. Hurt and guilt ripped through him like the claws of the beast that lived inside him. "I've been trying to get them away from my father for years. He's a brutal man, and brutalized me and my brother. When my brother died, and I left for the war, he brutalized them." Tears squeezed onto his cheek. "It's the greatest failure of my life that I didn't take them with me, and I didn't find a place for them."

Vidan rubbed his chest, his fingers brushing against mail. The feeling wasn't unpleasant, and Tristain felt a stirring in his groin. "You're still young. Your greatest failures lie ahead of you, I think."

"That's comforting."

He chuckled. "There's nothing we can do to control others. Your father is a bastard, it's true, but there's only so much we can control in this world. You say your mother and sister were stuck... but that's not up to you. They could've run, at any time."

"You're not one to temper your words, are you?"

"I don't see the point. We've only got one life in this world, until the gods take us again to fight in their eternal wars."

Tristain turned and kissed the man. "You're right. I might die at any time—life is short." *It's even shorter for a man with a demon inside, with hunters after him.* Thoughts of Selene shoved into the back of his mind, and Vidan let out a surprised grunt. Then he pressed in deeper, matching Tristain's enthusiasm. Hands made their way down to the loops and belts of their hoses and Tristain took Vidan's manhood in his palm, and Vidan did the same to Tristain. Tristain broke the kiss and moved to the captain's chin, neck, Adam's apple. Vidan let out a soft groan that sent a shooting thrill up Tristain's spine.

"Silence, you'll wake someone."

"Let them be woken."

Two days after, and they were on the road again, Tristain blinked his eyes open, squinting in the early morning sun. Fog still settled in the air. He started. He was cold, without a lick of clothing on him. This wasn't the barracks, nor even the keep, but he laid outside the walls, in a thicket a few hundred yards from the keep.

What in Sigur's name...?

The air smelled strongly of copper. He looked around. A black Vyahtken lay next to him. He got up and realized blood covered him down his chest. For a moment he thought it was Vidan's and his stomach turned until he looked at the dead creature. Its belly was cut open. Intestines lay strewn across the ground. *Gods... I did this...* Tristain's hands shook as he tasted blood around his mouth.

14

HUNTED

TRISTAIN STOLE BACK INTO the camp, bare arse in the morning sun. They camped on a bald hill, forest and mountains behind them. Yellow fields of broom-like wheat bloomed ahead of them. The air smelled crisp, while the porridge stodging over the fire warmed Tristain's cool skin. Caen and a few of the grooms laughed their heads off. "Breakfast," Caen yelled, "When the naked prince is ready!"

Vidan offered him a spare set of clothes. "I won't judge," he said. "Everyone's got their own interests."

Tristain turned red as he stuck his foot in the pant leg. "*In*—It's not an interest! I lost my clothes when I was bathing in the river!" Vidan murmured his agreement, walking off to check the fire. "I did, I swear!" He blew greasy hair out of his face in frustration.

When Tristain was dressed, he went to join them by the fire. Leon stopped him.

"Are you okay, lad?" he asked quietly.

Tristain scratched his cheek. "Not really. Can we talk more... privately?"

Leon nodded. They walked down the hill, passing behind a tree. "What is it, son?"

"Well... I went to sleep last night in the camp and woke up out in the forest. I rarely sleepwalk, so imagine my surprise when I find a fucking half-eaten horse at my feet."

Leon wiped a hand over his face, blowing his lips. "You're saying..." Tristain nodded shamefully. Leon took his arms in his hands. It was comforting. "It's high time we learn to control this, no?"

"*Control?* How?"

"Well... how does it normally happen?"

"The first time it happened, it was when I nearly died. But now it happens whenever I get angry, or sad, or-"

"Overwhelmed with emotion?"

"Yeah."

"I imagine it's like any other skill—it needs practice to master. Take your clothes off. Don't be shy, we've both been in the army, son."

"What are you..." Caen said, walking up. He was picking grains out of his teeth. He grunted in surprise, seeing the naked squire in front of him. "I'll leave you two to it, shall I?"

"Tristain slew a horse. I'm training him to control his emotions."

"Sig- *A horse?* Did he look at you funny? Don't mind their long faces."

"Corporal."

"Oh, that. What happened?"

"I woke up next to it," Tristain told. "It makes me sick. I ate its liver and heart, by the looks of it."

Caen leaned on the tree. "So? What brought it on?"

"I can't say. I don't remember having a dream or nightmare, anything that might make me angry or upset."

"I guess we'll have to kill you, then. What? That's what brings it on, right?"

"You better be jokin'," Leon glowered.

"Alright!"

"That's not a bad idea, though," Tristain said. "I can't believe I'm suggesting this, but... what if you attacked me?"

"Eh?"

"Hit me."

Caen wound his fist back. He sunk it hard into Tristain's stomach.

"*Ogh!*"

"Anything?"

"Harder."

Another uppercut.

"Harder!"

A jab to the chin.

"Wait! What if I lose control?"

"Don't worry about it!"

Caen pummelled Tristain, again and again. Leon kept him upright, so he didn't fall over. White pain washed over him. He clenched his jaw, pushing through it.

It was like a floodgate opened in his mind. Leon and Caen jumped backwards. Tristain felt a rush as he transformed. He loomed over the two men. He groaned, feeling the urge to thrash and destroy, but he calmed himself. *I'm... I'm in control!* He cheered inside.

Leon bellowed a cheer. "Ginevra be fuckin' praised!"

Caen glared, his face turning slightly pale. "Holy Gods! Fuck, up close..."

"Terrifying. That'll put hair on your balls."

"What d'ya think? Looks like a dog's face, right?"

"Bear. Or maybe a wolf?"

"Yeah... I could see that. Would explain the teeth. Can you talk?"

Tristain tried to speak, but his mouth and tongue were unfamiliar with the process.

"Yiiidddiot." It sounded a little like a cross between a moo and a yowl. The knight and the corporal howled with laughter.

Tristain's chest heaved, sniffing the air. Something wasn't right. He glanced around. His ears pricked up. Something rustled in the distance. A whooshing noise drew closer and closer. He dodged, feeling the slight brush of metal past his fur. The bolt thudded harmlessly into a tree.

Caen and Leon spun, drawing their swords. "What the hell was that?"

They're hunters, he wanted to yell, but it sounded more like a distended growl. The two men turned. Confused. *Fuck!*

Tristain ran. The two men cried out after him. Tearing through brush and forest, he tried to get a better look and head the hunters off. But if they were who he thought they were... well, he wasn't sure what he could do. But now he was in control, so maybe he could finally deal with them once and for all.

High in the branches of an elm, Tristain sniffed the air. Two of the hunters were heading this way. They smelled like sweat. Both of them had eaten soaked beans and barley meal for breakfast. The way they barely disturbed the ground as they walked suggested they were light on their feet. They moved like predators, back against back. There wasn't any way he was getting the drop on them.

A smell drifted into his nose. The smell of lavender and roses. Fresh herbs and Tanerian reds. The smell of silver maples blooming in spring. *What the hell? It couldn't be...* He shook his head, focusing on the task at hand.

He roared. Leaves shook. Birds scattered. The hunters came running.

Racing through the tops of the trees, he led the hunters away, howling every so often to draw them further away from Leon and Caen. He used thick arms and bendy branches to vault his way across the forest. He understood the movement implicitly, somehow, like his expanded hearing—he knew where and how the hunters came after him; which leaves they stepped over; which branches they snapped. The only time they became obscured was when they stopped moving, and Tristain had to rely on his less sensitive, but still improved, sense of smell.

He dropped onto a leaf bed. The hunters were lost; it seemed. They moved in circles, running into each other like headless chickens. He smiled, baring his teeth. *Now, to get back to camp.*

Click. A mechanism thundered to life. A clattering of metal and pulleys. His world spun upside down. Thick chains bit into his leg. Tristain howled. He swung there, helpless.

Shitshitshitshit—

The hunters came running. Tristain reached up, trying to work the chains free. He couldn't get any purchase. The chains were thick. He tried to wrench the links apart, but they were too strong, and he was too exhausted from running. He wondered briefly how far he had run—miles, and yet the hunters seemed to be around every corner.

They drew closer. *Fuckfuckfuck—* The chain loop caught around his ankle. He tried to wriggle his foot loose, but he couldn't get the angle. Then he had a stupid idea, and he reached up, and snapped his ankle in two. He groaned, blinking back stars that circled at the edge of his vision. Slipping free of the chain, he twisted in the air and landed on his side with a thump. He looked down. His foot dangled at a weird angle.

Using his arms to propel him along the ground, he ran on three legs. Even with a broken ankle, he still moved faster than running on two human legs. He made it back to the edge of the forest, the hill ahead. He looked around in a panic, hoping that Caen and Leon hadn't followed him or the hunters. But no, there they were, standing at the edge of the forest.

How do I transform back? Hm... he focused on his breathing. In. Out. In. Out. Slow. The urge to thrash and destroy was a distant memory. Slowly, he felt his chest relax, and his breath grow steady. He thought of his sister, and their childhood. A picture of Selene formed in his mind. A picture of them giggling as they tricked Bann—making him think their father wanted him at the stables, when he was really in his office. The look on his face as he marched back up to the house, of which Tristain and Selene had a prime view of from Tristain's window. Other moments, too, flashed in his mind.

Remember when you lost a horse's bit? Father was so furious. I took the blame, remember? You didn't see it, but he gave me a flogging. You owe me one.

He recalled the song his mother used to sing as she brushed his hair.
Oh, sweet child,
Oh, sweet child of Juniper.

Blessed that rests on her knee,
Never have I seen such a likeness,
But in the child before me.

Tristain looked down at his body. His arms had shrunk back to their normal size; his sense of smell returned to its usual mundane state. Black fur sheathed itself under his skin. It was a strange feeling. The Change was taking less of a toll on his body and mind now, he noted, as he did not collapse from exhaustion this time.

Pain bit into his calf. Caen and Leon looked up as the squire cried out at the edge of the forest. They raced over.

"Shit," Leon said, cradling Tristain's underarm on his shoulder. He had a shirt for him to put on. "C'mon lad. We'll get that foot fixed up."

"Hell of a thing," Tristain said, chuckling.

"Oye, what happened?" Caen asked, helping with the other side.

"They're miles deep in the forest still—I led them on a wild chase. But then they caught me in a snare. I had to break my ankle to escape."

"Gods be good."

When they reached the camp, the horses were already being corralled, and were ready to go. Clearly, the grooms hadn't noticed one missing. The captain nodded as they returned. The sky darkened as a drop of water fell on Tristain's cheek.

"SHUT THAT SIGUR-CURSED DOOR!" someone yelled. Their cloaks spilled with a deluge as freezing wind battered the inside of the taphouse. The captain closed the door behind them as he strode over to the barkeep, putting four fingers up, and joined the other three as they thumped down at a table.

"The ale's good here," Vidan said. "Have a drink. It's on me. Pay's in my chest upstairs. Give me a minute, though. I'll have to take a cut of the missing Vyahtken out of it." Caen raised his hand to ask how much that'd be, but the merchant's son was up the stairs and out of sight already.

Tristain wiped long wet hair out of his face. Water dripped from his sodden beard onto the table. He laughed inside. Seventeen years and not a whisker, and now it was practically impossible to get rid of it. It paled next to Leon's, of course.

Tristain glanced around. Two dancers twirled by the minstrel in the corner, dressed in vests traditionally with bells, tilting their hips in time to the music. They were muscular, more muscular than Tristain would imagine a dancer would normally be, with bulging shoulders and firm necks.

At a table next to them sat a merchant in fine clothes, speaking in strongly accented Osbergian. He was probably from the republics, the same as that bastard steward. Which one, though, Tristain was never sure. Alania, probably. The man across from the merchant had his lean, powerful arms crossed and seemed deeply uninterested. His long, dark hair streaked with white was tied back in a ponytail, while the scars on his face spoke to an interesting and dangerous life. Not wanting to linger on the tough, Tristain moved his eyes along.

Next was a farmer and his wife; their small child was in a swaddling basket alongside. The wife had a tansy flower tucked behind her ear, blonde hair framing a youthful face. She looked the part of a young mother, but something about her seemed uncertain, like she was expecting something to happen at any moment. In fact, both of them looked like they were waiting for something. Their food lay untouched before them.

Along from them stood the barkeep, who was wiping the same spot on the bar, compulsively, like he was trying to clean a year-old stain. Over by the door looming like an enormous shadow, was a man. A gigantic man, dressed in an oversized black cloak. The fabric blanketed him, darkness obscuring his face under his hood. Tristain glanced down. A steel sabaton poked out from beneath. He was a knight, like Leon. Others sat around, drinking alone. He hadn't expected the alehouse to be busy. *The ale must be good*, he thought. *So why is everyone so cross?*

The minstrel plucked a cheery tune, and the brawny dancers twirled again, though the patrons' faces remained unsettled. The barmaid came up to them with their tankards. Tristain thanked her with a smile. She was young, younger than himself. She would've been the innkeeper's daughter, most likely, though they looked nothing alike.

"Hey, lass," Leon said. The woman gave him a curt nod. "Any news of the war here?"

Caen added, "Must've been hard to see all the young men leave."

"Oh, been fine," she replied. As she spoke, her accent seemed strange for a southerner, speaking more with the refined tones of the capital. "There's no war here. Sigur protects this house." *Sigur? Sigur doesn't give a toss about travellers and alehouses. That's Eme's job.*

"Thanks, lass," Leon said. The barmaid walked off and joined the barkeep. She lingered her eyes on Tristain before someone else called for her.

Tristain took a sip of his ale. It was light and fruity, slightly sweet. It slid down easily. Soon enough, they needed another round.

"Where's that Sigur-cursed idiot?" Caen yelled, drawing a few eyes. "He better not 've gotten lost on the way to our money."

"Ah," Leon said. "He's probably hoping we'll get bored and piss off so he doesn't have to pay us. You know those burghers. They could sit on a pile of money and still have their hands outstretched, looking for more."

Caen laughed. "That one'll go to his grave with his hands outstretched, I'm sure."

Tristain got up after a few more rounds. He needed a piss. The giant man in the corner got to his feet in lockstep. Tristain froze. Gods, he was tall. The top of his hood grazed the ceiling. He was wide, too. His dark grey blanket, because that's what it was, gave him the appearance of a mobile wall.

It was only at that moment that he noticed the minstrel had stopped playing. Tristain sat back down. He leaned forward. "Something doesn't feel right."

Caen turned his head. "What?"

"Have you seen that giant by the door?"

Caen glanced backwards. "Hmph. He's big."

Leon rested his hand on his sword-hilt. "I see what you mean. Have you seen the state of those dancers? I've seen more agile lumberjacks."

"I've not heard that woman's baby cry once since we arrived," Tristain added.

Tristain gestured with his eyes. "And what about that merchant? Annaltian clothes, but Tanerian mannerisms? If he's Republican, I'm the Emperor."

"I think we need to go."

Leon nodded. They stood. Chairs scraped on the ground. The farmer and his wife stood. The merchant and his bodyguard. The dancers and the minstrel all came closer, moving to surround them. All of them stared daggers.

Caen drew his sword. "What are you lookin' at, ugly?" He directed his words to the farmer. As he drew closer, Tristain noticed he had nearly half his face missing. Mangled, like a dog had attacked him. Tristain pulled his longsword. Leon drew his sword and axe.

Laughter came from above the stairs. The treads creaked as a woman in a black cloak descended upon them. Tristain felt the blood drain from his face.

"Selene...?"

"You always were a little dull, cursed beast," she said. It was her, but different. Her raven hair came in waves, vibrant and lustrous, but her green eyes, once bright and curious, now stared at him coldly, completing a cruel sneer. A small, straight scar on her chin rounded the look, as if she'd dodged a knife or a sword a fraction too slowly. The way she carried herself was new as well. No longer the meek child. She pulled her shoulders back, commanding the room. And the biggest thing... it took Tristain a second, but he realised. He wanted to throw his arms around her, offer her comfort, but... *Holy gods! What happened to her arm?*

"It took half an hour for you and your little friends to see through our little pantomime. And I am Diana, a vessel of the holy martyr, and an inquisitor of the Sigurblessed Holy Order of the Golden Sword, and you'll address me as such, demon."

Tristain's jaw went slack. "Dem- What are you talking about? I'm your brother!" *She's the one hunting us. Gods, what happened to her?* Martyr and inquisitor... she was in the Order now, a Golden Sword.

Caen laughed. Leon scratched his neck with the sharp end of his axe.

"I knew that captain was a bastard liar," Caen muttered.

"Had us fooled," Leon remarked.

"That'd be Karl." She laughed, a bitter laugh that was completely foreign to Tristain.

"What do you want from us?"

"I'd want your heads on spikes if it was up to me," she replied, as calm as if she were giving directions. "But it isn't. So, will you come quietly?"

Tristain felt sick. "Heads on spikes... Gods, what happened to you?"

"I have been blessed, demon. I am a sword of the Lightfather, shield of the innocent."

Silence fell as he pondered the question. *Would he come quietly?* Tristain snorted, twisting his hands over the hilt of his sword.

"Sorry, Selene. I won't go with you... Step back. I don't want to hurt you."

She smiled. She *wanted* him to say that. "Oh, don't worry. You won't." A crossbow *twanged*. The bolt bit into Tristain's shoulder. A flare of pain shot up his arm to his neck. He grit his teeth, ignoring the pain.

He dropped to one hand, bursting forward with his sword. Selene moved aside easily. Tristain stumbled on his hurt foot. His vision blurred. The woman he'd grown up with, the woman he'd once thought he'd marry, grinned, wicked and cunning, as he collapsed to the ground. Tristain's body wracked with fire, prickling with needles.

The giant marched over. Caen swung his sword, cutting through the enormous cloak. The blade glanced harmlessly off the plate underneath. The huge man grasped Caen's face, lifting him easily. He brought the corporal up, then drove his head into the floor. The wood cracked. His eyes were glassy as his body went limp. Blood pooled from his head. Tristain could only watch in agony, helpless... unable to move or change.

Leon clashed with the merchant and his bodyguard, crying out in fury, until he took a sword in the chest. He collapsed to the floor, coughing dark red blood onto the wood.

"Take them," the inquisitor said, her face stretched out in a wicked grin.

VOLUME THREE

Pages from a leather-bound journal:

I was framed! Unbelievable. Albrecht will regret this. I've had to flee from the city, but I will return one day, to seek my rightful place as Lord Silberwald at the Archduke's side.

I was attacked on the road. I cannot see out of one eye, and my face hurts something terrible. I have lost my voice. Ditchborn bandits took a shine to the chain around my neck—I suppose it's only right. It was a gift from the Archduke, and I didn't deserve it. When I fought them off, one of them transformed into a monstrous creature.

Some Sigurian priest saved me. Gods. He's given me some drug to help with the pain, and slathered my face in a poultice, but my hands tremble as I write this. It's tiresome.

I woke up in a dingy stone temple near Etzen. He tells me that given a month or two, I'll be getting around again.

Some visitors came to the temple today. They were armed to the teeth, but stopped for no more than a chat and a waterskin. Golden Swords, even though they wore black. One of them eyeballed me. I'm sure he didn't know what to make of a highborn down on his luck as I am.

Getting around gets easier every day. I regained my voice, though it is still scratchy. I'm holding a sword again. Praise all the Gods I haven't forgotten how to fence. Only having one eye has affected my depth perception, but it isn't anything I cannot get used to. Maybe soon I can return to Ostelar, reclaim my rightful place. Though they'd probably run in horror from my horrible face. I was beautiful once. What a cruel joke the Gods have played.

The black-clads returned today. One of them came up to me as I was practicing. We sparred, and he complimented my technique, as I knew he would. He asked how I acquired my disfigured face. I told him of the beast that attacked me. He suggested I should join the Order. Apparently, they hunt the creatures. I was going to say no until I asked a few questions. It's incredible. They're rudderless. Unfocused. They only fight for tradition's sake. They have no idea what potential they have. The laws of men don't apply to them. They could do incredible things, and answer to no one. I was wrong. I won't return to Ostelar. No, the Order will suit my ambitions, just nicely.

15

TO THE CITADEL

FOLK PASSED DIANA AND the other Swords on the road north, young, old, little children, babes at their mother's teats. The south offered refuge, safety from the coming war. Some drove wagons, or carts as they did, their families walking alongside them. Most came on foot, their goods on their backs. They all wore hard looks. The men and the women carried weapons. Axes, scythes, sickles. Some gave lingering looks over their cart. The allure of the covered wagon might've been too much to deny if it were just Diana on her own. The inquisitor had silver at her belt. Even that might've been tempting enough, but the three other Swords deterred them from getting any closer. The armoured giant likely kept them away with his sheer size alone. He was practically a walking mountain, seven feet tall at least.

They stopped by a brook. Diana led Eda to the water for a drink. She brushed her fingers through the horse's chestnut mane, drawing it out, watching the hair fall, strand by strand. She reflected on the capture. *Did I go overboard? Eight seemed a little excessive for just three of them...* The four others had moved on—wardens sent back to their duties at the local preceptory. *It felt necessary, but I wonder if I was overcompensating. How many hunts have I been on? Fifteen, twenty? Why is it that one mention of family and I'm acting like a damn novitiate?*

"Brother, huh?" Tansy said. Diana turned. Her affinity for silent movement was enviable. She danced a bolt between her fingers, leaning against a tree. Her real name was Lena Ulnstadt, an arbiter and a master of the crossbow. Her name was a moniker, given because she always wore a yellow-petaled tansy flower behind her ear.

"What?"

"You heard me."

"Yes, the beast is my brother. So what?"

"No need to get defensive." She snatched the bolt from the air and walked up. Right into Diana's face. She had blonde hair, with viperous blue eyes, and the practiced, purposeful step of a professional. She was shorter than Diana and looked up. "I just don't want to let any attachments impede what needs to be done."

"Hm. They won't. And Arbiter... you step out of line again, and I'll string you up from your feet."

The woman smiled. "Evening, Inquisitor."

Diana breathed and released her jaw. *I'll have to watch her...* Lena had confronted her without regard for seniority. That meant trouble.

They continued on. Diana kept her gaze on the cart. Muscles in her neck clenched involuntarily. She took a deep breath, trying to calm herself and adjusted in the saddle. Eda shook her head, whinnied. Diana felt the creature pull at the bridle. She wanted to go faster. Diana obliged.

"I'm riding ahead," she declared as she cantered past. She gave a few flicks with the reins, turning the pace into a gallop. "Hyah!"

The horse pulled ahead, further, further, along the road, over a bumpy path, on damp grass, splashing over silver puddles, under leafy birches. A scared fox flashed its fluffy, bright orange tail as it disappeared into a bush. Wren, magpies, all sorts screamed into the air. Eda threw her neck forward as her strong back muscles worked between Diana's thighs.

They went further, further, until the wagon was long out of sight. Then Diana slowed, moving to a trot, then a walk. She sighed, looking around. She had a job to do. After all, she had the duty of protecting the cart. She could do that from here. Protecting them until they delivered the cargo to the citadel. *Protecting them from what?* The Lord Inquisitor wanted the Black Beast and The Strong alive. He clarified that if they were harmed, it would mean all of their heads. *Why?* That was a dangerous question. She buried it in the back of her mind.

The road was empty. The train of refugees had reduced to a trickle. Tristain was a monster, a horrible beast. The bodies outside the alehouse in Badonnia made that clear. *Galeaz reported a field of severed heads and body parts... he wasn't wrong. It was a massacre. It resembled how those children the tax collector killed looked, but on a larger scale... he's much more dangerous than Father ever was. He wouldn't be alive if I had anything to do with it. We may have shared a home, but... it was pure luck he didn't just claw my eyes out when he cried for Mother.* She squeezed the reins. Her face screwed up. Angry tears rolled down her cheek. *Now he's just a few hundred yards away, more than capable of killing again.* She could only hope that the sleeping drug held its sway.

She stopped, wiping her face. *But he is like Father. Cursed, just like him. Is it his family? Maybe it's what Sigur wants. His family was cursed, and I'm the only one who can save them.*

A strong wind blew through the trees, leaves whipping up into the air. Eda shuffled, got nervous. *Storm's coming... We'll need to make camp soon. I'll find the firewood and light the fire. Lena will hunt our dinner. Manus will lift the swingle-tree from the sumpter and undo the traces. I'll set up the tents, hitching the poles and setting the lines. I'll have to sleep with Lena tonight. It wouldn't be proper for the men to share our tent.*

And then... then we'll have to deal with them.

T RISTAIN DREAMED HE LAY with his face pressed against timber, the deck of a ship in a nameless ocean bobbing up and down in the waves. His body ached. He went to speak, but nothing came. He glanced behind. The sea he was sailing on rippled with green forest and grey rock. His mother stood in the centre, staring back at him, holding her eyes in her hands. Her sockets were dark pits, but he could feel them boring deep into his soul. She turned her back on him. He ran through the trees, crying out all the while for her, again and again, until she disappeared.

Stabbing pain in his shoulder thrust him awake. The world was blurry, bloody. Every roll of the wagon's wheel was pain, his head pounding. He concentrated, trying to change, but he couldn't. There wasn't anything he could do—he was as helpless as a drowning man begging for air. Things went black as the motion of the cart and drowsiness took him again.

He dreamed he was in camp again, delusional as he was. Propped up like a deserter on the rack, bent low by a whip. The crowd egged him on. Caen and Hopia, Leon the Strong, Andrea and Maria from Badewald, Lombas the Small, Herrad and Caspar... all dead, and hollow. The noble knight had a hole in his chest, sucking air. Andrea had her head split in two. Caen had his tongue cut out. They howled for him to help them. Unending... their howls wracked his skull until he cried out for them to stop.

A pure-white lion came and ate them all, eating the entire world until it was nothing but a void. Tristain fell, tumbling down and down, to the deepest pit below it all. Everything was black. *This is Hell.* He knew it in his heart. It wasn't a pit of fire, or death, or demons. *Black... unending black, for eternity. Cold nothingness.*

His breath was icy in front of him. A chill passed over his body. His blood felt icy in his veins. The pulsing of his freezing heart in his chest, beating faster and faster and harder and harder until it ruptured, tearing and gnashing with wild teeth through his skin. He screamed for it to stop. He screamed for his mother.

"*Squire!*" a voice from the bowels of the earth said. Tristain groaned, fluttering his eyes. The wagon came into focus. It was Leon. *You're alive!* He went to scream, but found he couldn't talk. His mouth was gagged and refused to cooperate, anyway. The walls spun as he sat upright. His head felt like it was made of lead.

"Squire!" The knight's muffled voice. A foot shoved his shoulder. "Oi! *Sal'brath!*"

"Sigur, be quiet," a woman yelled from outside the wagon. Tristain tried to move his arms. They wouldn't cooperate either. He looked down, his head unsteady; unable to support its own weight. Thick ropes resolved around his wrists and ankles. Leon was bound in the same way.

The wagon slowed, then stopped. Heavy clanking feet came to the back. The flap opened. A giant, towering and immense, stared at him, then reached over and scooped him up. He carried him with ease, as if Tristain weighed as much as a feather. The giant propped him up against a tree, orange light coming from a crackling fire. Tristain's head slumped. The giant laid down Leon next to him like a sack of potatoes.

A green-eyed, raven-haired, lithe, vicious looking woman sat across from him on a log. She leaned over, staring at him. She'd tied her hair back in a tight knot, while a dagger and crossbow sat at her tooled-leather belt. A black boiled leather jerkin over her top, and black trousers under a black cloak. She wore a brooch of a flaming sword at the fold of her cloak. One arm was missing, a metal plate over the shoulder. It did nothing to tame the savagery in the look she was giving him.

A strong wind chilled him to his bones. She said nothing. She simply stared.

"So," a blonde woman with a yellow flower tucked in her hair said, squatting down next to him. It was the farmer's wife from the alehouse. She wore a similar set to Selene, though without the brooch of a flaming sword. *No, she's not the farmer's wife. That was a fiction. This woman is a Sword. She hunts my kind.* Tristain narrowed his brows as she eyed him up and down vigorously. She had freckles and pale skin, and a taut scar down her cheek in the shape of a crescent. "He's a pretty one," she said. "But skinny. Hardly a beast. Shame. I like my men with a bit of meat on them."

"This one's for His Revered, Arbiter," the silver-haired, broad-shouldered, handsome one said, walking up from the horses. "If we gave him to you, Tansy, he's apt to end up like the last one."

"I'd like to get him to the Citadel in one piece," Selene said.

Tansy stuck her chin out. "His Revered like young, pretty boys?"

"I don't concern myself with the Lord Inquisitor's predilections, and neither should you. Enough. Let's just eat."

The big one wasn't a giant, after all. In Tristain's much less deluded mind, he was just an enormous man. Though he was taller than any man he'd seen before. The big one cooked three skinned rabbits over the fire as the sun went down and a strong wind whipped up. He turned them with care, roasting them until they were golden on all sides. He wore his plate even now, next to the fire.

Tristain glanced at his shoulder. A bloody bandage had been wrapped around it, and the bolt was gone. They had stripped him of his mail and sword. He looked around. The hilt of it stuck out from under one horse's saddle. Clearly, one of them had thought it was worth something. Perhaps they would sell it.

"Do we give them some?" Tansy said, munching on her rabbit. She nodded to Tristain.

"Give him a nibble. Enough to keep him going," Selene replied.

What happened to her?

The woman did as she was told, taking Tristain's gag off first.

"How could you, Selene?" Tristain's voice came hoarse and strained. They looked at each other and laughed, a cruel laugh.

"Just take the food and shut your mouth," Selene said.

Tansy chuckled and shoved the roasted haunch into his face.

Tristain took a bite begrudgingly.

"There, was that so hard?"

"Gods curse you."

Tansy's eyes flashed with excitement. She smashed him across the face with the back of her gloved hand. He cried out and blood dripped into his mouth.

She laughed. "You demons... it's always the same thing. All bark, no bite. Some morel berry, and you're as weak as babes at their mother's tit." She tapped him on the nose with the half-eaten rabbit leg. "Any more of that, and we might just forget to feed you." She yanked the gag back into place.

Leon watched what happened. He was silent and ate without complaint. *I'm sure he figures they'll let him go, eventually. They'll have to. He's a knight of the empire, a hero, even disenfranchised as he is. If the archduke or the emperor were to find out they have captured him...*

Tansy sat down next to the fire, picking up her lute as the others ate. She plucked gently, singing as the fire popped and the dark overtook them. She sang, like they sat at a minstrel show. *"Brigida and Dietrich, they slew the heretic..."* Her voice glided over the melody. The silver-hair joined in. Selene just leaned back on her log. Her expression was... content? It was hard to tell, but she certainly hadn't been broken up about killing someone—or an underling killing someone on her orders. Who was this monster that sat before him?

She's gone. The girl you knew, the girl you relied upon, could count upon, could understand you... loved you... she's gone. The Order has taken her. They've taken her humanity.

Tristain saw Caen singing along with them. He blinked, and the corporal was gone.

16

SEA OF BLACK AND RED

A SEA OF BLACK and red surrounded the city. They arrived in the afternoon, orange light falling on the gathered army, tens of thousands strong. The estuary around Ostelar was a bustle of soldiers and knights, camp servants and followers, all wearing the Annaltian colours. They were laying siege to the city. *No smoke... they haven't assaulted it yet.* They were surrounding it. In preparation, she was sure, but they'd been there long enough to set up earthworks and a palisade around the camp.

She wondered how it would go—what would the Swords do if the Annaltians invaded the city? The Order, as an arm of the church, was apolitical, uninterested in choosing sides between the conflicts of men. In theory. Many examples of usurper archpriests and inquisitor assassins in history stood out in practice.

A cadre of riders cantered past them, scouts on the Imperial road. The captain eyed them as they rode past, the four Golden Swords with their wagon in tow. Diana wondered if they would turn around, demanding to see what was inside. They could easily believe it was supplies, or vittles for the people, and it would be entirely reasonable for them to do so. Though it was entirely within their rights as Swords to refuse, it would be much easier to avoid the scrutiny of tens of thousands and an Imperial prince.

The hooves of their horses and the rattle of the wagon's wheels echoed over a freshly hewn bridge. *There wasn't a river here before...* She gasped. From the surface of the water poked roofs, structures, poles. They'd flooded the Outskirts. A mile north, a huge curved dam of stone buttressed against the Tibor, diverting it down constructed trenches, emptying the river out to sea a mile further east than it would normally have been. It also had the side effect of submerging the low-lying Outskirts in two feet of water. It wasn't clear what happened to the people who lived there, but they weren't here now.

The earthworks were incredible. Normally, Ostelar sat at the confluence of two rivers, the Alba and the Tiber. This made it incredibly hard to siege, as only a narrow strip of land permitted entrance from the north. Normally. Somehow, this Prince Reynard had changed the very landscape in order to bring all of his thousands to bear.

Swift hooves clattered behind, and over the bridge after them. *Here we go...*

"Halt!" shouted the riders' captain. They stopped and turned. The riders approached swiftly. There were twelve of them. The riders were going too fast to see before, but they were very well-dressed, too well-dressed to be scouts. They prickled with lances, while one of them carried a black lion standard. Diana saw Manus lift one of his giant hands off the wagon's traces, placing it on the hilt of the greatsword sitting next to him in the driver's box. It had a cloak over it, but the shape and size of it were undeniable.

"Who are you, and from where do you ride?" The captain spoke with a strong northern accent, and in Osbergian for the sake of the group, though Diana understood and spoke Annaltian just as well. Not that different, though some verbs differed slightly, and which particular syllables were stressed.

"Who comes?" Soren calmly straightened himself in the saddle.

"I, Prince Reynard the Second of Annaltia, have."

Soren bowed his head. "Your Serene Highness. We are servants of the Most Holy Order of the Golden Sword. I am Inquisitor Sorenius, and this is Inquisitor Diana, Arbiter Lena Ulnstadt, and Arbiter Manus Ironhand. We come from Avercarn, important cargo for the Lord Inquisitor in tow."

The prince returned the bow with a slight bend in his neck, representing their unequal footing. "Well met. Lord Inquisitor, hm."

Diana looked the prince over. He wore a fine, embroidered burgundy jacket over a breastplate, undone at the front, tabs fluttering in the wind. He had a lance in his right hand and a decorated sword in a scabbard at his side. A handsome man, like most of the Imperial family, with hair cropped close to his head, bright blue eyes, and high cheekbones. His helmet was hooked to his saddle, a bascinet with klappvisor, like the rest of his retinue.

"Can you verify this information?"

"We wear the badges of our office, Your Serene Highness *Raginardus*," Inquisitor Diana said in Annaltian, turning on the charm by using his High Istryan name. "We are simply what you see before you."

Soren gave her an amused glance.

A clever grin spread across the prince's face. "Yes... you are, indeed, Mistress Inquisitor. Fortunate I should make your acquaintance. Please, all of you, dine with me. The caprices of camp upkeep can wait."

The Swords fell in line with the retinue, moving at a gentle pace. Reynard moved alongside Diana. Soren kept an eye on him.

The prince kept his eyes trained on her, only correcting the courser between his legs when it drifted out of line. "Whence do you hail, Mistress Diana?"

She kept her eyes forward. "Invereid, Your Serene Highness."

"Please, call me Reynard." She gave a brief nod. There was a brief pause. The prince chuckled. "That iciness could freeze smoke, Inquisitor. Come, tell me... where was it you said you were riding from? Avercarn? I have but a small confession to make... you take those, don't you? A confession for Sigur's ears, or as close as it gets." He laughed. Diana couldn't help but smile. "I don't know my brother's province very well. Where is Avercarn?"

"The south, Serene Highness," one of his advisors said. "Near the border with the Alanians."

"Thank you, Anselm. And how long did that take? A month? You must be terribly exhausted, Mistress."

Soren snorted. If the prince heard, he didn't react.

"I'm fine, thank you, Your Highness," she said.

"No, you must rest. I can hear it in your voice. You must stay for the night, at the least. Enjoy a fine meal, a hot bath. I'll have the servants prepare one for each of you at once. Though the big one might need a horse trough and a scaffold."

"Excuse us, Serene Highness, but we are carrying important cargo that must be delivered expeditiously. If you'll but let us pass."

"That's no way to talk to your soon-to-be liege lord. Please, join me in my tent. At least long enough for a drink."

Diana sighed inwardly. She was itching to get rid of that damn wagon, and what was inside. But she would humour the prince. "Very well."

They passed through the palisade gate; the perimeter of the siege camp. The camp was a set of rings, the eastern side of which sat in the depression that was the former riverbed. At the fringes stood the tents for the men-at-arms, and the camp followers. Campwives scattered throughout, cleaning pots, washing linens, sweeping built-up ashes from campfires, and delivering stew and strongale by the cask to the men. Inside fenced yards, soldiers drilled with spear and pike formations. Further inside sat the cavalry's tents, the knights, and their lieutenants. Beyond that were sets of trenches alternated with rows of spiked poles facing towards the walls, deterring any sallies of defenders from the city.

"This siege ought not to last," the prince said. "My brother's walls will come crashing down soon enough."

She saw what he was talking about and let out an involuntary sigh. Three giant trebuchets, over a hundred feet tall, were being erected in the centre of the ring, a few hundred yards away. On the road, they'd passed teams of woodsmen felling trees by the dozen, and now she knew what he was using all that lumber for. Carpenters and craftsmen clustered like bees around a queen, lifting, hammering, tying and nailing pieces into place. They were nearly finished.

"Your Serene Highness must have dazzling engineers," she said.

"Thank you. You are *very* agreeable, Inquisitor. From which house do you hail?"

"You wouldn't know them. They are but a minor house."

They arrived at the prince's tent; a marquee large enough to house a company. In the centre, in front of them, stood a parquetted oak table, flanked by high-backed oak chairs set with rosewood inlay in the shape of a lion roaring. Both the table and chairs had carved feet in the shape of lion paws. The tent was empty apart from the dining set, other than an armour and weapon rack. Diana supposed it would've been for assembling, when all the knights and generals met for battle preparations. The two inquisitors filed inside after the prince, while Manus and Lena were told to wait by the wagon. The prince noted their absence, but Soren told him they should keep watch over the wagon.

"What are you hauling in there, prisoners?" the prince asked as they sat down. Soren didn't answer. "I get it, important cargo. Besides, that's not the reason I called you here."

Diana leaned over the table. She cringed a little inside. She was ignoring decorum on purpose, but her training throughout her youth had given her hard-to-break habits, and that all came rushing back in this lauded company. "And what is the reason, Your Serene Highness?"

"I *am* fond of the Order." He leaned forward as well, letting the moment draw out. Diana wondered if she was too obvious, that he could misconstrue her behaviour as disrespectful. "It's important work that you do. I believe very much so. In fact, that's why I allowed you into my camp, allowed you to see my fortifications, to see where I store my supplies, to tally how many soldiers I have, to examine my siege-works, and it is why I will let you travel onto the gates when we're done here."

A servant came over with a tray of drinks, placing a goblet of wine for each of them on the table. Reynard picked up his cup and gave it a slow swirl. "I truly believe it. That's why the Order in Annaltia has flourished under my patronage, and it would disappoint me very much if the Order in Osbergia did not."

"I'm not sure what you mean."

"My patronage, of course." He took a sip of the wine. Diana's and Soren's wine stood untouched. "I believe we can end this war, you and me. My profligate brother must answer for his crimes, but I have no wish to throw the lives of his people away. You, you could be heroes, lauded for your efforts in preventing bloodshed, and praised as loyal servants of the Emperor."

"Prince Reynard," Soren said.

"Please! Why don't you have a drink? You—" He slapped his head softly. "Of course! My apologies, I'll rectify this at once. Anselm! Two apple juices, please!"

"Yes, Serene Highness."

Soren looked back at the prince. "Prince Reynard. The Order does not answer to the Emperor."

The prince smiled. Gods, it was a cunning smile. Diana got a little frustrated with that perfect smile and perfect teeth.

"Inquisitor, please. Don't take me for a fool. I know well that the Order is loyal only to Sigur himself, and I have no problem with that. I do not wish to interfere with that. But, as the largest patron of the Order in Annaltia, I am deeply familiar with its inner workings, and its reliance on donations of both men and money from its lords and its princes. Not to mention the land that you lease for your citadels and your preceptories. It is but a simple request. I ask that you to deliver a message to your leader—the Lord Inquisitor Rotersand. Ask him to throw open the gates on the fifth day of the next week, and he shall have all the men and money he could ever want."

The servants brought out apple juice. Still, she didn't drink. Who knew if it was poisoned? "And if he doesn't?" she asked.

"Well, then... nothing. Nothing immediately obvious, of course. But after a few years, a crack might appear in the walls of your great fortress. Nothing major, nothing that cannot be put off. Then another appears, and it's larger, possibly structural. But there're no funds to be found to fix it. You might find that you must choose between fixing a wall and purchasing an alchemical reagent to fight the demons, and we both know which you would choose. On and on it goes until you find that your great fortress has fallen out from under you and buried you within it. Who knows, it might even fall into the bay. Wouldn't that be something?"

Diana's face grew hot. She glanced at Soren. He nodded. *We have little choice.* "I think we understand," she said.

"Good." The prince clicked his fingers. "Anselm, have whatever the inquisitors need brought to them. If you require fresh horses or waterskins, please take them. Whatever you need." The prince stood, and the others followed.

"Thank you, Serene Highness."

He walked them to the opening of the pavilion. He talked directly to Diana now. "It is truly a shame you can't stay the night. I loved the stories my inquisitors in Annaltia would tell me. I can only imagine yours are just as entertaining. What a night we could've had."

"A shame indeed, Serene Highness, but we must be going."

"Very well." He bowed deeply, deeper than he should have. "Sigur be with you."

"Farewell." Diana matched the bow, and came to her horse. She threw her leg into Eda's saddle and up and over, and they began the final length of their long journey to the citadel.

Her chest released as they walked over the trenches, over the makeshift drawbridge the prince had lowered for them. She glanced back. He was smiling at her. She looked away. *Thank the Gods I didn't become a courtier.* She screwed up her face involuntarily. *I might've married a man like him.*

"What's wrong with him, Inquisitor?" Tansy asked. "He's a bit too pretty for my liking, but he looks just your type."

"I'll remind you, Arbiter," Soren said. "Our codes strongly forbid physical intimacy."

"Who said anything about intimacy? I meant fucking."

"Who approaches!" a voice boomed from the top of the wall. A row of guardsmen pointed their crossbows at them, tense-jawed, ready to fire upon them at any moment.

"Inquisitors of the Order," Diana yelled back. "Returning to the Citadel!" There was no answer for a while. Then the gates opened, chains rattling as the mechanism pulled the great metal-reinforced doors wide enough for three wagons astride.

On the deserted, cobbled stone road, the Strand Osterlin, stood a man in a black cape. He had it wrapped around his throat, passed over his shoulder. Black hair slicked back with oil, his vulture-like eyes examined them. It was Galeaz, Lady Adolar's former steward. Their agent.

"Come," he said. "The Lord Inquisitor waits."

17

REUNION

T HE COVE SMELLED LIKE mucky sand and seaweed. The smell
matched the face that Tansy was pulling—waiting in a damp, smelly
place after such a long journey was the last thing Diana wanted. *That
makes two of us, Tansy.* Crates lined the walls of the smooth, black hollow,
stacked on the rough-hewn wharf. Sunlight reflected off the waves, slosh-
ing up against the stone. Out in the harbour, the tri-masted carrack *Iustitia*
anchored, its impressive black sails rolled up and away. On the water, a
twenty-man tender was rowing to the wooden jetty that extended out from
the wharf. On it was the Lord Inquisitor, dressed in a raiment of white and
gold. The skipper threw the rope, catching it around a pole, and pulled
them in. Rotersand and his retinue stepped off the boat. The jetty creaked
under their weight.

"Inquisitors," he said in his smooth voice. "Well met."

Diana bowed.

"How was Isterrand, Revered One?" Sorenius said, bowing.

"It's always a pleasure. We have much to learn from our cousins in the
north. Have you heard of black powder? A new invention. They say it
comes from beyond the Vyahtken wastes. Very impressive. And my deliv-
ery?"

"Yes, my lord. The beast waits for you in the prisons, given the venom as
you requested. The other waits in the eastern tower."

Rotersand turned to Diana. He smiled, or at least the closest approximation of a smile he could manage. "Very good. I'm thrilled to hear that. I'm retiring to my quarters, for now. Inquisitor Diana, please see me as soon as possible."

She nodded. "Yes, my Lord."

"My Lord," Galeaz interjected. "May I speak with you?"

The inquisitor sighed. "Galeaz... I'm afraid I'm much too busy."

"But, my lord—"

The Lord Inquisitor turned and walked from the cove. Galeaz cleared his throat, pivoted, then pushed his way past the inquisitors. "Out of my way."

Diana stepped aside. She wondered for a minute what happened, then decided she didn't really care.

She climbed up the levels, up to the top of the citadel, passing under a portcullis that kept any prisoners from escaping. It was solid steel, thick enough that it could resist even a full demon. Beyond that, a spiral staircase took her from the cove through storerooms, the prison, the training halls, overseers' offices, and finally to the top of the eastern tower, where the Lord Inquisitor's office was. Her legs burned. She looked through a window as she reached the top. The sun was bright over the bay. A gentle breeze washed over her face. It was peaceful. She could almost forget about the army that surrounded the city and the brother that lay drugged up and caged so many feet below.

"Good morning, Diana," the lord inquisitor said as he entered. Diana thought of home as she walked in, and forced the thought from her mind. He'd changed into a white velvet robe with gold trim. The finery was a little overkill. She had only ever seen the Archduke wear such nice clothes. She bowed her head in greeting.

"Have a seat." Diana forced her nerves down. He waved to the chair in front of his desk. His office was circular, like the tower, lined with bookshelves stuffed with papers and books.

The room overlooked the ocean. Hanging on the back wall was the standard of the Order of the Golden Sword—a golden sword pointing to the sky on a black background. Light rays shone from its base, symbolising the penetration of the night by the golden light of truth. In truth, it was quite phallic.

She took her seat. His desk was in a bit of a state, papers and files scattered all over. Clearly, the man didn't have time for organisation. There was an unassuming leather-bound journal that stood out, though. There were no marks on the book to identify it and he had cleared papers to make space, as if he took particular care.

"I must congratulate you, Inquisitor," Rotersand said. Diana breathed a little sigh of relief.

"Thank you, Revered One," she replied. She told of the events, how she'd captured the Black Beast, and Leon. She told of their return to the city, and Prince Reynard's offer.

"Yes, the Inquisitor Commander told me of your meeting," he replied. "Very interesting. I should reflect on this."

She blinked. "You're considering it?"

"And why shouldn't I? If it can avoid... needless bloodshed."

"Because the Order's impartial. We rise above the muck of politics and war and pledge ourselves to a higher calling."

The Lord Inquisitor smirked. "Yes, we do. Now, this knight, Leon Vorland. Is he cooperative? Do you detect evil within him?"

"No, my lord. No trace of the beast within him. I checked with the archivist. No traces of it in his heritage, either. There were many moons between Avercarn and Ostelar, and I did not drug him with the morel. If he was going to transform, he surely would've done so before now."

"Did you cut him?"

"Cut? No."

He tsked. "If a devil has sufficient control over his abilities, he may suppress his transformations. An adequate emotional stimulus, such as the removal of a finger or an ear, something vestigial so as not to cause premature death, should provoke the metamorphic response. No matter. If you believe he has no trace of the Great Devil, I believe it. Should you talk to him, turn him to our side, he could be a valuable ally. He is highly respected in the courts of the land, and commands a sizable force in the Hills under his white eagle banner."

"Did Galeaz not try to destroy his reputation, to sow discord in the ranks?"

The Lord Inquisitor's eyes darkened. "Who told you that?"

"A rumour, Revered One. I should know better to ignore such trifles."

He sighed. "Yes, he did. A mistake. I did not know Reynard was marching on Badonnia not as an ally, but as an opportunist. Thankfully, Galeaz failed."

"Reynard is a snake," she offered. The Lord Inquisitor nodded. "Should we trust him at his word?"

"I saw the great siege engines from the deck of my ship as we were pulling into the harbor. The walls *will* fall within a fortnight. If his threat is genuine, we could find ourselves without a patron, and we would wish our heads decorated the palisades with the archduke and everyone else in the White Palace."

"Is it that serious?"

Rotersand rubbed his temples. "I cannot say. Talk to this Leon. He may know something we can use. If not, he could be a bargaining chip. Convince him to join our side. Who knows, if we can get him close enough to the prince, perhaps he can solve the problem."

Is he suggesting... "Y-yes, my lord."

"Good. We've made him comfortable. I have a feeling he'll come around quickly. Now, please send for the jailor. I wish to pay someone a visit."

T RISTAIN WOKE UP, BLOOD stinging his eyes. The dark room he sat in was blurry. His throat felt numb and his tongue swelled in his mouth. He coughed.

"Ah, you're awake," a voice said. A rag wiped his eyes and the dark stone walls of the small room came into focus. A broad-shouldered man in a white and gold robe stood before him. His eyes were familiar, like he'd seen them before in some half-dream. The man was wiping his bloody hands with a rag.

"Tristain Florian Oncierran, second son of the Count of Invereid," the stranger pontificated. "First a son, then a squire... now an abomination. Or was it the freak all along?"

The man came closer. He seemed to appraise his work. Tristain tried to move and found he could not. His arms and legs were numb. Strength completely fled from them. This differed from the other drug. His torpor seemed deeper, and there were no chains or ropes on him. There was no need.

"You'll find yourself unable to move, and much to my benefit, my black beast: unable to synthesise."

Tristain tried, but when he concentrated, the wall in his mind was still there. He went to speak, but his lips seemed unfamiliar with the action. He twisted his lolling mouth to form the word: *how*? It sounded more like, *oooh*, but the Inquisitor understood his meaning.

"The Gods were truly sadistic," he said. "Handing us this corrupt world they created, and all the horrific things within it. Have you ever heard of the sand adder? A nasty creature, from the northern dunes of Saburria." The slick-haired inquisitor held a glass syringe in front of him—white liquid glistening off the tip. "Dreadful, isn't it? Can't move a muscle? Can't blink or even swallow? Don't worry, it's not fatal to wukodlaks, at least not at the dose I have given you. Although... that does not mean you won't be uncomfortable. Following paralysis are spasms and hallucinations. Uncontrollable feelings of terror. Grinding of the teeth. It will be so bad you may even break a few. You may think... it must wear off at some point? At some point, it will release you from your torment?" He let out a rattling laugh. "Indeed. But I inject you again and the process begins anew. It will only stop when I say." The Inquisitor grabbed Tristain's jaw, wrenching it forward. "And only when I say."

Tristain fury bubbled underneath, under a layer of helplessness.

"Poor boy. I can see it in your eyes. You want to kill me."

Tristain went to move but found he could not. His body was unresponsive. Painful tingling spread through his legs and feet. The tingling spread through his body and up through his body to his jaw. His eyes glazed over, and his teeth started gnashing together. Something in his periphery darted by. He looked over. Only black mould and dark stone. Another shadow moved in the periphery. The stranger's throat rattled when he breathed. It was nearly imperceptible normally, but to Tristain's ears, it sounded like a thousand thundering hooves. He thought his head might burst from the pressure, and he whimpered inside. The experience was wholly disconcerting. Ribbons of white light danced down by his nose and up towards his brow. The ground shook and bubbled up before him, as if it had turned liquid. The black stone floor rose like liquid foaming in a cup, and popped right in front of his face. His jaw hurt from the grinding. Shivers ran up through his body, shivers that he could not control. Hours passed like this, hours of Tristain's mind straddling the edge of insanity. The stranger watched him the whole time. Finally, the ringing in his ears subsided. He wiggled a finger, cautiously. It moved, and Tristain rejoiced internally. Strength was coming back.

"I see you're recovering," he said, looking down on Tristain.

"Fuck *yooo*," Tristain mumbled, tongue still taking up far too much room in his mouth.

The stranger's countenance shifted slightly.

"I should kill you for what you've done," he spat. "What you've done to our family."

"*Ouurrr fami-lee?*"

The stranger's face twisted into a grin. His grin called to mind white maggots wriggling in a carcass. Roaches squeezing through gaps under doors. Fat horseflies infesting an abscess.

"Do you not recognise your own brother?"

The floor fell out from under him. His jaw went slack. "*Noooo... mmmmyy bbbb-*"

"Died? I nearly did." He turned his head and peeled back a flap of skin—the skin wasn't real, somehow. It was a mask. Beneath the skin, revolting scars ran pink and split, raised flesh and taut skin, circling from the left side of his face to the back of his head. It was then that Tristain noticed he was blind in one eye, the iris grey and milky. The other eye was bright green, just like Tristain's. "The work of one of your kind. You're surprised? I suppose you would be. I took excellent care to cover my tracks."

"*Whyyy?*"

"Because I have plans, brother. Plans that cannot be interfered with. Plans for our family."

Tristain started trembling. "No..." The stranger took the syringe and stuck it into Tristain's neck. "*You whore-sooo...*" Then he went as still as a corpse.

18

DECEIT

DIANA STRODE INTO THE room with purpose in her step. The knight sat unchained by the window on his bed. It was a narrow bed, with a hair-thin mattress, but the room was well-supplied, with fresh apples on the table, and a trunk by the wall full of fresh clothes. A gentle breeze blowed into the room, a salty smell filling the air.

"Making yourself comfortable?" she asked, pushing the door shut.

Leon turned to face her. "Selene, is it?"

She smiled. "Diana. Inquisitor-"

"You can keep your titles. I'll have my freedom if you're offering."

"Very droll. I won't mince words. Consorting with a demon is a serious crime in the eyes of Sigur. You will be tried in the eyes of the Lightfather, according to his laws."

He scratched his chin through thick red beard, making a rasping noise. "Hm. Tell me, can you see the army from here? Humour me."

She glanced outside the window. The army were still there, static, fixed, gathering around the walls like a sea of tar. "They're still there."

"I think I've seen fewer Annaltians in Annaltia. What do you think is going to happen when those walls come crashing down?"

She walked to the table and sat down. "They won't harm us. We won't fight on either side, so they'll have no reason to."

"Could be. D'you really think the prince will believe that?"

"He has no reason not to. Besides, I didn't come here to give my opinion on politics."

"No, you came here to talk me into joining your cause, didn't you?"

Diana smiled. "You're smarter than you look."

"Of course. What other reason would you have for keeping me alive?"

"A fair hearing. You will have the chance to defend yourself."

Leon crossed his arms, waving a hand to punctuate his point. "And Caen? Did he get the chance to defend himself?"

"That was a mistake. We believed him to be a demon."

"It's hard to tell, isn't it? They, we... we all look the same, we all bleed the same..."

"Don't be ridiculous. They're uncontrollable beasts. Left to their own devices..."

"Aye, and your brother?"

"He was never my brother."

"I'm sure he's thinking the same thing. Not my sister, not anymore. You know, he never stopped talking about you. He used to say when he got home, he would bring you a gift. Pearls or something. Never stopped thinking about you." He leaned back on the bed. "I imagine he's going to be burned at the stake, or whatever you bastards do."

"Yes, I suppose so."

"And you're just fine with that... all fine and dandy. Thanks Tristain, for all the childhood memories."

"You speak as if our childhood were honey and roses. His father was a demon, too. He killed his mother and gave me this. My biggest regret is that I haven't run my blade across Tristain's neck yet."

"Aye, but can't you see? That's what they do. The Order. They prey on the meek, the dregs. People that have been left behind by war, or death. They turn you. They make you believe that what you're doin' is right, and good, when really, you're just doin' everyone else's biddin'. You never had a moment of hesitation? Never had a moment where you've really asked yourself, *is this right?*"

Diana sighed inwardly. *I don't think he's going to be convinced.*

"Y'know the name Palerme?"

"No. I suppose you're going to tell me."

"Aye, lass, an' you'll listen. Palerme's on the border of Alania and Osbergia, in the mountains. Yonder, it was a trading post. But then the traders started havin' children, started t'settle down—buildin' shacks, then houses, and it grew into a vibrant little community. The people even pooled their money together and had a watchtower built that their sons and grandsons turned into a keep. Palerme became *the* border crossin', but Duca Alberracin took notice. The Duca thought they were cutting into his profits too much when people could just come to the border for their Alanian wine, Argedian oranges, or their Tanerian pepper. In those days, trading by boat was unheard of. But you know what they say—never come between an Alanian and their coin. So, what did he do? What else? He paid off the Order to invent a fallacy that they were harbouring demons, and the Order did what they do best, declarin' a cleansing. No defence. No fair hearing. Extermination was the cure for a disease that never existed.

"But, here's the thing. The people of Palerme were tough. They fought back. Lots of 'em died. The rest retreated to their keep, high in the mountains, and waited the Order out. They'd stockpiled for the winter, and there were only a dozen left, so they had enough for years. Or they would have, had the Order not thrown their dead over the walls. We threw them over in such quantity... faster than they could bury them. The people inside got sick. Very sick. The last merchant threw open the gates in desperation, begging for the Order to spare his life, treat his young son for the corpse sickness... and they cut his throat. Just like that. We burned the son at the stake."

Diana started rolling an apple between her slender fingers. "You expect me to believe that?"

Leon shrugged. "I don't expect you to believe it, lass, but it happened. I was there."

"Horseshit."

"It's true. Speak to Velstadt."

"Velstadt? Lord Inquisitor Velstadt? He's dead. Elias Rotersand is the Lord Inquisitor now."

"Rotersand, huh... Well, go look at the archives. It's all in there. Some of them in grey robes kept records of it. I saw it. It's going back, uh, twenty years now, yeah. Ten-twenty-three it was."

She tapped her fingers. "No, I don't think I'll do that." The man seemed convinced of his own lies. The bell rang for noon. They would serve luncheon in the west wing, if she remembered correctly. "Excuse me," she said, unlocking the door and leaving. Leon didn't say a word. She sighed, locking the door again. *I really don't think he's going to be convinced.*

L EON'S WORDS WEIGHED HEAVY on Diana's mind, even a week later. She practiced alone in the training hall, shooting her crossbow at targets idly. Memories like decanted wine had come pouring back. Leona, Salim, Ebberich, Ruprecht... the moments spent together in this place. Half of them were dead, the others, she wasn't sure. They could've been, too. Of course, she'd done things she'd regretted. Leona was dead because of her, all because the girl just wanted a friend. Diana had killed that.

She killed Salim because the Order told her to. She remembered now... the rector threatened her life. *No... that was me. I could've refused. I might've been punished, but I wouldn't have been killed, no. Soren would've stopped that before it could happen.*

Other names flashed into her head. *Lorena-Maria. Baltas.* She remembered every name, every demon she'd killed. Some were outright murderers, but others... others were less certain. *I wonder... I wonder if we left the herbalist alone, would she have just lived her life in peace?* She nocked another bolt, mechanical in her movements. She squeezed the trigger, not caring if it hit the target or not. *It can't be true... the Order helps people, they saved me... well, Soren and Father Radomir did. Soren found me, saved my life. One of many times.* She paled, realisation washing over her. Everything they had taught her, the self-realisation she felt... it was all him. She let the crossbow fall by her side.

Palerme... if that was true, there'd be records of it, surely... The Order recorded everything. The archives were a trove of information, but they were tightly controlled. The archivist had eyes everywhere, his assistants. No records could leave the halls. Only inquisitors or higher ranks even had access. She would have to be careful. Leon's words weighed heavy on her mind.

THE ARCHIVES BUILDING SAT atop the immense Osterline Hill, opposite the White Palace. Diana shivered, pressing her arm closer to her jacket as she ascended the stairs. The Inner Ring's stone architecture and vast thoroughfares funnelled wind, making it chilly most of the time, even in summer. Their height at the top of the hill did not help matters, funneling the wind even further.

Diana turned. From here, she could take in the entire palace. The curving form of its arches and buttresses gave the structure a sound foundation, while the tops of its towers extended into fine parapets, where even finer gold-and-red pennants flew from their tops. White birds circled the sky-piercing structures. A bronze statue of the Istryan the Conqueror stood imposing above the central doorway. The man was a visage of strength—one hand gripping the haft of a winged spear, the other by his side. A huge brazier burned in front, evoking comparisons to Sigur and his golden lantern.

Diana walked into the archives. They paled compared to the palace, though it was nice enough. Beyond the columned front, the Neo-Alanian style placed an open-air courtyard of sandstone in the centre of the building. Sets of assistants and notaries in their grey robes stood in quiet conversation about the latest gossip or the latest discovery. She asked for directions, and they pointed her to a stairwell off the left side. Down she went, following signs to the records section. Through a candlelit hallway, she came upon a large, dimly lit room filled with row after row of bookcases. In front of her sat a man at a desk, his head bent over a piece of parchment. She was about to speak when she saw his hands as he wrote. They were pinkish and misshapen. They seemed to shake whenever he took them off the page. The left side of his face was heavily scarred and seemed to melt into his neck. She cleared her throat. The man looked up. He laughed, putting his quill down.

"Selene, is that you?"

Diana narrowed her eyes.

"It's me, Ruprecht!"

"*Ruprecht?*" This was the man confirmed before her, and she had heard nothing from him for years. "Gods, it's been..."

"Years! Sigur, time has been kind to you. You're as beautiful as ever. Meanwhile, I'm just... anyway, what are you doing here?"

She smiled gently. It was exciting to see him again, even if it was like this. "I... I didn't know you were an archivist."

"Assistant. They transferred me here after... well, after this." He pointed to his face. "A case of hot pitch exploded in my face. My fault, really. I was setting a trap, and overbalanced."

"Gods... I'm sorry."

"No harm. I wasn't cut out to be a Sword. I prefer my books, anyway. But you—Inquisitor! When did that happen?"

She laughed, feeling giddier than a month-old pup. "Ah, not that long ago, really. A few months."

"Well, it suits you. From the day you landed that knife flick on the second try, I knew you were heading places."

"Thank you."

"How about this siege, eh? They say the Archduke's in talks with the prince. We can only hope brotherly love wins the day, eh? Well, you didn't come here to let me talk your ear off about politics. What are you after?"

"I... I suppose I don't know. Do you know of a place called Palerme?"

"Palerme... no, never heard of it."

"It's on the border with Alania. What about... operation records, from ten-twenty-three?"

"Ten-twenty-three... ten-twenty-three... there was an operation down that way, but I can't recall if it specified where exactly. It's over there, third row in. Operation Heregeld, I think it was called."

She found the book, a thin wafer of calfskin, bound with twine. *Operation Heregild...* She found a seat in the reading area. The room was quiet. She and Ruprecht were the only ones in the room. Though that didn't mean there weren't eyes watching from the walls.

She flicked open the first page. *Hmm... Operation successful... locals grateful... ten inquisitors, twenty prosecutors, thirty arbiters, forty wardens... an auxiliary of mercenaries, under a Leon Vorland—sum-total one-fifty, led by His Revered Lord Inquisitor Velstadt.* Diana hesitated. The knight had been right. He was there. This was a major operation. There were over a hundred Swords in total. *And I thought I was being absurd by having eight of us... Surely someone this big would've caused a stir.*

She turned the page and snorted. Someone had taken to it with a quill, scoring deep lines of black ink across the surface. Someone wanted to cover their tracks—the depths of their guilt as black as the ink itself. She could barely read any of it. Only fragments remained, and nothing useful. The next page was like this as well, and the next. On the last page was a table of financials. She checked if there was a payment from the Duca, but there wasn't. The seal of Lord Inquisitor Velstadt sat at the bottom of the page, along with a signature in his hand.

She sighed. *Useless. There's nothing here.* She heard footsteps. She turned, hand shooting to her dagger.

"You'd do me a favour by killing me," Ruprecht said. "But I thought you might want to see these first."

Diana relaxed. He carefully placed a pile of assorted tomes, books, and ephemera on the table.

"Everything I could find that talks about a place called Palerme in ten-twenty-three. Census reports, business transactions, deed transfers, law proceedings, you name it. Now, you want to tell me why you're so interested in this place? And why you were all but ready to cut my throat for sneaking up on you?"

She rubbed the side of her face. "It's... it's nothing."

"You're a terrible liar, Selene." He sat down at the table. "You don't have to tell me, but you're going to need help if you're going to get through all this before sundown."

"It's Diana, now," she whispered.

He grabbed the first book off the pile and started flicking through. "Hm?"

"Never mind."

She flicked through them. None of them had anything useful. *Legal proceedings of a M. Talbert and D.F. Chamfer regarding steel tariffs... Financial records of Palermean Holdings, blah-blah...* Surely, if the whole town had been wiped off the map, there'd be some trace of it. Everything looked right. All the legal records wanted to talk about were trading and inheritance disputes, while all the financial records itemised in excruciating detail the income and outgoings of twenty different trading companies in the area. Two hours later, and she was getting nowhere fast.

She tried the next book—*Census Records of Osbergia, 1023*. It wasn't an overly large book, but it was comprehensive. She rolled her thumb over the thin pages. Ostelar had twenty of them alone. *Come on... O...O... P... Paarville... Paen... Palberg... Pale... Palerme, finally.* She glanced down the page. *Records count three men married of chief means, eighty men married of moderate means, four men married of low means. Twenty men unmarried of chief means, six men unmarried of moderate means... twenty heads of cattle, blah-blah... here. What's this? Records could not be confirmed in the following census?*

She looked up. "Ruprecht, is there a ten-twenty-four here?"

"For the census? They do it every three years. I'll go get ten-twenty-six." He winced, favouring his right side as he left the room. She frowned in pity. *It must pain him so... it looks like it was his hands and the whole right side of his body. I knew those traps were dangerous—I've used them. To think, one moment of inattention and that could've been me.*

Gods, it was silent in here. She could've heard a pin drop. Her heart was in her throat. The still, underground air seemed to want to choke her for even stepping foot in this place. The roof seemed to bow and press down on her, crush her under the stone. Eventually, after an ungodly amount of time, Ruprecht finally returned. She breathed a sigh of relief.

"Here," he said. "What is it?"

She took the book he offered, flicking to the P's. "Here... but... there's nothing. Paarville. Palberg. Pale. Passtadt. Perm. No Palerme."

"That can't be right."

"Here, look... the page is missing."

He looked at the pages, flicking back and forth. He flipped it over, inspecting the spine. "It's aged, but it's fine. No pages missing."

"What does that mean?"

"They skipped it. Either... the census wasn't able to be done, or... or the town no longer existed."

"*No longer existed*—what in the hells?"

"Selene, what is this?"

"Ruprecht... I think I've found something I shouldn't have. I don't think I can tell you, though. It would put your life in danger."

"Alright... but please be careful. I would hate to think *I've* put *your* life in danger."

She sighed. "Thank you, Ruprecht."

"Anytime. If you need anything else, you know where to find me. Good luck, Selene."

She nodded and bid him farewell. She walked back to the Citadel. The night-time streets were a blur around her. She didn't even notice the nearing autumn celebrations of Eme; bawdy girls and innkeepers in the street alike bellowing for patrons, fragrant lavender and rosemary being burned in every window in every street, and the men and women alike ignoring usual modesty and going around in nothing but their boots. No, she didn't even notice the excessive drinking and celebrating going on around her, as the city wanted to break free of the bondage that the siege brought upon them, and she especially didn't notice the great flaming ball of hay and pitch soaring through the air and dashing into the side of the White Palace.

19

THE ATTACK

THE STREETS OF THE city were in a panic around her. People screamed, running to get to nowhere. There was no escape. The Hill burned, and the Port. Another ball of fire soared over her head, crashing into houses a few hundred yards away. The flash was incredible. The heat of the explosion nearly knocked her off her feet. She threw her hand up, covering her face. Crowds gathered in the street, trying to see what the commotion was. Young children wailed, unable to grasp what was happening. Women clutched at their husbands, begging them to run, but there was nowhere they could go. They'd have to run to the sea, like rats diving from a sinking ship. They could only watch their city go up in flames.

Diana raced up the hill to the Citadel, her legs burning. She burst into the cavernous cathedral. A procession was happening, burning censers filling the air with sweet smoke. No one seemed to realise what was happening outside. She bolted down the hall and up the stairs. She had to find Leon. The sky lit up again. Screams and smoke drifted into the windows of the stairwell.

She threw open the door.

Leon snorted, waking from his sleep. "I'm up!"

"Knight, you see what's happening out there?"

"What—Ah... 'tis time, then. What are you doin' here?"

"Palerme, it's real. It was a cover-up. They wiped a town off the map, and everyone just forgot about it. We have to do something."

"Of course, it's bloody real, girl! Now, calm down. We're not in any danger here. What's your plan?"

"I... I'm not sure."

"Well, what do you want to do? I won't lie. I'm hopin' whatever you say gets me out of 'ere, lass."

What do I want to do? "This isn't right. This isn't what the Order should be."

He turned to face her, coming to the edge of the bed. "Althann. That's what us Hillmen call 'em. The demons. Althann are friendly spirits, ambivalent to humanity. If you left him alone, he'd leave you alone. There are even stories of him helpin' humans out if they got lost in the mountains, like givin' 'em healin', sup, and water."

"Like the herbalist."

"Who?"

"Doesn't matter. But wait, you said you were in the Order?"

"I didn't say that. They hired mercenaries. Paid us enough to keep our mouths shut. Don't look at me like that, lass. I weren't always Sir Leon the Strong, and I'm opening my mouth now."

"So, these Althann... Hillmen were here before the Empire, weren't they?"

"Yeah. We got absorbed as Istryan and his armies pushed east."

"It's known that Sigur came with Istryan. If the Hillmen have stories of the demons that predate Sigur... maybe that's what they originally were. Friendly creatures, who were forced to adapt to a changing world. Their descendants are what we see as demons, forced to live in a world that was never meant for them. And they made the curse up to justify hunting them. Althann, huh..."

"Might be. Might be nonsense. But I *know* Tristain. He's like a son to me. He killed no one that didn't deserve it."

She slumped in a chair. "What do we do? He's locked up down below, and I don't have the keys—" *But Sorenius would.* "I know what to do."

S ELENE BIT HER LIP as she opened Soren's door. His room was austere, just as hers was. A nightstand sat next to an armour rack, where a boiled leather jacket sat. Two sets of white robes were draped over hooks on the wall. A narrow bed sat in the opposite corner. She glanced at the nightstand again. On first pass, she hadn't noticed them, but there they were, a set of iron keys on a thick ring.

He sat there, on the bed, shirtless, sharpening a dagger by a tallow candle. Her eyes lit up. Gods, he was handsome. His shoulders and chest rippled with taut muscle. Powerful arms curved enticingly. Silvery hair filled out his chest and stomach, framed by two rosy nipples.

He looked up. "Inquisitor? What are you doing here? Have you seen what's happening out there?"

Selene shut the door behind her. Her mind swam with possibilities. Wonderful possibilities. This could be the last time she would ever see Soren again. She wanted the key, and she wanted him. She wanted him more.

She strode up to him. He placed the dagger and sharpening stone on his nightstand. "What are you—" She grasped the side of his face, and pushed in with her lips, and straddled him with her legs. A jolt shot up her spine.

He pushed apart. "Selene, we shouldn't do this."

She let go, and undid her nightshirt, and her hair knot. The lacing slipped effortlessly, sliding down over her breasts and belly, past her waist until it settled around her hips. She tousled her hair. Her raven curls bounced past her shoulders, cascades of flowing black. Her green eyes twinkled in the candlelight. His mouth gaped slightly.

She smiled teasingly, enjoying his gaze passing over her. "Haven't you ever broken the rules?"

He regained his wits. "Not in a long time."

"Allow me, then." She leaned in, her locks brushing gently across their faces. She grasped him tight, and he gave in, pushing deeper and deeper into her, tongues wet, pressing against each other, breath heavy and hot. He tasted like salt and honey, and her mind buzzed with excitement. He grabbed her with both hands. If it was a jolt before, this was a storm. It felt incredible. *Soren and I had so many months together... why weren't we doing this the whole time?*

She moaned as she ground herself against the swelling in his trousers. His rough hands danced across her neck, shoulders, back, arse. She felt her wetness slipping onto his hard belly. His engorged cock begged to be freed. She obliged, undoing his trousers and lowering herself onto him. Her body wracked with pleasure. She rocked her hips and pushed him back onto the bed. She brought her head down and took his nipple in her mouth. He let out a moan. It stirred something deep inside her. Neither of them cared they were no longer quiet. She felt his body jerk beneath him, and the same feeling swelled within her. They writhed and spasmed and quivered together, and fell exhausted onto the bed.

They were silent as they filled the room with their hot breath. Selene turned to him. He looked back at her. His grey eyes like the ashes of a long-dead pyre begged her to ask. Begged her to ask him to come with her. The belfry rang midnight, tolling across the black cape and out to sea. She sighed. *I can't ask. I can't do that to him. The less he knows, the better.*

"What is it?" he asked.

"Nothing. I should get back." She wiped herself off with his covers and got up from the bed. *I should get back. It's nearly time.*

"Is something wrong?"

"You've never asked before, so I don't know why you're asking now," she said as she threw her nightshirt back over her head, deftly palming the keys.

"Is this about—that was a long time ago. I apologised, didn't I? And it's never happened since."

"It's not that. Really, I'm fine. Look, I should get back before anyone sees I'm out after curfew."

"Stay here, then. I have a spare robe. You can leave in the morning."

"No... Please. I have to go."

"Diana." She turned her head. He waited for her to say something. She didn't. They stared at each other. She forced herself to leave. The door latched as she walked into the hallway.

Right... now to get Leon.

She avoided anyone in the hallways, and her room was as she left it. Her armor was on the rack, waiting for her. She threw it on, clasping the jacket closed, belting her trousers and pulling her gloves on. She dropped her dagger into her belt frog and hooked her crossbow to her belt. Three morel juice vials in her beltpouch, and the antidotes, along with ten bolts and the iron keys, and she was ready to go. Ready as she could ever be. Her hand hesitated as she reached for the doorpull. *Come on, Selene. Do this. He's counting on you...*

She pulled open the door slowly. No one was outside. The halls were empty. They were all still in the cathedral. *Good.* She crept along the narrow hallways, avoiding the major thoroughfares and sacristies. She knew the way, had trod these halls for a year in her training, and this last week refreshed her memory of the place. *Ten more paces, then a right. Fifteen paces, there's the candelabra with the one broken arm. Twenty paces, then down the stairs.*

20

BREAK

L EON HEARD A SOFT knock on the door. His eyes shot awake. He was just resting them. He wasn't sleeping, really. The lock mechanism clicked. The door opened slowly. Leon crept behind the door, chamberpot in hand. A woman strode into the room.

"Leon," she whispered softly.

"Oh, it's you," he said. Selene looked unimpressed. He expected her to be frightened that she was standing behind him, but no. She had nerves of steel. *Good. We're going to need them.*

She held out a set of black robes for him. "Put this on. You're overly all too big and recognizable. Keep your head down, and pretend like you're not four feet wide, and they might not know who you are."

"Alright," he replied, throwing the robe over his head and his hood up. "I'm not sure how I'll pretend to do that, but I'll try."

S ELENE CREPT ALONG THE tiled floor. Leon was in lockstep, keeping his back pressed to the wall, light on his feet, and his head down. For a knight famed for his honor and known for his bluntness, he seemed well-accustomed to subterfuge.

They walked down the spiral stairs as if they were inquisitor and novitiate. She took a candle from a candelabra on the wall. Down here, it would just look like they were a mentor and apprentice situation, perhaps a little later than usual, and Diana the Inquisitor was just taking the novitiate for a tour of the prison. *During an assault on the city... who am I fooling?*

Selene heard shuffling from a cell. One of the prisoners must've been awake. Hushed tones and whispers alighted her steps to the door, and she lifted her candle, lighting up the room through a small grate at the top of the door. Selene peered inside. A little girl snuggled up to her mother, both trying to negotiate the chains shackled around their wrists. The girl looked up at Selene and huddled closer to her mother. They were both shivering. The mother looked at Selene with a sense of sad weariness. Selene felt a twinge of guilt. She thought back to herself as a little girl—the one who felt scared and alone. She felt for the girl in the cage, but what could she do? Tristain wouldn't rescue himself. She left them alone and moved on.

They rounded the corner. The silence buzzed in her ears, and she smelled the stink of the bay below. The hairs on the back of her neck stood on end. Turgid with a hollow, reverberating quiet, something slinked out of the darkness. Sharp cheekbones, lips that could charm the pants off a queen, and eyes as white as the brightest white silk resolved from the shadow.

"Selene," Soren said, his arms crossed. He was in his own armor now, estoc sitting at his belt. "What are you doing here?"

"You followed me?" she asked.

"You weren't acting like yourself."

"And you know me?"

"Of course, I do. I know you better than anyone else."

She placed her hand gently on Leon's back as the knight tensed up. "Why do you suppose?"

"Please don't tell me... You're going to rescue your ward's son, aren't you? I knew it... as soon as family comes back into the picture—"

"Hang on, just-just... hold a minute." *If I can convince him...* "It's not just about my family, Soren. I can't do this anymore."

"So, you turn your back on us? After all we've done for you?"

"*We?* What about you? What do *you* want? Come with me. They *deserve* to be free. The Order just wants to exterminate them, the devils. See, I don't believe that's what they are. I may have once, but not anymore. They're victims. Victims of a thousand-year-curse that is passed down, generation to generation. A curse that turns the rest of the world against them, for nothing other than their difference. They've done nothing to deserve what they get—"

"*Done nothing?* What of all the families and good folk that've had their lives utterly destroyed by the creatures? What of the innocent, Inquisitor? The children?"

"They... they can't control themselves. The Order makes it worse, as it is. We hunt them, force them to hide their powers, rather than seeking help. The world hates them, but we could be different, show the world that there's a different way, a better way. We could *protect* them. There is no chance that they would harm anyone if we offered them a place to change in a controlled way. We know more than anyone else about them, and we can use that knowledge for good."

"What about someone like the tax collector from Annaltia? He escaped his bonds and slaughtered *everyone* in that village. You don't remember that? He nearly killed you, too!"

"Of course, I remember that. But it's no worse than what we've done. Have you seen what's in the archives? We burned whole towns to the ground for the sake of a few likely harmless beasts. What about Lorena-Maria, the herbalist? What about the blacksmith? They were just living their lives until we came along, and we destroyed them. The Order is rotten. The way we do things, it's not right. We need to change it for the better."

"I see you've been reading that *Truth*, gross falsehood. No, Selene, now come, I know you. You don't mean this."

"It's rotten to the top, Soren. You know, Leon here, Rotersand just wants to use him to assassinate Prince Reynard." Leon turned his head. He hadn't known that. "I can't... *pretend*... like what we're doing here is good and right, not anymore."

He clenched his jaw. "No."

"I... please, Soren. Please, you have to."

"No, Inquisitor. I'm sorry." He drew his blade slowly. "I can't let you do this. Surrender, and I won't harm you."

She felt a tear go down her cheek. "I know you won't." She closed her fist around the dagger's hilt and unsheathed it. Leon backed up. The dagger felt heavy in her palm. "I'm sorry, too."

They came to blows. Lunging, thrusting, parrying. Selene did a half-turn, lashing out with a kick. He caught her leg, and she quickly did a spin to get out of his grip. He brought his thin blade around for a low blow. It skewered her calf. She yelled.

"Stop, Inquisitor," Sorenius begged. "Surrender, and we can forget this ever happened!"

"No," she spat through ground teeth.

"You won't win. I taught you everything you know." He withdrew his blade. Blood spurted onto the stone, black. She cried out. "You'll throw it all away for someone you barely know anymore. You've spoken of your ward's son *how many times* in the years I've known you? No. Your place is here. Now, I'm going to the belfry to sound the alarm. They should know there's someone trying to escape here." He eyed Leon pointedly. "You should go back to your room and pretend like none of this ever happened."

No. She would not let that happen. He passed her. She lunged.

Sorenius clutched at the blade in his heart. His eyes went wide. His voice was weak. "What..." She let go of the blade as his legs gave out from under him.

She kneeled next to him, head hung low. She started to cry. Soren swallowed hard, then coughed blood. He grasped her hand weakly. Then his face relaxed, and he died.

Leon rested his hand on her shoulder. "I'm sorry, lass."

She sniffed, letting the silence draw out. The air hung heavy with sadness. Minutes later, she spoke, "Me too... I... I loved him."

"We all lose those we love. It's part of life." He released her and stepped past and down the hallway, peeking around the corner. "Lass, I'm sorry, but... we have to go. Grieve after, but please—"

Selene got to her feet. She wiped her face, sighing. "Yeah." *Tristain waits for us...* They couldn't linger here. She looked at the silver-streaked man with the grey eyes for one last time.

"S ET HIM DOWN HERE," she said, the red-bearded man nodding as he gently placed the Tristain's gaunt frame onto a long crate. The storeroom down the hall from the cells would do for now, but they needed to move soon. She tended to him, uncapping her waterskin and putting it to his mouth. Tristain's eyes were glassy, unfocused. He was muttering nonsense.

"Sigur! What is wrong with him?" Leon was watching a line of drool that had worked its way out of Tristain's slack mouth.

"How long has he been like this?" she wondered out loud. "It looks like he hasn't eaten in... Ginevra knows how long." She glanced over his skeletal form, bones poking from scarred flesh, covered in a layer of grime. His thick beard was home to all manner of dirt and things she did not want to put a name to.

She stepped back, watching Leon try to feed her poor brother. Tristain muttered something, and Leon put the piece of apple in his face again. He flinched.

"I'll shove it down your fucking throat, Squire!"

Tristain remained unresponsive.

She looked back at her guardians' son, her childhood friend, and her lip quivered. She had a flashback to the last time she'd seen him. Tristain was the magnificent knight in his armor, the great tournament, the battle of two lords; a song for the minstrels. That man now sat before him, propped up not by his own strength, but by another's. Dark, greasy, matted hair, and sunken eyes. There was nothing behind them, they were just bloodshot, lifeless. Her hands trembled, then her breath quickened. She stumbled backward and landed softly on a box. Leon glanced at her and said something, but she did not hear him. A cascade of thoughts assaulted her mind.

How long has he been like this...?

Her breathing became quick, and her hands cold and damp.

Who did this to him...?

The colour drained from her face.

The Order did this to him... They're not the only ones... All those people... What I've done in the Order's name...

She lost her bearings, and the room spun.

All those terrible things I've done...

She tried to control her breathing, cradling her head in her hand. Desperate tears spilled onto the ground. A vicious thread between the thoughts ripped her to pieces. The thread did not have a name, but sobs wracked her body as it ran her through. An inordinate amount of time went by.

"Lass!" Leon cried out, finally reaching through. She jerked with recognition, fuzzy eyes darting towards him. "Where are we going?"

"There's... there's a ship." The *Iustitia*. The Lord Inquisitor's ship. It was the only way out. "Out in the bay. We can take a boat from the cove."

"Well, are you coming?"

It took all of her will to force words out of her mouth, but she finally said, "Yes."

21

LIFE AND DEATH

THE STEEL GATE WAS down, shut tight. Thick steel barred their escape to the cove. The inviting sound of gently lapping water sat tantalisingly out of reach.

"*Raaaaggh!*" Leon booted the gate in frustration. "*Sal'brath!*" He yelled louder than he should have, really. He limped, juggling Tristain as he hopped around on one foot.

"It's no use," Selene said. "This is made to keep demons—Althann—from escaping."

"There's gotta be some way!" He put Tristain on the ground. "Come on, lass, give me a hand!" He lowered himself, gripping tight, his thick back muscles flaring as he tried to budge the gate. It didn't move a hair. He yelled, giving up.

"Shit... what do we do, now?"

Selene strained her mind. There must've been something. *A novitiate's body cut to pieces... a soft splash...* "The arena!" She grimaced. "You might not like it, Knight. We might have to crawl through some awful things. After they train novitiates, they test them in a Trial, a test against an Althann. They dump the dead ones from a chute."

"Oh, *sal'brath!* And you really thought the Order was good? Sorry, lass, I'll leave it. Ah, shit... If it gets us out of 'ere, I'll crawl through Sigur's arsehole."

"That's... vivid. But reassuring. Let's go. We'll have to go back the way we came."

"Lead the way."

"Arms tired yet?"

Leon laughed cheekily. "I'm used to carrying his weight."

They walked back through the dark halls of the prison, moonlight contrasting starkly on the basalt. The air was tense. Selene imagined coming around the corner to a full complement of arbiters and having her body filled with crossbow bolts. She soothed herself, tugging on her hair.

"*Wait!*"

She turned her head, stopping dead. Leon bumped into her. "You hear that?" Leon shrugged. The silence stretched out.

Someone poked their head up from behind the barred viewing window. It was a shabby-bearded man in sackcloth, naked from the waist down. Clearly, the guards hadn't thought it important to give him pants. "Oy! You're not Order, are you? We saw you pass before, the stark-raving one with you-"

"Who the hell are you?"

"Frischeid, son of Frischeid. Call me Frix."

"But what are you doing in there?"

"Oh... they thought I was a demon, didn't they? I mean, I am. But I did nothing wrong. My business partner, *that bastard*, told on me. Was given a fat reward, I'm told."

Behind them, another person stuck their head up. It was the young mother from before. "You heard the screams, milady? What's going on out there?"

Selene swallowed. *Shit... these people are going to die. If it's not the Prince's men, it'll be the Order... or maybe they'll forget about them, and they'll all starve...* "What's your name?"

Leon tugged her along. "Lass, we have to go—"

"It's Meszel, milady."

"Meszel, Frix... I'm going to get you out of here."

They breathed a sigh of relief, thanking her profusely as she pulled the set of iron keys out of her beltpouch. *Now, which one is it...*

Frix offered unhelpful words. "Nope, I think it's that one—No, try that one—Ah, turn it the other... Okay, not that one."

Leon put Tristain down, leaning him gently against the wall. Selene glanced at him. He was still unconscious. A line of drool ran onto his sackcloth shirt. *Come on, Tristain... you have to wake up eventually...*

"*Ahah!*" Frix yelled.

"Who's there!" someone called harshly, out of sight. They were near. Selene swore under her breath.

"Shit, shit, shit," Leon swore louder.

"Here! Take the keys!" Selene threw the keys past the bars into Frix's cell. They would have to free themselves. "Let's go!"

Leon scooped Tristain up and ran. They ran through dark halls, past cells, over hard stone, up stairs, down stairs. Finally, they reached the tunnel that led to the pit. Selene swallowed as they entered the sandy, dimly lit killing ground. Blood still stained the sand. The circle smelled of terror, and piss. A bleached finger-bone stuck up from the tan-coloured earth.

The giant iron door roared to life above their heads. Selene looked up. It was quickly coming down on them. They dived forward. Leon landed hard on the sand, trying to stop himself from crushing Tristain's frail body.

"What in the hells?"

The sound of clanking plate filled the smooth-stone circle. A giant stepped out of the darkness. Above, the brazier roared to life, scattering light across the room. The light reflected down onto the sand, giving the giant a reddish-orange hue. In hulking plate, he glared. Manus Ironhand.

"Gods, I'd forgotten how big that bastard was," Leon said. Behind the metal giant, the iron door slammed shut. The soft sound of a lock being turned. Selene looked up as a rasping voice spoke.

"Hello, Selene."

"Lord Inquisitor," she said.

The man grinned wider than seemed possible. He stretched his face to absurd proportions. He let out a chuckle, and his voice dropped its harshness. No, it was his authentic voice. It more than resembled her guardian father's in passing. "My father's ward."

Tempered by the realization that it should've been obvious in hindsight, she smiled. "Bann."

"I see you've finally realised, after all this time. I must admit, I thought my act was very good." He yanked at his face, pulling skin. Scars revealed themselves under the false skin. He rolled the skin up in a bundle, like dried glue, and tossed them into the arena. The wad hit the sand with a gentle *plop*. "You enjoy my work? Brother was always entirely too much of *himself*, wasn't he? Butter-boy always needed to be taken down a peg. I'm only sad we were too far distant by age, that I could not have more time with him, to work on him, to mould him. Ah well, needs must."

"*You* did this to him?"

"You're lucky he's still alive. Sorenius told me what happened with Father. He gave you that freakish stump, didn't he? Where is your lovesick puppy, anyway?"

"Dead. I killed him." She spotted someone coming up the stairs next to Bann, taking up position, crossbow pointed towards them. Someone with blonde hair, and a tansy flower tucked above her ear. *Lena.*

"You... Selene! That's cold. I really thought you loved him."

"I wouldn't expect you to understand, Bann."

"Yes... well, this is getting tiresome. It's about time you dropped these heroics and kill the knight, already. He's lived well past his usefulness."

Leon sent a glance to Selene.

She raised an eyebrow at Bann. "Why would I do that?"

"Because if you don't, I'll kill Tristain, and then I'll take my pleasure in taking each of your fingernails, one by one. Oh, I suppose I'll have to settle for toenails as well. Five is entirely not enough. And *then* I'll kill you."

"You're insane."

"*Insane? Insane? Father is the insane one! He did all of this! He turned us against each other! The great hypocrite!* Blabbing on about family, and honour, and respectability... while he murdered and ate his own wife, the Godsdamned *monster!*"

"No, *you* did this. The Order... was it just a means to an end? What end?"

He chuckled. "Yes, I suppose it was... but what end? Power, of course. Control."

"Power is never for power's sake," Leon mentioned quietly. Selene nodded.

"But I digress. Regardless, this is the ultimatum I present. Kill the knight, and I'll let you return to your duties in the Order. I'll let you live, and forget the disrespect you showed me."

She looked at Leon. The man still held Tristain in his arms. The knight wiggled his jaw, cricking his neck. He nodded.

She unhooked her crossbow and shot at Bann.

The shot was quick. Bann was quicker. All the spryness of his youth was now undisguised. He threw himself out of the way. Tansy let out a shocked cry. Selene swore.

"*How dare you!*" he screamed. "*Kill them!*"

Manus stalked up to them, his giant two-handed sword at his side. His dead eyes seem to light up behind his faceplate. He raised the greatsword, ready to strike. Leon placed Tristain in the sand gently, drawing the axe at his belt and the shield from under his robe. "Let's go, you big *sal'brath* bastard!"

Selene bolted for the gate behind Manus. It was the only way up to Bann. The sand pounded under her feet. Ironhand swung a wide arc. Selene barely ducked underneath it. Gods, the sword was enormous. The brute swung it far too fast to be human. *What the hell is he?* Suddenly, the sword was bearing down on her again. She jumped out of the way. She scanned his armour, looking for a weak spot. There wasn't much. A small gap under the helmet, maybe. She had to try something.

LEON BELLOWED IN FRUSTRATION. Manus kept them both at bay with wide sweeps. The ground felt warm under his boots. He kicked up, sending an arc of sand into the air. The giant stumbled. Leon jumped, driving his axe forward. The axe slammed against the plate, glancing off harmlessly. Leon pushed his advantage, driving his heel into the brute's knee. Manus didn't budge. *Fuck.* The greatsword came behind Manus's head for a cleaving blow. Leon threw his shield up high. He swallowed. The moment moved in slow motion. *No, it's going to go right through it!*

Leon changed his footing at the last moment. The shield turned aside the cleave, using its own momentum. The sword kicked up sand. Leon's arm felt stiff, sore, but he smiled. The brute had overbalanced. The back of his neck stood exposed. Leon brought his axe down. Flesh split. Blood gushed from the wound.

The giant didn't seem to notice. Suddenly, Leon's vision spun. A sharp pain hurtled through his chest. He thumped into the sand.

Leon coughed and spat. He lost his bearings for a moment. His vision swam. He narrowed his eyes, focusing on Manus. Bright red blood gushed down the giant's breastplate. *He should be dead... but, sal'brath, I just tickled him.*

He went to get to his feet. A bolt glanced off the sand near Tristain's head. Leon looked up.

Tansy was laughing. "You've left your pup to fend for himself, red-beard! There's scorpions in the sand!" Leon grunted in surprise. He threw himself over Tristain, shield ahead. A bolt planted itself in the shield. Another one. Another. The woman's laughter grew manic. She pinned Leon down.

Selene cried out. She flew past his eye, crashing into the sand. She spat up blood. Leon clenched his jaw. *Fuck... some help... some help would be nice... we're gonna die... a man-wolf would be nice right about now...*

"Squire, wake the fuck up!"

THE PRESS OF DARK trees loomed over Tristain. The air hung heavy with mist. His feet pounded unevenly against the slippery dirt. He could feel something approaching. His breath came hard and fast. He wasn't sure where he ran, and where he came from, but he knew he had to run. As fast as he could.

A familiar scream rang in his ears. He spurred himself on. His heart felt like it might burst from his chest.

"Selene!" He waited for her reply. Nothing. He threw himself over an uneven embankment, sliding in the mud. He burst through a bush and caught his breath. A little girl with dark hair sat before him, cradling her knees, and crying.

"Selene," Tristain said, giving her his hand. "Let's go."

They ran. Tristain looked behind. Something large moved between the trees. His eyes went wide. "Faster!"

Their breathing grew panicked. Tristain tripped on a rock. He groaned, face bleeding. A giant wolf pounced on Selene. She screamed. Tristain pulled himself to his feet.

He charged. "*Get away from her!*" The beast slapped him aside with a powerful throw of its shoulder. It loomed over Selene. It licked its chops. She cried.

It spoke with Bann's voice, "*I'm going to kill you, you horrible little urchin, and I'm going to enjoy it.*"

Tristain went pale. The wolf took her by the collar and ran off. "*Selene!*"

She screamed for his help. Tristain was too far away. *No! You're not taking her away! Not now, not ever!*

He felt the familiar pit in his stomach. A burning began in his chest. Fire rippled through his lungs, his nerves, his muscles. The pain was welcome. He knew what came after. Sigur came to him in that moment. He remembered himself thinking about what he might've done to deserve his damned fate, Sigur's curse. This was no curse—this was *strength*. He was *might*, given flesh. Power surged throughout his body. Fur glided from his skin. Snout grew from jaw, nose and face re-formed. Teeth grew finger-sized, sharp as a wolf's. His hot breath curled in the forest. The air seemed to tremble as he rose to his full height. He took a deep breath, filling his lungs with night air. It was the freshest air he'd ever smelled in his entire life. A bellowing roar rattled the trees and shook the ground.

He blinked. He was no longer in the forest. Hysterical laughter filled his ears. Sharp grunting. He felt the sand under his feet. The surrounding walls were high, but he could see the top, and no longer would fear affect him. He sniffed. The blonde woman started shrieking. With his sharp hearing, he heard a derisive grunt behind her.

The steel-covered giant turned from his fight with Selene. Tristain leaped and crashed into him. Smashing through the gate, he sheared the iron gate off its hinges.

Tristain ripped his helmet off. Bright, luminescent eyes widened as Tristain tore his throat out.

T HE GATE HUNG OFF its hinges. Selene darted in behind. She flew up the stairs, turning a pirouette as a bolt skimmed her arm hairs. Tansy screamed in surprise.

"*Wait, Se—*" The blade under her chin cut her off. The venomous woman finally died.

Bann backed up. "Selene, you know me... kill me if you have to. Everything I did, I did for our family."

She cried out, howling in pain. Her dagger pierced his chest again and again. He fell. She saw herself from above, taking his life, wound by wound. When it was over, her hand felt stiff, and Bann's blood covered her jacket.

"No!" It was Leon.

Selene turned. She ran to the stairs, and froze. She slumped on the wall. Her eyes glazed over.

Tristain was impaled. The giant two-hander had run him through when he'd charged at Manus. Tristain drew his lips back, snarling in pain. A deluge of dark blood ran down the steel, saturating the stone. He looked at Selene, his jaw going slack. He stumbled and collapsed. Leon rushed to him.

"*Pleeeaaase!*" he cried out. His voice was ragged. "*Not again!*"

Selene fell beside them. Tristain's body shrank and his fur receded. His face turned back to the glowing child she remembered. She shrieked, pleading for his apology.

He couldn't have heard it. He was already gone.

22

THE ARABELLA

A SOFT KNOCK FROM behind the heavy iron door broke the desolate silence. Selene wiped her face and picked up her dagger. She hoped desperately they weren't Order. She didn't think she had it in her to fight anymore.

"Let us in," Frix's voice came. "Someone help!"

Selene gasped. She raced up the stairs, and the mechanism thundered to life. A loud clinking of chains and pulleys, and the door raised slowly. Threadbare and unkempt, they threw themselves under the door, flooding in. Forty, fifty of them. Selene smiled through the pain she was feeling. At least they were still alive. Leon shut the gate when the last one came through.

"Milady," Frix said, his pale legs in full view. "'Tis good to see—" He cut himself off, looking around. "What happened?"

She didn't answer. People were getting restless, wondering out loud if this was another dead end.

"Let us help you, milady," Meszel said, her daughter at her side. "Is there anything we can do?"

She turned to Leon. "Come with me," she said.

People gasped, looking at the carnage in the stairwell. The body chute was off to the left, and that was where they headed.

"Down here," she said. Her lip quivered as she tried to organise her thoughts. Leon held her shoulder. His touch was calming. "It'll take you to the sea. Be careful, though. I don't know what it's like in there."

"What is this?" someone asked. "A corpse chute?"

Selene didn't answer. Frix shrugged. He spoke to the crowd. "Milady, if this is our only way, we'll take it. Better than burning at the stake, or getting slaughtered by Gods know what, right?" They all murmured in agreement. "Let's go, then. I'll do the honours." He crawled into the chute. "It's dark!" He cried out. "But it's metal, and smooth-*woah!*—" He landed with a soft splash. "*It's fine! Bit cold! Oh, don't mind the bodies!*" came his voice.

The prisoners murmured with uncertainty. "It's our only chance," Meszel said to her daughter. "Come, Gretel." They followed Frix into the chute, screaming as they fell. *Splash.* They were fine.

They formed a line, following one after the other. It was easy after that. Finally, the last one made it through, and Selene was next.

"I'm taking him with me," she said to Leon. She looked over Tristain's body. The greatsword was still planted deep within him. Her lip quivered again. "I can't do it on my own."

Leon nodded. "Of course, lass." He grabbed the sword's quillons, pulling while Selene put her weight on Tristain, closing his eyes quickly. She glanced at his soft neck, his bearded face. His body was warm, still. He looked like he could be sleeping. She blinked back tears, trying to focus on the task.

The sword pulled free. Leon stumbled back. "Gods, how did that fucker carry this, let alone swing it... it's gotta weigh thirty pounds..." He let it fall to the stone with a clatter.

They put Tristain in the chute.

"And your other brother?" Leon asked.

She clenched her jaw. "He made his choices. He can rot in this horrible place for all I care."

Leon nodded. "He won't need this anymore, will he?" He had cut Bann's purse from his belt. It looked heavy.

Selene shook her head. "No, he won't."

She pushed Tristain forward as she crawled into the dark tube. Forward, forward, forward, until it fell out of sight. She swallowed, taking a deep breath. There was enough room to manoeuvre. She threw herself, feet first. It was a sheer fall. She shrieked, not knowing how far she would plummet. But then soft orange light came from beneath.

Water engulfed her. The fall was only twenty, thirty feet. She swam to the surface. The prisoners swam to a nearby ledge, helping each other up. She looked up. Bright orange light filled the black sky. The air smelled of ash and salt.

Selene pulled Tristain's body along with her as she kicked her legs. The sea was calm enough to swim with only her legs. Eventually, she made it to the ledge. Frix was there, helping everyone get up.

"Take him," she said. "Take him first."

Frix called for help, pulling Tristain out of the water while Selene pushed. They groaned with the effort. Once he was on solid ground, Frix helped Selene out. Leon wasn't far behind.

"What now?" Frix asked as Selene wrung her raven locks of seawater. The others shuffled, not sure what to do. Meszel kneeled down, shushing her daughter, wiping her face. The girl was crying.

"There," Selene said, pointing to a shadow on the horizon. "We can escape on the ship."

"How do we get out there?" Leon asked, Tristain cradled in his arms. "I ain't swimmin' that far, not with him on my back."

The prisoners murmured with hesitation.

"Around there," Selene said, pointing to a curve in the cliff. "There's a cove. Should be a boat there."

They followed the curve of the cliff, rounding the corner. Water sloshed around their feet as the wind picked up waves. Selene shivered. She wasn't the only one.

The cove stood ahead of them, bathed in light. Men in short sleeves and shabby trousers were loading crates into moored boats. A man in a red coat and peaked wool hat was barking orders. They did not look like Golden Swords.

"That crate! No, Sev, leave that one! Too heavy! Yeah, we can always use more rope!" He turned his head, squinting into the darkness. "Oye! Blades!"

His men drew their swords, axes, and knives, dropping whatever they were holding.

"Who's there?" he cried.

Selene drew her dagger, and stepped out of the darkness.

She lifted it into the air. "I'm unarmed," she said, stepping onto the stone wharf. She threw her dagger aside. "We're looking for a way onto that ship."

The leader looked at his men. They all laughed. "Good thing, mistress. You've found it."

"I'm Selene. Are you the crew?"

"*Her* crew. The *Arabella*, or the *Iustitia*, as that pompous fuck calls her."

"What are you doing here?"

The leader waved for his men to sheath their blades. "Gods honest, men, keep loading! I swear, they'd trip over their damn noses if I wasn't there to tell 'em where to step. Mistress." He bowed. "Captain Bennington Stuart Albrich Chesterfield, formerly of Marberg, now of the high seas. The city burns, and the Order with it. We're taking what we can from this place and leaving." He rested a hand on his sword hilt. "I trust there's no issue?"

"Gods, no. Come, everyone. It's safe." She waved to the group behind her. They filed into the cove. She glanced behind the captain and breathed a sigh of relief. The steel portcullis was still down, so it was likely no one else would stumble upon them.

"Selene. Just Selene," she said, shaking his hand firmly.

"Well, Just Selene, we're—"

"*Leon!*" someone cried. Selene turned her head. A man with a silver earring clapped him on the shoulders. "It's Lorrin!"

"Sailor," he greeted.

Lorrin looked down. "Oh... is that... Shit. I'm sorry."

"Me, too."

"I'll see you on the ship," Lorrin said, and went back to loading crates.

"Let's go, men," the captain cried. "Mistress, we can offer you passage, but... are you this many? I'm afraid we'll have to ask for some compensation."

She gave him Bann's coinpouch. He flipped the heavy bag over, inspecting a single coin. "Yep, that's enough. Too much, in fact. Here." He handed it back. It weighed about half as much.

"Into the boat," she cried. The boats could hold twenty of them, with all the other sailors and crates. They would have to make at least two trips. It got heated.

"I'm not fucking staying here," one prisoner yelled. He had greying brown hair, and a thick-set body, with the asymmetrical musculature of a blacksmith. "I've spent a year in this place. No fucking way am I spending one more second!"

A man shoved him. "Back off! Let the women on first!"

"Bullshit!"

"Aye!" Leon bellowed, getting between them. "We're in no danger 'ere! This ain't right! Fighting amongst ourselves gets us nothing!"

Frix chimed in. "Lackwits! Can't you see the Order 're laughin' at us? We have to stick together!"

"What about a lottery?"

"How the fuck we do that, Heinrich?"

"It's just an idea, Gregor!"

"First on, first off!"

"Oy!"

Gregor the blacksmith threw a punch. It missed his target, smashing Leon in the face. He reeled, but kept his footing.

"That's Leon the Strong, you idiots," Frix yelled.

Selene strode up to him, worrying. She reached out, checking his cheek. "I'm alright, lass," he said. "I've taken harder drinks. How do you know me, Frix?"

"I saw you at the August Griffin Tourney... oh, three years ago? *Phwoar,* you were incredible. Unseated Gustav Vredevoort three times, he did. See, lackwits, that's who you're messing with. He'll drop you faster than a sack of potatoes."

Gregor turned red, giving him a stiff bow. "Sorry, Sir. I'm ashamed."

"That's alright, lad. Now, we'll have to draw lots or something."

"No, I volunteer," the blacksmith replied. "I'll take the second round." The man he was arguing with, Heinrich, volunteered as well. Then ten others did, then another ten.

"Right, well, anyone who didn't volunteer on the boats," Selene said.

The captain took up the helm, barking for the rowers to pull. "*Pull,*" he yelled rhythmically. "*Pull! Pull! Pull!*"

T HE *ARABELLA*'S DECK WAS a flurry of activity when the second wave of boats arrived, and soon everyone was on board. The reddish-orange sky grew brighter, and the smog was getting thicker. Selene coughed, leaning on the railing.

"*Haul anchor! All hands away,*" the captain yelled, and the black sails loosened. The wind inflated them, and the ship moved out to sea. Selene looked around. As the ship reached its cruise speed, the deck mellowed out. She walked up to Leon. He stared off into the distance, still holding Tristain in his arms.

"I've decided," she said.

The knight looked up.

"We're going to Palerme."

Leon nodded. "We'd better bury him."

She bit her lip. "Yeah."

They had Tristain wrapped in a shroud, and a bag of sand tied around his ankles. His face was left uncovered. Selene kneeled next to him. She placed her hand on his chest and closed her eyes. She apologised with all her heart. But she knew. She knew she would have to beg for his forgiveness for the rest of her life. *I'm so sorry...* A tear fell from her face, soaking into the canvas. Her heart hurt. It seethed in her chest.

The deck was silent as they lowered his body into the water. The knot was slipped, and Tristain sank. The sea swallowed him whole.

Selene had to look away. She found her solace in up. She watched as the sails distended in the gentle breeze coming off the coast. The backdrop of the burning city behind them grew distant. Topsails floated like clouds in the night sky. The very top sail, the skysail, appeared to touch the heavens themselves, free from human hands. The water was so still and the breeze so steady that the sails looked like sculpted marble hanging there, pulling the ship through the water effortlessly. It was breathtaking. She stood there a while, taking it all in.

Her lip quivered. She couldn't resist her grief any longer. It came unbidden. She leaned on the railing, unable to move. Her soul poured onto the timber. Like a piece of wood already burned and turned to ash finally crumbling at the slightest touch, Selene broke. She gasped as pieces of herself scattered to the seabreeze, sobs wracking her body as she cried about everyone she had lost, and a small voice inside her wondered if anything would be left.

EPILOGUE

"**C**OME, MAMA!" SANNA CRIED. "It's just over the ridge!"

"Sanna, wait! Don't race ahead," Ottille cried out after her. The frost was coming, and this high in the mountains, it was easy to get lost. The smell of coming snow filled the air. Ottille's feet were cold. Snow was soaking through her boots. "Come back!" She groaned. The girl disappeared from sight.

She walked over the ridge and sighed in relief. They had arrived. "Come, Ma," Ottille cried.

The old woman grunted, clambering slowly up the stone. "The spirit of youth," she croaked. "Impatient, no matter the age!"

Ottille helped her mother over a rock and onto the ridge. "A welcome sight, Gram."

"Indeed. I was afraid we might get lost, and I'd have to eat you to survive!"

Ottille laughed. "Now, where's that girl gone... ah, there!"

Sanna had raced ahead, and talked with a man in a thick brown cloak. He had a bright red beard, and his shaved head reflected the pale sun. Ottille and her mother walked gingerly down the ridge, which hadn't proved a problem for the young girl, but Gram's brittle bones and stiff joints had her lingering.

"...and who do we have here?" The wide man in the brown cloak said, his beard building up a little frost.

The girl spoke, "This is my ma, Ottille, and my Gram."

"They have lost my name to time, boy," the old woman replied.

Ottille rolled her eyes. "Her name is Lucia. We're from Invereid."

The man bellowed with laughter. "You'll have to meet our leader, then. She's from Invereid, herself." He bowed his head slightly. "Sir Leon Vorland."

"*Leon Strong!*" The girl cried. "Wow! I saw you fight every time you came to Invereid! Well... I peeked through the fence, but I still saw you!"

"Well, ain't I glad to have such a dedicated admirer? C'mon, warm yourselves in the keep. This ain't the time to be outdoors. Winter's almost on us."

They followed him up the hill and beyond the stone wall, into the bailey. The circular keep was seventy feet tall, capped with merlons, and flanked by a smaller tower to the right. The stink of horses drifted over from a squat building next to the smaller tower. To their left, a heavy-set man was tanning deer skin, the tanning solution making Ottille's nose itch. Next to the gate, a blacksmith was hammering away, making pickaxe heads. His apprentice was peaning the shafts, jamming the heads into place. The heat of the furnace made Ottille hunger for a place to warm her feet.

They passed through the wicket door of the keep, the person-sized door at the foot of the wagon-sized main doors. The knight closed the door behind them. The hearths blazed brightly. Feeling heat wash over her, Ottille breathed a loud sigh of relief.

"Thank the Gods," she said.

"Thank Althann," came a woman's voice. Ottille hadn't seen her sitting there on a chaise by the fire. "For that is what you are." She got up slowly, with one hand. The knight rushed over. She waved him off. Ottille snorted. This woman was superior to the knight, that was clear. He answered to her, but why?

"Welcome to Palerme," the woman said, walking over.

The girl cried, "*Baby!*" and ran up to the woman, throwing her hands on the woman's plump middle.

"I'm sorry, milady, she loves babies," Ottille apologized. She eyed the woman. Under a loose red samite and wool dress, her belly was round and full. Her young cheeks were rosy from the heat of the fire, and long, beautiful black locks hung down past her generous chest in waves. A grey silk cape covered her shoulders, hiding her left arm. Clearly, she was of means.

No, she wasn't hiding her arm. The woman only had one arm. Ottille's heart poured out for her.

"'Tis a welcome blessing, milady," Lucia said. "Expecting in winter, a bountiful harvest in spring."

The woman chuckled light-heartedly. Ottille breathed a smaller sigh of relief.

"It's quite alright," she said. "Hello, little one. What's your name?"

The girl grinned. "Sanna. What's your name?"

"Selene. I'm very pleased to meet you."

"Selene is our lady," Leon said, lifting his head in respect. "Our lord."

"I don't appreciate that word," she replied. "But yes, I manage the keep and its surroundings, as well as the day-to-day running of the place."

The old woman's countenance shifted slightly. "What was it you said before, milady? Althann?"

"Althann, from the old Hillmen tales. In truth, we don't know if he was a god, or who he was exactly. But he was a friendly spirit, we know that, and if you've found your way here, that means you are too."

"Hah! Brilliant!"

"Come, sit, warm yourselves."

Ottille sat down by the fire. "Sit here, Sanna." The girl ran over, sitting by her mother and Ottille ran her hands through her yellow straw-like hair. "Sir Vorland said you were from Invereid, mistress?"

Smiling briefly, Selene replied, "Yes, once. I consider Palerme my home now. So, why did you come here? Other than the obvious, of course."

Ottille stroked the back of her daughter's head. "My husband, Dietmar, was hanged by a mob out for blood. Even our old friends. They knew we were them demons, and we lived there in peace our whole lives, minding our own business, but that didn't stop them."

"I'm sorry, truly."

"Tis a shame. People are angry, ever since the capital burned. I know how they feel, but that doesn't make it right."

"Kings and emperors have failed us for centuries, for millennia. It's time we took our destiny into our own hands."

The wicket door swung open with a clatter, sending a cool breeze inside. A man in a woollen coat and fur-lined cap strode into the room, shutting the door behind him. "Frix," Selene said.

The man bowed deeply, dropping his hood. He was clean-shaven, with dusty brown hair, and had a broad, freckled nose. "Mistress Selene, we've found the iron."

Leon clapped his hands, letting out a bellowing laugh.

"Excellent news," Selene joined in the celebration. "I knew there would be some in these hills. Gregor'll be happy he won't have to buy iron from the Duca anymore."

The mood in the room shifted. A candle blew out without a breeze. Ottille turned her head, and found the old woman's hand on Selene's belly. Tense seconds drew out as Ottille paled at her mother's lack of tact.

Lucia grinned, gaptoothed, wrinkled, and genuine. She spoke with the self-assured nature of a long life. "It's a boy. I feel it in my heart. He's destined for great things. May Ginevra keep him hale and healthy."

Ottille went to speak, "Mother—"

"Oh, he's certainly hale," Selene cut her off with a radiant smile on her face. "So hale, he keeps me up at night with his incessant kicking." She winked at Senna.

The girl looked at her mother with anticipation.

Ottille sighed. "Go on."

The little girl ran up, throwing her hands on Selene's belly. She squealed, balling her hands up in excitement. "*Ahhh!* I can feel it! He's kicking!"

Everyone laughed.

"If it's a boy, as the wise woman says," Frix asked. "What will you name him?"

"I think... I think Tristain would be nice."

LIST OF CHARACTERS

- Tristain – second son of Count Sebastian of Invereid, squire to Leon Vorland

- Selene – fifth daughter of the Baron of Greifswald, ward of Count Sebastian

- Leon Vorland – knight of the realm, known as Leon the Strong

- Caen – corporal

- Sorenius – inquisitor of the Order of the Golden Sword

- Palia – rector of the Order

- Elias Rotersand – lord inquisitor of the Order in Osbergia

- Ebberich, Ruprecht, Leona, Salim, & Raul – Order novitiates

- Gida – lieutenant

- Andrea, Maria, Herrad, Caspar, & Lombas the Small – Leon's men

- Bann – first son of Count Sebastian of Invereid, missing, presumed dead

- Erken – Leon's son, died in the Battle of the Giant's Footfalls

- Vredevoort – knight of the realm, known as Vredevoort the Grim, commander of Count Andreas's regiment

- Andreas Pagehald – Count of Verania

- Reynard – Duke of Annaltia, third son of Emperor Franz II

- Ilse Adolar – Duchess of Osbergia, general of the Osbergian army

- Albrecht – Archduke of Osbergia, first son of Emperor Franz II

- Lorrin & Bean – marooned sailors

- Chesterfield – captain of the *Arabella*

- Roupert, Marie, & Luka – Badonnian refugees

ACKNOWLEDGMENTS

I WANT TO THANK Matty Parkin and Bjorn Burgher, for playing the DnD game this novel spawned out of. I had the idea of making a world where all humans are werewolves, but it wouldn't have been realized had I not had players to explore it. Megan Campbell, for being a reader and wellspring of encouragement. To all my other readers, as well. My ARC readers as well – thank you for doing what you do out of love and for taking a chance on an unproven author. Shannon, for being my first and foremost alpha and beta reader, and for her support. This novel wouldn't exist without her time, care, and love.

About Author

NC Koussis was born in Perth in 1993 to Greek and Kamilaroi ancestry. He has moved all around Australia, settling in Newcastle for the moment, where he lives with his wife, son, and staffy dog, Nala. He's been writing fantasy books since he was a little boy, after falling in love with Lord of the Rings and Harry Potter. He decided to publish a book in 2019, and it only took him three years. He considers himself an enthusiastic amateur of medieval history, historical battles and tactics, and food. When he's not writing, he's making sourdough bread and working on a PhD in neuroscience.

For more, check out art of characters from this book, and a high-resolution version of the map at https://nikitaskoussis.com. Sign up to the newsletter to receive a free story!

Lightning Source UK Ltd.
Milton Keynes UK
UKHW010708070223
416609UK00001B/243